Until the Last Dog Is Hung

Until the Last Dog Is Hung

Chris Craig

ISBN: Softcover 978-1-5434-5542-7
eBook 978-1-5434-5543-4

Cover art, concept and design by Ed Simkins
www.etsy.com/shop/Kinographics

To contact the author:
Twitter - @craigman20
e-mail - chriscraig20@gmail.com

Other novels by Chris Craig available online and at bookstores:

- Show Pony
- Lawn Darts of Fate

This is a work of fiction. Names, characters, places and incidents either are the product of the author's imagination or are used fictitiously, and any resemblance to any actual persons, living or dead, events, or locales is entirely coincidental.

Print information available on the last page.

Rev. date: 11/07/2017

To order additional copies of this book, contact:
Xlibris
1-888-795-4274
www.Xlibris.com
Orders@Xlibris.com
762511

I poured the gasoline over the bodies.
"They're not dead, Arch."
"They will be."
"Ever worry about Hell?" Spaceman asked.
I tossed the can to the side.
"I worry there isn't one."
I grabbed the unconscious man's Bic and spun the wheel.

1

The last job was brutal.

It paid well, but so had my back.

On my stomach, in the heat, waiting patiently for a clean shot.

People everywhere.

Carousing.

Schmoozing.

I knew guys that would've painted the house with hollow points hoping to hit their target.

Bush league.

I was a professional.

I was a professional. And that meant waiting.

Seventeen hours.

Waiting.

The last time I was in Malibu, I was playing paddle ball with a faded B-movie actress on Zuma Beach. This time I was laying prone on a rocky ledge beneath a poorly ventilated ghillie.

I was as sharp as I'd ever been. Knew more breathing techniques than a Buddhist with Scuba certification. But after twenty-five plus years in the saddle I'd begun to let my mind drift a bit. I passed the time remembering funny skits from *Saturday Night Live*, considered taking a new multi-vitamin and pondered the unfortunate trajectory of Billy Squier's career.

And then…

It all stopped. Nothing else mattered.

My mark walked out on the balcony. A cigarette in one hand and a martini in the other.

I gave him a moment to take in the view.

Maybe he'd had a hard day. Perhaps he was lonely or feeling introspective.

Whatever he was thinking, it ended precisely at 18:37, when the pink mist from his exploding skull contrasted beautifully with the sinking sun.

2

I went where the job took me.

No question.

But flying?

Flying meant dealing with undesirables.

I liked driving.

On the freeway, I could blow by anybody.

In the air, there was nowhere to run. You were stuck.

Stuck next to some overfed sweat machine or conversation starved stranger hoping for a new friend.

There were crying kids.

Bad cabin pressure.

Teens with loud headphones.

Overstuffed bins.

The stewardess that only gave you half a can of ginger ale.

I considered myself to be a tolerant person to a point, but sometimes, damn.

The flight was LA to Chicago.

I'd just taken my seat in first class when a blob of a man wedged in next to me. He waited until we were cleared for takeoff before he went down into his plastic bag and came up with an enormous egg salad sandwich. It had been improperly refrigerated. The rancid smell filled the cabin within seconds.

The bread was soggy. Boiled egg and mayo oozed over his fingers.

Various bits of goo flew out of his gaping maw.

A snot whistled in his nose.

I had seen and done things in combat that would've made an iron-stomached Viking sick, but this guy's sandwich nearly brought me to my knees.

The man's body odor and unkempt appearance were unfortunate. His egg salad on sourdough? Unforgivable.

He washed the thing down with a Coke and began flipping through the latest issue of Model Airplane News. Each page read was capped off with a small burp until he reached the cover story on executing perfect barrel rolls. Then he unleashed it, a roaring, trachea rattling belch trailed by a putrid stench.

"Whoa ho! That is nasty." He chuckled to himself.

We touched down at Midway.

"Excuse me," I said, attempting to step out into the aisle.

"Easy," he said. "We're going the same way."

He remained sitting. Blocking my way to freedom.

"Excuse me," I said. "The aisle is clear. Time to get off the plane."

He turned and looked at me. "When I'm damn good and ready."

The obesity anti-shaming movement had made these people bold. Rude even.

He belched again. Laughed.

"Last time," I said. "Move."

He mumbled the word asshole and slowly squeezed out of his chair.

I looked at the back of his head. He shaved it, but had missed a large area in the fat folds. When he looked down at his watch his neck sprouted a bushy soul patch.

We exited the plane. He continued to belch and fart up the jet bridge to the gate.

I should have let it go. Probably would have normally, but the painkillers and three martinis hadn't done much for my sore back.

"Hey Egg Salad," I called out.

He turned.

"What in the hell do you want?"

"I need you to apologize."

"For what?"

"Your lack of consideration for others."

He pinched dried mayonnaise from the corners of his mouth and looked at me.

"My lack of consideration for others?"

"Yeah. And for being an unbearable asshole in general."

He looked around the gate to see if he could get away with taking a swing.

"Fuck you!" He said.

He worked up another ozone depleting belch.

I followed him to the bathroom. He threw his bags on the floor by the sink and went into a stall.

I looked around. No one.

I slid a credit card out of my wallet. It was one of those hot shit, *look at me I'm rich* metal cards. I kept the bottom corner razor sharp.

I kicked in the door of the stall. It drilled Egg Salad in the forehead then swung open wide the other way.

"What the-"

I stepped in and swiped my card across his jugular like a hippie throwing a frisbee for distance.

I slipped my card back into my wallet and was out the door.

Egg Salad bled out in the last stall of the men's room between Hudson News and Harry Caray's in the main terminal.

It was all over the news.

V called later pissed off.

"Unacceptable, Arch. Stupid."

I explained I had been compromised.

V called bullshit, so I copped to it.

"What are you going to do? Kick me off the company softball team?"

I was the best guy V had. Top two anyway.

"You're far too smart to be that stupid."

"Okay, it was a little impulsive, but, honestly, who eats deli on a commercial flight?"

"You need to disappear for a while," V said. "Middle of nowhere."

"Any preference?"

"No. Just keep your ass out of bars and your dick in your pants."

"Easily done."

"I'm serious."

"Me too."

V sighed, "Keep being careless, Arch, and you're going to get yourself killed."

Guys in my line of work had a hideaway, a hunting cabin, a lake house, somewhere they could lay low until their next job. I did too, but the whole Walden Pond vibe was getting old.

Predictability got a man killed in this business. I liked to move around.

I chose my random get out of dodge locations on a whim. My last one was Lawrence, Kansas after hearing *Dust in the Wind* come on the radio.

Lawrence was a neat college town. I wouldn't have minded attending KU had it been an option when I was younger. It wasn't. I bought a hat from the bookstore instead.

I got a cab from Midway and went straight to the nearest used car lot on Cicero Avenue. I paid cash for a beat-up Ford F-150. I asked the salesman where he was from. Biloxi, he said. Fourteen hours later I found myself on the Mississippi gulf coast playing blackjack in a dive casino.

The drinks were watered down.

The dealer kept throwing me losing hands and seemed happy about it. I scooped up what I had left of my bankroll and bailed.

Two hours down the road I stopped for gas at a place called Hickok Beach. It was a small patch of sand that sat in front of a half-boarded up town called Meemaw.

The town had one attraction, a Wendy's with a huge revolving Frosty on the roof.

There was a bar called the Last Straw. It was a dusty honky-tonk full of booze soaked patrons fist pumping to Blake Shelton.

"This town still manufacture mufflers?" I asked the bartender.

"Nope." He stabbed at his gums with a toothpick. "Nowadays, we just make boredom."

Boredom.

It was perfect.

"What can I getcha?"

"Gimme a diet green tea ginger ale."

"We got Bubble Up and Royal Crown Cola."

I tried V.

I tilted back five or six bourbon and waters, had some popcorn and shot some pool.

Down the road I found a beat-up motel called the Sandpiper. It was like a 1960's Howard Johnson's with fifty-seven years of solid abuse. The proprietor was an older woman named Enid.

I plunked down enough for a weeklong stay.

My room was a dump. The following morning I fixed the shower head and reset the door on the hinges.

That afternoon Enid offered me a job.

Cash only is what I said.

3

My first few days in Meemaw had been just what the doctor ordered.

Quiet.

Easy.

Uneventful.

I was sipping coffee at a laminated menu joint called Pat's Spatula and met a guy named Elmer. He mentioned he was the janitor at Meemaw High School. I told him I worked at the Sandpiper.

"That's downwind of the school. Sorry if the odor gets to you," Elmer said. "I just varnished the gym floor."

"Must be some kind of varnish."

"Toxic and cheap. Fits the school's budget. I left a bunch of windows open to air the place out."

It was good information to have.

Later that day I slipped into the school library for a few books. I read anything but period romance and Nicholas fucking Sparks.

My favorite place to read was on top of an old metal shed behind the Sandpiper where the only sounds were the sea gulls and Spanish moss filtering the breeze.

It might sound strange, but it was the most peaceful place I'd been in years.

There wasn't a man alive that could lay on top of that tin roof for more than an hour and not doze off.

I didn't want to die, but I wasn't afraid of it either.

If dying in one's sleep felt anything like those afternoon naps atop that shed then I welcomed it. Not eagerly, like an anticipated houseguest, but more like an understanding nod to a delayed delivery man.

"You up there, Arch?"

There were three things I never used; an electric razor, liquid smoke and an alias.

"Nope."

"Then how come this book is on the ground?"

"What book?"

Enid grunted and bent over. I imagined her lifting her glasses and squinting at the title.

"*Flowers for Algernon*."

"What makes you think it's mine?"

"It's lying in the same spot where the other one landed earlier."

I opened my eyes, stretched and hopped down.

"What can I do for you, Enid?"

"Bathrooms look great. New toilets are real nice." She held out her hand. "I wanted to give you something a little extra."

"That's not necessary."

"I insist."

Enid handed me some crumpled bills. I put them in my shirt pocket without looking at them.

"Thanks, but that chicken you fried up last night was payment enough."

"A home cooked meal for you anytime."

Enid smiled. She was short and slight of frame. Her face had pruned from decades of going without sunscreen, but she had a spark. A bounce in her step.

Enid tried to think of something else to say.

"Well, I'll let you get back to your reading."

"Railings will be done this evening," I said. "Figure I'll let them dry overnight."

"Sounds good. You're getting everything done a lot faster than I thought you would."

"I'm not a union guy, Enid. Honest day's work for an honest day's pay."

"You keep it up and I may have a buyer."

"Hanging it up, huh?"

"Time to retire. Live a little."

"Good for you."

I climbed back onto the shed and stretched out. The tree branches split the sky into shifting chunks of blue.

I briefly considered retirement.

Nah.

There was nothing else.

I made it through another chapter before dozing off again.

4

On the outside chance I missed a shot, I had shoved a shop towel between the busted rim and the backboard lest I wake the Sandpiper's few guests.

I was doing some circus shots when a young black kid stopped on his bike to watch me. I sunk 'em over the backboard, backwards, one handed over the shoulder, worked in some no-look hook shots.

"Wow, mister. You Larry Bird?"

I put my index finger to my lips and winked.

"Yeah, you fulla gas man."

The kid laughed and rode off.

I was putting up moon balls when a poorly aging Lexus with a white trash makeover blasted into the parking lot and skidded to a stop in front of me. I ignored it. Held my form and watched the ball swish through the net.

The driver hopped out. Squatty, stout. Thick red hairs attempted to sprout from his adult acne. A filthy gray chain hung around his neck. I put him at thirty something with a seventh-grade education and less than adequate ass-wiping skills.

"Luck," he said.

"Cherry ride," I said.

Acne looked me up and down.

"Who the hell are you?"

"I'm the handyman."

"You don't look like no handyman?"

"Yeah, we voted to quit dressing like Schneider at our last convention."

"Who?"

"Nothing."

"What are you doing with that basketball?"

"This basketball?"

I gave it a spin on my middle finger.

"Yeah."

"Thought I'd play a little tennis."

Acne spit on the ground.

"Listen motherfu-"

Enid burst out of the motel office then slowed upon seeing Acne.

"Lonny?"

"Sup, Aunt E?"

Lonny walked over and attempted an awkward hug.

Enid looked ill.

"What? How'd? When'd you get out?"

"Thrilled to see you too." Lonny smiled. "Kicked me out of the cage free and clear. Can you believe it?"

Enid shook her head. "No."

"Turns out there are bigger assholes in this mean old world than me. Thanks to good behavior and overcrowding here I am."

He stepped forward for another hug. Enid recoiled.

Lonny chuckled. "Come on now. I ain't that bad."

"Where you plan on stayin'?"

"Why right here of course."

I looked at Enid.

"I beg your pardon, Enid. Who's this dapper gent?"

Enid clutched the neck of her shirt like something evil was swarming her.

"This. Is. Lonny."

"Her nephew," Lonny spat. "Who the fuck are you?"

"Archibald Moses."

I reached out to shake Lonny's unoffered hand. He didn't take it, just stood there and sneered. I held it there for dramatic effect. One second. Two seconds. Three seconds.

"The hell asshole. Something wrong with you?"

"Sorry. Silly custom."

I put my hand back to my side.

"Arch has done wonders with the motel. Fresh paint, new plumbing, new carpet-"

"Good," Lonny smiled. "I can't wait to see my room."

Enid sighed. "You don't have a room here anymore, Lonny."

"Oh, really, and why is that? This dump looks as empty as it ever was."

"My insurance doesn't cover known felons as guests."

Lonny laughed. "Now, Aunt E. Are you cookin' up another batch of your world-famous horseshit?"

"It's true," I said. "Known felons can't be guests."

"Says who?"

"Your aunt."

"Well, it's a good thing I'm not a guest then. I'm family. You mind if I take a look around. See what Arch here has done with the place?"

I didn't care. Enid looked skittish.

"I'd rather you didn't," she said.

"But I need to get into my room."

"It's no longer your room," Enid said. "Arch is staying there now."

Lonny spat on the ground.

"What about all my stuff, my personal belongings?"

"I boxed them up when you got put away. It's all in the shed."

Lonny chuckled. "Damn, outta site, outtta mind. Hurts if I'm being honest with you."

"You haven't been honest a day in your life," Enid said.

"You still sore about those cookies I stole when I was a kid? You know in prison I learned to forgive and forget. Sometimes, when people are locked up, they get to thinking a bit more. I bet you could do all kinds of thinking in an old folks' home."

"You've got no claim on this property. Nothing." Enid glared.

"Oh, I know that Aunt E. I was just thinking what if you got hurt around here?"

I raised an eyebrow. "How would she get hurt?"

"Place is run down," Lonny sniffed. "What if she tripped on the cracked pavement?"

"She won't. I'm almost done with it."

"If you ain't done, why're you out here playing basketball?"

"I'm waiting for a skid of concrete to be delivered this morning."

Enid smiled.

Lonny sniffed.

"How much you bleedin' her dry?"

"Arch gives me the receipts for all the materials he buys and I pay him fifteen dollars an hour. Plus, I give him a free room."

"Fifteen dollars an hour?" Lonny said. "Hell, I'd do it for that."

"You didn't," Enid said. "Never asked or tried."

Lonny stared at me. "You get done you hit the road."

"That's the plan," I said.

"And no more basketball neither."

Enid stepped forward. "Now Lonny, you're not in charge here."

I smiled. "C'mon, Lon-bronoven. How about a little horse?"

"Shee-yitt." Lonny coughed up a pancake of green phlegm and sent it flying.

"A Mucinex then?" I said.

"How about you go paint that fuckin' sign?" Lonny pointed.

"How about you spring for a new basketball goal?" I said.

"What, you the director of recreatin' around here now too?"

"I think it'd be nice," Enid said. "Some guests might enjoy playing."

"Are you kiddin'? They can shoot hoops in Indiana or wherever the hell else they're from." Lonny tossed a thumb over his shoulder. "Beach is right over there."

I smiled at Enid. "Geography major. Impressive."

"Hardly," Lonny said. "But I know a cop when I see one."

"Cop?"

"Hell yeah. What kind of handy man wears flip-flops?"

"Like you said, the beach is right over there."

Lonny looked me in the eye.

"Whoever you are mister, I'll find out and you don't want to be here when I do."

"Just doing a few repairs for your aunt."

"We'll see about that. Everything better be up to code."

"To the letter," I said.

"Better be," Lonnie said.

"Don't you have some other things to do?" Enid said.

"Yeah," Lonny snorted. "I gotta take a piss."

Without an 'excuse me' or a 'may I', Lonny stepped past us and walked towards Enid's apartment.

"Neat guy."

Enid frowned, "Been a thorn in my side ever since I promised my sister I'd watch over him after she died."

"How long ago was that?"

"Twenty-two years."

"What? He's an adult. I'm sure your sister would understand you cutting the cord."

"I've tried. He won't leave. That boy is nothin' but bad news. Sticks around like napalm."

Lonny kicked open the screen door to Enid's place and strolled out.

"That your jacket on the chair in there handyman?"

"You mean the navy blue windbreaker with the zipper hood?"

"Yeah, that's the one."

"Nope," I said.

Lonny spit another five-star loogie.

"You two churnin' butter?" Lonny snickered.

"Excuse me?" Enid said.

Lonny slid his index finger back and forth inside his hollowed fist.

The smack from Enid was lightning fast. Lonny rubbed his chin and smiled.

"Oh, so you just wish he was."

It was my turn. I swung a thick open palm across the other side of Lonny's face nearly sending his eyebrows on a permanent vacation.

Lonny was stunned. He held his throbbing cheek in his hand.

"I should kill you for that."

"It was more than deserved. Keep it clean around your aunt."

Lonny whipped out a butterfly knife and did the cute twirlie thing with it.

Enid stepped behind me.

Lonny stared at me. Gave the air a few stabs.

"Put it away, Lonny, or I'm calling the police," Enid said.

"You don't need to do that Aunt E. Looks like you already got 'em here."

"Put the knife away, Lonny," I said. "You just got-"

"Shut up, faggot!" Lonny did his fancy twirlie thing again with the knife then put it away.

"You've got three days to finish the work. Got it?"

Lonny got in his polished turd and tried to start it. It wouldn't turn over. He slammed his fist on the dash. Pulled the key out. Shoved it back in. Tried it. Still no go.

"Give it some more dash," I said.

Lonny gave me the finger.

Suddenly the engine roared to life.

"Kiss my ass cop."

Lonny looked back over his shoulder and hit the gas blasting dust and gravel towards Enid and I. For a moment, he lost control and fishtailed nearly hitting my little black friend on his bike.

"Watch it nigger!" Lonny yelled.

Enid gasped.

I watched the kid's shoulders deflate. I jogged over to him.

"Don't worry about him," I said. "He's an ignorant-"

"Redneck," the kid said.

"I was going to say dead man."

"So, you a killer too huh?"

I put my index finger to my lips and winked.

The kid smiled. "You fulla gas man."

5

The rules in my line of work are simple.

Plan precisely.

Execute flawlessly.

Disappear without a trace.

The post-assignment rules are simple too.

Lay low.

Keep to yourself.

Mind your own business.

Things like being social, making friends and hitting the town weren't options.

Provided of course, you weren't bored to tears in a speck of a town called Meemaw.

It had been three days since Lonny's ultimatum and I still hadn't seen him.

"Let's do it again, Tonya."

I was bellied up at a sandy dive called the Lost Sole. A single flip-flop was nailed into one of the shack's support posts. Old Mil was on tap. I was doing vodka.

I had a few hits and pondered my next move.

I had bounties on me in Miami and Seattle.

Maybe I'd ask V for something overseas. It had been awhile since I got some ink stamped on my passport.

Tonya handed me the darts.

"Here ya go."

I walked over to the board and began throwing.

I had two in the bullseye when they came up behind me.

"You the handyman at the Shit Pipe?"

I turned around. Two goons I'd never seen before gave me their best tough guy looks. One had a tattoo of a bluebird on his neck. The other had a nose piercing with a chain that ran to an earring.

"No. The Shit Pipe guy left a while ago. I work at the Sandpiper." I drained my drink. Crunched on some ice. "Do I know you guys?"

They both took a step towards me.

"All you need to know is that you need to leave town," Nose Piercing said.

"Travel agents huh?"

Neck Tattoo looked at Nose Piercing.

"You could say that."

"See, I'm waiting on a new pool pump, so I can't go anywhere. Once I get that in, I should be gone when I'm damn good and ready."

"You're leaving today," Neck Tattoo said.

"You know gents, I have to tell you, as a consumer, the aggressive sales approach has never really worked for me."

On cue, out of a bad 80's action movie, Neck Tattoo turned his neck and popped it.

Other than me and the two goons, the bar was empty. Tonya was the only witness. Still, I didn't want to take any chances. I looked at Nose Piercing. He had a pack of menthols in his shirt pocket.

"Cool. Cigarettes," I said. "Care to step outside so we can have one?"

Nose Piercing looked confused. "Uh, we can smoke in here, douchebag."

Neck Tattoo rolled his eyes and sighed. "We'd be happy to step outside."

I put my glass of ice down and followed them out.

I walked to the back of the place by some beat-up trash cans.

"Here's the deal guys." I looked at Nose Piercing, "Wait, can I have that cigarette now?"

"You serious?" He said.

"Give it to him. It's his last request." Neck Tattoo laughed.

"Sure, okay. Whatever," Nose Piercing said.

He went into his pocket. I brought my left foot up high and down forcefully, caving in his left knee. Nose Piercing screamed and fell forward. As he came down I brought my other knee up into his head and felt his nose explode.

Neck Tattoo whipped out a butterfly knife. It was the same kind Lonny had. I imagined the two of them laughing at the bad guy Christmas gift exchange, *Hey, I got you the same thing.*

Neck Tattoo held out the blade. It was sharp. Shiny.

A dead front tooth hung out of his top gum.

"You're fuckin' dead."

"So's your central incisor," I said.

He lunged at me. I did a quick side step, grabbed his arm, swung under it, brought it around and broke it at the shoulder. One throat punch and he was down.

I picked up his knife, walked over to Nose Piercing and grabbed his leg.

"You guys with Lonny?"

Nose Piercing uttered a weak *fuck you.*

I leaned down, pulled his foot back and sliced his Achilles tendon to the bone.

He screamed in agony.

I walked over to Neck Tattoo.

"You with Lonny?"

Neck Tattoo struggled to breath. Not wanting to lose face to his pal, he choked out a *fuck you* as well.

I grabbed him by the hair and shoved a dart into his ear canal. Thanks to his crushed wind pipe his screams were barely audible.

I squatted down and lifted Nose Piercing's head by his greasy hair. Now he had a new name. It was Cheap Jewelry Driven Deep into Nasal Cavity.

"Listen to me closely. Come at me again and you two will be wearing each other's scrotums for shower caps. Got me?"

Cheap Jewelry Driven Deep into Nasal Cavity nodded.

"Good. Tell Lonny, I said I'll leave when I'm damn good and ready."

I went back inside the Lost Sole.

"I gotta go," Tonya said into her phone with a surprised smile. She hung up. "You're alive."

"One smoke isn't gonna kill me."

"I thought one of theirs might," Tonya said.

"Who? The travel agents?"

"Do you have any idea who those guys are?"

"Looked like a couple of dicks with ears to me."

I had a few more drinks and watched an episode of *Jeopardy.* I hit both Daily Doubles, but would've lost it all on Final Jeopardy. Category: Unreal Estate.

"What do I owe you?"
"No charge, hon."
"What? C'mon. That's crazy."
"No, really. My treat."
I tossed a hundred on the bar.
"What's this for?"
"What I figure I owe, plus tip."
"It's too much."
"Keep it. I lost one of your darts."

6

Cherry cut hair. For an extra twenty she'd do it with her top off.

She also gave massages. If your shoulders weren't sore you could ask her to skip straight to the happy ending.

Cherry wasn't like most whack-off palace queens. She was legit pretty. Had that rockabilly chick thing going on. Swept her hair up in a bandana. Tied her gingham shirt at the waist to show off her flat stomach and pierced navel. She wore guy jeans and let them hang low on her hips showing off her lower back.

Cherry said she didn't feel any shame in what she did. Said women in Africa go topless most of their lives. That the human body was beautiful. People were too hung up on nudity. And more succinctly, if God didn't want her to show off her tits he wouldn't have made them so perfect.

Cherry's reasoning was similar for the handjobs. Gynecologists in the late eighteen hundreds used to get women off all the time, she said. Women would go in for what was then called hysteria and have the doc massage their clits with a vibrator until they came. They considered it a legitimate medical treatment, a way to relieve a woman's frustrations.

She said she did the same thing for guys.

"Some men get lonely and need a release. Some are stuck in dead marriages. All I do is tug on a piece of skin. There's no sex, no touching me, no kissing. Just the jerk, the load, and a handful of cash."

Cherry kept it discreet. Only offered her VIP services to certain customers. She kept a pistol in her top drawer in case – pun intended – things got out of hand.

Her real name was Teresa. As a kid she went by Teri, but after reading S.E. Hinton's *The Outsiders* she changed her name to Cherry after Cherry Valance.

Cherry loved celebrity gossip weeklies and watching rom-coms. To relax she liked to get high and listen to Willy Dixon.

Cherry told me all of this in the span of the twenty minutes it took her to cut my hair.

"How'd you hear about me?"

Cherry worked the scissors with precision and speed.

"I was shooting pool with Elmer the other night."

Cherry popped her gum.

"Elmer. The high school janitor?"

"If you want to be crude about it. I prefer custodian."

Cherry gave me a playful punch and popped her gum.

"He came in here once. Think the menu freaked him out or maybe embarrassed him. He's sent me some good customers though. Hold your head down."

I heard the shears work for a second longer, then Cherry spun me around.

"Whatcha think?"

I looked in the mirror. "It's shorter."

"Are you kidding? You look hot."

I looked again. "Well, I'll be damned."

Cherry laughed. Popped her gum. Hung her tits in my face.

They were nice alright. Of the seventies Playboy variety, natural, heavy.

"What's your boyfriend think about your vocation?"

"Baby," she said. "My boyfriend is battery operated. You can watch me do that too for an extra seventy-five." Gum pop.

"Not today, but thanks for the cut."

"Oh shit."

"Excuse me?"

"I just offered to play with my puddin' and you passed? Nobody does that. You a cop?"

"No."

"Hah. I'm supposed to believe a man that looks like you is really a handyman?"

"What do I look like?"

"You look intense. Like you have an agenda."

"I'm just a handyman that likes seeing the country."

"Oh really, and you wanted to see Meemaw?"

"I did. Read a great travel piece about it in *The New York Times*."

Cherry stuck her chin out. "Oh yeah? What did it say?"

"Come see depression done right."

Gum pop with a smile. "You're full of shit."

"Enid found me on Angie's List."

Cherry moved a brush through my hair along the top of my scalp. Her heaving cleavage was an inch away from my nose.

"You know her nephew?"

"Lonny, the oozing pored wonder?"

"Careful. He's crazy. Stay away from him."

"Trust me. If acne was contagious I'd be wearing protective coveralls and a gas mask."

"He skeeves me out."

"Please don't tell me he's one of your customers."

"Oh, God no! Never. See those locks?"

I looked at Cherry's door. She had given it the six deadbolt treatment primarily reserved for young women in big cities.

"Well, thanks for the cut." I stood up.

"Nothin' else I can do you for?" Cherry smiled.

"Nah. That's it."

I handed her some bills. She looked at the cash.

"With a tip like this you don't need to leave."

"I've gotta a lot of work to do at the Sandpiper."

"Okay then. Well, come see me soon."

"I'm afraid I'll be long gone before I need another haircut."

Cherry popped her gum and smiled.

"Who said anything about a haircut?"

7

Hickok Beach was flanked by rotting docks, empty warehouses and boarded up industrial buildings. There were cleaner areas to the east and west, but for the most part the water wasn't fit to swim in.

I took a seat in the sand.

The juice was Tropicana. The champagne was pure shit. It didn't matter. When I could do a mimosa on the beach I did. To remember them.

I poured the booze into the ice bucket from the Sandpiper followed by the small carton of OJ.

The sunset had turned the busted pier into a stick silhouette.

It looked like something a kid might draw with a black crayon on a pink piece of construction paper. Something she might have drawn.

I drank from the bucket like a prisoner on a chain gang. I wanted the headache that came from the cheap booze, something else to ache other than what was inside of me.

I could smell them. See them. Hear them.

They were beautiful. Perfect.

I pictured her little strawberry blonde bob and seersucker jumper. Her little hand wrapped around my pinky asking me where all the sand came from. My other hand holding her mother's, a Kentucky knockout, with a soft southern accent and even softer skin.

I remembered that day. Remembered it so clearly.

I remembered thinking, God must not exist for a man like me to be so blessed. To have two people I loved so completely.

And then they were gone. Taken away by another man's gun. And it was clear, that there was a God, and he was giving me exactly what I deserved.

Or was he?

Maybe this whole living thing was some kind of twisted cosmic lotto. Traits, handicaps, gifts all doled out randomly and left to chance. Perhaps things like intellect, disease, wealth, illness, family, fame, madness were all tossed into a wind of uncertainty and however they landed on soon to be born souls was the way it was.

I was no scholar or theologian, but given the business I was in, it was good to have some kind of take on the afterlife. After what I had seen and read, the cosmic lotto thing seemed to make as much sense as anything else.

But, if there was no God, then there was no devil. No devil. No hell. No hell, no punishment for the wicked.

And that's where I came in.

"Hey, mister!"

Three approached.

"You the piece of shit fucking my old lady?"

They were bikers. Looked like they'd just walked off the set of a Billy Jack film.

One had a chain. One a lead pipe. The other a knife.

I hadn't been laid in months, but these guys didn't seem to be interested in the truth. I looked in the bottom of my empty bucket then stood up and gave a grin worthy of Warren Oates.

"Fuck yeah I am."

I tossed the bucket and let 'em close in.

Then I went to work.

8

When Enid wasn't feeding me her delicious home cooking, guests were feeding her compliments about the improvements I was making at the Sandpiper.

More and more people were checking in for longer stays. There was happy chatter around the pool again and with the jacuzzi back up and running, everyone had a solid shot at an STD.

I was changing the oil in my truck when two Mexicans in cowboy hats with roosters on their boots walked up.

"Hola, amigo. You see an ugly gringo with red hair roun' here?"

"Does he drive a polished turd and go by the name of Lonny?"

The Mexicans looked at one another and smiled.

"Si."

"I haven't seen him in a day or two. If I had to hazard a guess, he's probably cruising the Piggly Wiggly parking lot for tail. You guys old college buddies?"

"No," the Short One smiled. "But we do owe him a lesson."

"You work for him?" The Tall One asked.

"Sir, I'm a gentleman, but if you insult me like that again-"

The Tall One smiled, "I kid. If you see him, tell him we're looking for him."

"Who should I say is calling?"

"Beans and Rice," the Short One said.

"Those are your names?"

The Tall One shook his head no.

"It's what Lonny called us the last time we did business," the Short One said.

"I don't know about you guys, but those monikers border on being racially insensitive."

They both looked at one another.

"How do you know him?" The Tall One asked.

"Just my luck," I said.

"What is it that you do?" The Short One asked.

"Excuse me?"

"Why are you here?"

"I ask myself that question every morning."

"No. Like here at the motel. What do you do?"

"I train the flea circus in room 205."

They looked at me. Then back to one another. Then back at me.

"You policia?" The Tall One asked.

"Nope."

"You look like policia."

"You guys look like Penn and Teller do Tijuana."

"So, you're comedian or something?"

"Are you guys magicians?"

"No."

"I work for Lonny's aunt. She pays me to put chlorine in the pool to keep Lonny's pee-pee from making people sick."

The two men chuckled.

"You're funny," the Short One said.

"Comico," said the Tall One.

"Thanks fellas. I like your sideburns. Is there a message you'd like me to give Lonny Donny Ding Dong if I see him?"

The men nodded.

"Tell him, we are very happy to hear he is out of prison," the Short One said.

"I'll do that. Anything else?"

"That's it," said the Tall One.

Beans and Rice looked around one last time, tipped their hats and got back into their Lincoln.

Dinner no doubt would be served soon. And it looked like the starter would be toe tag tortillas with pico de Lonny.

9

It was almost midnight.

I was sucking on a pint of Kessler and reading a little Kurt Vonnegut when there was a loud banging on my door.

If it was the kid in the frat pack in 211 whining about losing another quarter in the vending machine, he was going to receive a colonoscopy with his own head.

"Who is it?"

Another obnoxious pounding.

It wasn't Sigma Alpha Douche. Sure, he may have been rude and drunk, but he wasn't deaf and dumb.

I put the book down and tilted the bottle up.

More loud knocking.

I didn't think Lonny had the guts to show up alone, but if it was him I was ready to take him apart.

I swung the door open.

It was Cherry. She was crying and smelled like low end kush.

"Oh, thank God."

She stepped inside and threw her arms around my neck. She was trembling like a scared dog. I held her. Closed the door.

"What's wrong?"

She collapsed on the bed in tears.

"I can't tell you. They'll kill me."

"Who?"

I grabbed the pint and took a seat on the bed. By the time Cherry finished her story I wished I would've had a fifth.

Cherry's mom had been a topless waitress. Her dad was a musician. They met one night when his band rolled into town. Some couples pay tens of thousands of dollars for medical procedures in hopes of getting pregnant. Cherry's dad saved a quarter on the rubber machine at the Stop-n-Go that night and knocked her mom up on the first try.

They decided to make a go of it.

Both found jobs on the strip in Biloxi. Dad dealt cards in between gigs, while mom delivered tall cocktails in a short skirt.

Dad split a few years later to become a rock star and/or hang drywall in LA.

To supplement her income, Cherry's mom soon began bouncing between hotel rooms. Depending on the situation, she'd sometimes bring a big tipper home to her own bed.

As can be expected without a parent in the home, Cherry grew up fast. Her early natural physical development made her desirable to fellow students as well as teachers. She dated both. Sometimes her mom's strays crawled into bed with her.

Drinking on a fake ID at nineteen, Cherry met the man she believed to be the love of her life. He wore a suit and drank scotch and soda. He laid on some lame pick-up line Cherry had never heard before. Took him for a poet.

His name was Dean. He was an accountant. After a couple dates Dean told Cherry he loved her. Four months into their marriage Cherry found out Dean had another love, blackjack.

Dean had markers out at various casinos. Sometimes he'd take out a less than legal loan to cover his debts.

One night there was a knock on the door. It was a man with a gold tooth. He asked for Dean. Cherry said he was on a business trip. The man asked Cherry if she had an envelope for him. Cherry said no.

The man looked Cherry up and down. He told her he'd knock off a hundred bucks of what Dean owed for every time she gave him head. Cherry tried to slam the door, but the man put his foot in front of it. He told her he'd be back in twenty-four hours. By then either Dean would materialize and have his money, or he was going to take his pound of flesh from Cherry.

Dean called Cherry that night. He said he was in Arizona on his way to Mexico. He wanted her to meet him in Nogales. She told him about the man with the gold tooth, the debt and what the man had said.

Dean laughed. He told Cherry to tell those guys to go fuck themselves and get on a plane.

That night Cherry packed a bag. On her way to the airport she was run off the road. It was the man with the gold tooth again. This time with three friends.

They had her call Dean.

She told Dean they were going to kill her unless he paid the men back what he owed.

Dean said he'd be back with the money in two days. He never showed.

The man with the gold tooth told Cherry he worked for Stefan LeVoux. The name didn't register. The man took Cherry to meet Stefan.

Turned out Stefan LeVoux was one of the big swinging dicks in the Confederate Cartel aka the Dixie Mafia aka People Not to Stiff on Loans.

Stefan had short clipped gray hair, wore tailored shirts and silk ascots. He favored leather kilts. His eyebrows were sculpted and he always wore black eyeliner.

Dark-skinned young men in jockstraps delivered Stefan's martinis to him on a tray.

Stefan told Cherry she had a choice, give him what Dean owed in full, or pay it back with interest.

Cherry told Stefan the truth. She had nothing.

Work it was then, Stefan told her.

Cherry started working sex parties for Stefan's associates. One night, as she was being transported back from a party, the driver stopped and picked up some friends. They gang raped Cherry.

The parties, Cherry said, took an emotional toll, but as far as wealthy scumbags taking advantage of an illegal sex ring go, they were gentlemen.

Her rapists? They were savages. Rough and proud of it. Cherry was hospitalized.

She tried to kill herself, but Stefan took pity on her. He put her up in a small apartment across town. Told her she could pay the money back anyway she wanted. But when she healed, he'd need her for the occasional business soiree again.

"I didn't have a choice," she cried. "That's why I do what I do. Otherwise, it would take a lifetime to pay back what Dean owed."

"What happened to the guys that raped you?"

"One is still in prison. One just got out. Stefan killed the man with the gold tooth."

"Why didn't you run?"

Cherry sobbed. "I've tried. They have eyes on me at all times. They said they put a tracking chip in me."

"In you?"

"They said they implanted it while I was drugged."

Poor thing was just a kid. A scared kid controlled by abuse and lies.

"They're lying. At most they have a GPS tracker on your car. Did you drive here?"

Cherry shook her head no.

"That's good."

Cherry bit her bottom lip, tilted her head down and stepped toward me.

"You're saying I'm safe here tonight?"

Her v-neck sweater revealed her ample cleavage.

"You're beautiful," I said. "But I'm not a guy you want to be around."

Cherry's blue eyes looked into mine. She rubbed her hand on my crotch.

"Why not?" She playfully frowned. "You gay?"

In seconds Cherry's hand had me harder than a Kryptonite dildo.

"Does it feel like I'm gay?"

"No," Cherry smiled.

She closed her eyes and went in for a kiss. I leaned out of the way.

"I'm sorry, but you can't get mixed up with me."

"Why? The age thing?"

"No, because…wait, the age thing?"

"Yeah, you're like fifty something right?"

"I'm forty-six."

"So. Two decades? Big whoop."

"It's not my age. It's just not safe."

"Safe? Are you kidding? Like my life can get any worse."

Cherry stepped back and pulled her pink mohair sweater off over her head. Her bare breasts were perfect. She shoved me down on the bed and leapt on top of me. She spun around with her head over my crotch. In seconds, she had freed me from the constraints of my zipper and had my cock in her mouth.

She wrapped her lips tight around my throbbing purple helmet before ramming her head all the way down to the base, taking my full length into her throat.

Her ass hung right above me.

My dick and brain fought for common sense.

Emotional collateral was a no-no in this profession.

Cherry's hot mouth, however, was a yes-yes.

I yanked Cherry's Daisy Duke's down and buried my face between her rounded ass cheeks. Her lips were long, moist and pliant. I sucked on each like stubborn oysters refusing to disconnect from their shells. I drank her in. Her hips jiggled and shook involuntarily as she moaned.

I considered a condom for a millisecond before Cherry gleefully mounted me. I hadn't given her consent, but decided I'd let it slide. And slide she did. Up and down my swollen shaft with the fury of a fat kid trying to murder a pogo stick.

We pounded into one another all over the room for what seemed like an eternity. Afterwards, a quick glance at my watch informed me our passionate fuck-a-thon had clocked in at just over four minutes.

Nonetheless, spent, Cherry fell asleep in my arms.

I let out a long deep breath and looked up at the ceiling.

Nice work genius.

10

I woke the next morning to find Cherry digging in my pants.

"Help you?"

She turned startled.

"Oh. Morning. I'm sorry. I didn't want to wake you. Just need a dollar for the Coke machine."

"You're going to walk out there naked?"

"I was gonna get back in bed if you didn't have any money."

I flipped my pillow over to enjoy the temporary cool.

"Just hit the Mello Yello button. I got it set up for free Cokes."

"What if someone wants a Mello Yello?"

"Nobody drinks Mello Yello, but Lonny."

"Forget the soda," she said. "Roll over. Let me give you a massage."

"I'm good," I said.

"No really."

I begrudgingly flipped over and waited for the-

"Oh my God!"

"What?"

"Your back."

"I told you all about it last night."

I hadn't.

"I don't remember. Tell me again."

The scar was approximately fifteen inches long. It was pink, purple and white. It was a crooked line varying in width, running diagonally across my back from my left shoulder blade to right kidney. It rose above the skin and was crossed with crude stitch marks.

Cherry ran her fingers over my shoulders, sides.

"Oh my God. What happened?"

"Power tool accident."

"It looks like you fought in a war."

"I was painting. Fell on a metal sculpture."

"Where?"

"Some project."

"In Mississippi?"

"North Carolina."

"You travel a lot?"

"Where the work takes me."

"What's in North Carolina? Did you go to college there? Family?" I could feel Cherry's swollen nipples on my back as she leaned forward and squeezed my biceps. "You're in amazing shape. You're sure you're not a cop?"

"I'm sure."

"US Marshal?"

"No."

"One of those NCIS guys on TV or something?"

I spun around beneath her and grabbed her wrists.

"What's going on?"

Cherry started crying.

"I can't do this anymore. They're making me ask. They think you're down here to bust them."

"Who is them?"

"Lonny, he works for Stefan. It's mostly two-bit stuff, but now that he's out he's getting aggressive. Looking to move up."

"You know this how?"

"Lonny was one of the men that raped me. Stefan had him framed for a two-year swing as punishment for disobeying. I'm promised a chunk off my debt to Stefan if I find out who you are."

"I'm nobody. Just passing through."

"Oh please. You show up in dead-end town like Meemaw looking like you do and take a job working at a shitty motel?"

"Trust me. I'm beginning to see it as the piss poor decision others do. Believe me. Look, tell them whatever you want to tell them. Tell them anything you'll think they'll buy."

"I don't want to tell them anything. I just want to get out of here now. For good."

"So, go."

"I can't."

"Why?"

"You don't understand."

Cherry leaned down next to me and lifted her hair. Behind her left ear was a small brand.

"I'm property to them. They move us girls around."

"What about you?"

"Stefan keeps me in town."

"The other girls are run by Stefan's crew?"

"Yes," she sobbed.

"How many?"

"I don't know. Some local politicians and business guys are in on it. One girl ran off, but they got her back."

The incident with Egg Salad had made national news. As much as I wanted to wipe out an entire southern fried sex slavery ring, I didn't have the means nor time to kill everyone involved.

I took a deep breath and looked at Cherry.

Far too many flowers got steamrolled in this world. It was against my better judgement, but the words came out before I could think.

"Pack a bag."

Cherry sniffed. "What?"

"Pack a bag."

"You're going to help me?"

"Get you out of here at least."

Cherry threw her arms around me.

"Oh, thank you, thank you, thank you," she sobbed.

I wrapped my arms around her and looked at our reflection in the mirror.

I was no savior. Not even close.

But if I had to save someone's ass, I was glad it was one as firm and round as Cherry's.

11

After begrudgingly accepting Cherry's thank you sex for rescuing her, I dropped her off with instructions on where to meet later.

I was bummed I hadn't run into Lonny again. My message must've come through loud and clear after I tuned up his goons.

Perhaps it was selfish, but I wanted one final reading session in my favorite spot before I was ready to put Meemaw in the rearview.

I walked up and down the hallways of the empty high school.

Poked my head in a few classrooms.

Went into the gym to check out Elmer's handy work on the court. He'd done a nice job. There was a basketball in the corner. I picked it up, dribbled some, took a shot or two.

I hit the library, spied Flannery O'Connor's short story collection *A Good Man is Hard to Find* and grabbed it.

I crossed the lawn and made my way back to the Sandpiper.

I was happy.

I'd tear through some quality short stories then grab a nap.

Maybe it was time for me to retire? Get out before I got sloppy or worse killed.

Where was the shame in reading poolside for the rest of my life, especially, if I had someone like Cherry in a bikini stretched out next to me?

There were worse thoughts.

Twenty yards from the Sandpiper I wondered if an inexplicable fog had rolled in.

Was I having a stroke?

Losing my eyesight?

I blinked my eyes. Rubbed them.

Maybe I had finally lost my mind. I looked again.

No such luck.

It was real.

Someone had torn down the shed.

My shed.

Its contents were strewn across a large pile of dirt where a deep hole had been dug.

I tossed Flannery over my shoulder. A good man was hard to find, indeed.

But, a bad guy? A bad guy was easy to find.

Especially, if his name was Lonny.

12

I went by the office to see Enid. She wasn't there, but her car was in the lot. I rapped on her apartment door. Nothing.

I knocked a few more times and listened. I could hear muffled sounds coming from the front room. I put my back to the door, brought my knee up high and kicked it open. The place had been tossed like a salad.

Enid's mouth was duct taped. She had a black eye and was tied to a wooden chair. Tears streamed down her cheeks. I counted to three and ripped the tape off her mouth.

"Who?"

Enid sobbed. "Lonny."

"Why?"

"He said something about drugs. Thinks you took them."

"He hid them here?"

Enid nodded. "Thinks you must've found them."

I untied Enid. Looked at her eye. It was swollen and blood had gathered around her pupil.

"He hit you?"

Enid shook her head yes.

"Anything else you can tell me?"

"Yeah. There were two other men. Mexican cowboys."

"Did they hurt you?"

"No, but it looked like they had beaten on Lonny."

"And that coward hit you?"

Enid nodded.

I looked around her modest apartment. A curio had been knocked over. All her glass figurines were broken.

I put some ice in a baggie and handed it to her.
"Do you need me to take you to the hospital?"
"No," she cried. "I'm so sick of him and the burden he's been on my life."
"Sit tight," I said.
One unburdening coming up.

13

I whipped into the parking lot and ran up the stairs to Cherry's apartment.

If I was right, Lonny and his pals were there waiting for me and planned on using her as a bargaining chip.

In spite of years of experience in hostage negotiation, I was hot enough go in blasting. The problem was dead bodies meant disposing of dead bodies. It also meant cops, headlines and investigations. Which also meant an Olympic-sized ass chewing from V.

I had a Bersa .380 concealed and a Judge revolver loaded with .410 shotgun shells.

I knocked on the door. No answer.

I tried the knob. It was unlocked.

I put my shoulder into it and pushed. The obstruction. Two dead Mexicans.

Beans had taken a bullet in the head. Rice had gotten it in the chest. I stepped over the bodies.

A bedroom door was closed. I heard struggling.

"Pizza guy!" I said.

The door cracked open.

A sliver of face appeared on loan from Liberace.

"Well, well. You must be, Arch. I'm Stef-"

I put everything behind my shoulder and drove it into the door. Stefan went down. His forehead busted open and began bleeding.

"Careful there now," Lonny said.

I looked up. Lonny stood behind Cherry. He had her bound to her barber's chair. Her mouth was duct taped. Lonny held a hunting knife to her throat.

"Drop the piece hero."

"Let her go."

"I promise, I'll kill her right now if you don't drop it."

"If you kill her, Lonny, then it'll be just me and you and I don't see you faring well in that one."

Lonny smiled and moved the blade two millimeters. Enough to give Cherry a tiny cut."

"Put the gun down hero."

I did.

"Been expectin' you," Lonny said. "You know for DEA you've been pretty handy over at Enid's."

"I'm not DEA."

"FBI, whatever. You're somethin'. I seen what you done to my boys at the Lost Sole. Time for some payback."

"You send the bikers too?" I said.

"I don't know nothin' about any bikers."

It seemed silly to lie now. Whatever.

Cherry's makeup ran down her face. I looked at her, then Lonny.

"Let her go. You can call in more thugs from Pascagoula. Give me what I've got coming."

"Oh, I plan on doing that, but first I want my cocaine."

"What cocaine?"

"The cocaine I ripped off from the spics. The cocaine that somehow went missing between Enid moving my stuff from my room to the shed."

"I don't know anything about any cocaine."

Lonny laughed.

"You expect me to believe that? Hell, you were guarding it."

"Guarding it?"

"Acting like you were napping on top of that shed."

"Acting?"

"Not to mention sticking your dick everywhere it don't belong."

"I had pot roast, a few meals with Enid. Nothing more."

"Oh, you've had more than that. Like this stuck-up whore right here." Lonny did a Gene Simmons with his tongue and licked Cherry's face. "Been far too long since I've had this one."

Lonny wrapped his arm around Cherry's neck and cut the top button off of her blouse. He brought the blade back up to her throat. Opened Cherry's shirt with his hand and freed her left breast.

"Ooowee!" Lonny brought his mouth right next to Cherry's ear. "Look at these happy handfuls of fun. Damn shame I have to see them this way. If only you'd just given me the full salon treatment like everyone else."

Lonny kept the blade next to Cherry's throat. He reached down and squeezed her left nipple.

Cherry shot up in her chair against the duct tape.

Lonny laughed. Looked at me.

"So, where's my coke?"

"Let Cherry go and I'll take you to it."

"Haha. Right. I ain't going nowhere." Lonny pinched Cherry's nipple again. She jumped. "I'm staying here with this wildcat until you get back."

"You want me to go get it? I could come back here with a truckload of agents."

"You could, but you'd also come back to a dead Cherry."

"Okay, so-"

"So, you're gonna go, but you're not leaving alone."

I followed Lonny's eyes above my head. I turned around just in time to see Stefan's fist in my periphery. I ducked and backed up.

Stefan was much bigger than I pictured him to be. In fact, much, much bigger.

"What's the matter?" He hissed. "Never seen a football player with a flair for fashion?"

"Football player," I said circling. "Where?"

"Delta State," Stefan said. "Linebacker. All Conference."

"No pro?"

"Blew out my ACL."

"Oh really?" I said. "Which one?"

Stefan looked down and pointed.

"This one."

"Thanks," I said.

I reared back and delivered an explosive foot strike straight forward into Stefan's knee cap. I could hear his ACL snap as his knee hyperextended.

"Hey," Lonny yelled. "Hey!"

Stefan screamed in agony and fell to the ground. Before I could reach him, he magically produced a Glock from under his kilt and squeezed off two errant shots.

I did a piss poor dive roll, but still managed to come up in time to grab Stefan's shooting hand with my left and deliver two devastating throat chops with my right.

"Now goddammit," Lonny said. "Hey, hey!"

I grabbed Stefan's gun and kicked him over on his stomach. He gasped for air.

"Hey!" Lonny yelled. "Drop the gun. I'll kill her. I swear."

"Kill the bitch," Stefan hissed.

"Quiet, sweetheart," I said.

I emptied a slug behind each of Stefan's knee caps.

Lonny's eyes were wide.

"Jesus Christ! You can't do that. You're-"

"A killer," I said.

I brought up the Glock and sent the back of Lonny's skull into the wall.

Cherry's eyes were as big as saucers.

I went over and freed her from the chair. Took the tape off her mouth.

Cherry ran over to Stefan and began stomping on him.

"You sick fuck!"

In a flash, Stefan pulled a switchblade out from under his kilt. He slashed at Cherry's feet and legs. The blade just missed, but cut deep into the rubber toe of one of her Chuck's.

I stepped over and brought my boot down on Stefan's neck. Once, twice, three times.

I looked at Cherry. "You okay?"

Despite the tears, she nodded that she was.

"We gotta move."

Cherry got her things together and packed a bag.

"You got any hairspray?"

Cherry bent down, opened a bottom cabinet and tossed me a full can of Final Net.

I turned the gas stove on high.

"Get to the car."

I waited until the fumes were almost too strong to take then put the can of hairspray in the microwave and cranked it.

I hustled down the stairs and considered briefly - for the benefit of Cherry- to do the *badass slow walk away from the explosion thing* like in the movies.

But I didn’t.
I ran.
And it was a good thing I did.
The place went up like a NASA launch.

14

In order to alleviate suspicion, Cherry and I stuck around Meemaw for a few days.

She played dumb for the cops while I put up a new awning over Enid's office.

With the end result being four dead bad guys, the fire department and local authorities poked around just enough to validate their worth to the taxpayers. No tears were shed.

We met Enid at Pat's Spatula on our way out of town.

"The coke fell out of a shoe box while I was moving his stuff to the shed. Can you believe it? A shoebox? What kind of ignoramus puts that much blast in an empty shoe box? Anyway, I sold it to a long-haul trucker I used to date. Thought I'd launder the cash by fixing up the Sandpiper then selling it. Move to Arizona before Lonny got out."

"Solid plan," I said.

Enid shook her head. "I just can't believe it was a lover's spat with that gay from Pascagoula. Thank God my sister wasn't alive to see that. That damn Lonny had disappointed her enough."

"Investigators said it was hard to speculate what happened exactly."

"Speculate?" Enid exclaimed. "The one was wearing a skirt, makeup and no britches underneath."

"I was told the fire crisped them both up pretty good," I said.

"Not good enough," Enid spat. "Fireman told me they found Lonny had gone wristwatch deep in the fairy."

That was Cherry's idea. She had staged Lonny's prostate check on Stefan while I wiped the place down and rearranged Beans and Rice.

Neither of us had a problem with homosexuals, but Lonny did and after what he did to Cherry, she knew the gay rumor would be his final humiliation.

"So, you're thinking Palm Springs?"

"That's what I'm thinking," Enid said, "but who knows? I could get out there and hate it. What about you, Cherry?"

Cherry smiled and threw her arm around me.

"I'm going to tag along with this guy as long as he lets me."

"Where to?" Enid asked.

Cherry shrugged, took a sip of her lemon Coke.

The waitress brought our change.

"Thanks again ya'll."

I left the bills on the table and picked up the solitary quarter.

I tossed it high in the air and flipped it over.

A bronco busting cowboy looked up at me from my palm.

"We're going to Wyoming," I said.

15

We ditched the beat-up truck for a road weary Mercury Marquis in Yazoo City.

The Marquis was old, but had tons of room and an ancient tape deck. The dealer was a sport and tossed in a well-worn cassette of Van Halen's *OU812*. I pushed the tape in.

Other than the occasional semi, the road was clear.

Cherry slept with her head on my lap while I drove.

I liked driving at night.

It was quiet.

I could think.

Meditate.

Cherry didn't bat an eye when I killed Stefan and Lonny. Instead, she just hugged my neck and said thank you. The things she must have endured.

Now they were gone and she was free.

I put the cruise on seventy-five.

I ran my fingers through Cherry's hair and tried to figure out what in the hell I was doing.

Part of me wanted to save her. Be with her. Maybe fall in love with her.

The other part of me knew it was impossible.

People in my line of work that had personal relationships were selfish. Their fear of loneliness put the innocent in harm's way and often got them killed. I knew it all too well. I vowed to never let it happen again.

I had just rolled over a hundred miles out when my phone rang. It was V.

"Let me guess. You were in Mississippi."

"What makes you say that?"

"A minor league crime lord found torched in an apartment with an ex-con? Two known goons disfigured and maimed. Three dead bikers. The Vaqueros twins of the Guadalajara cartel shot to death."

"I know what you're thinking, but it wasn't me."

"What I'm thinking? What in the hell were you thinking?"

"Honest to God. I was minding my own business down there."

"Did you stay out of bars and keep your dick in your pants."

"Absolutely. I don't know any other way to be."

"You're a horrible liar.'

"Please. Tell me," I said, "How is it you always know where I am and what I'm up to? I can't be that predictable."

"I run a crackerjack organization, Arch. That and you make Sherman's March to the Sea look like a Sunday afternoon stroll."

"Fair enough. When's my next job?"

"Depends."

"On what?"

"How long you're going to be with the girl?"

Unreal.

"What makes you think I-"

"Before the cops interviewed her, they thought she was missing. I saw her picture. Cute."

"It's a friendly lift to Wyoming," I said. "I'll call you in a few days."

"Wyoming?"

"Don't ask."

"Why? Because you don't have an answer?"

"No. Because my methods are my own."

"Be smart, Arch."

"Always am."

I cranked up Van Hagar and hit the gas.

I was a horrible liar.

V knew it, too.

16

It was around 9PM.

We were eating at a greasy truck stop with more flies in the dining room than patrons.

Cherry took small bites. The strawberries in the photo on the menu were far more impressive than the red canned goo they had dumped on her waffle.

I chased a mouthful of gravy covered gristle down with hot black coffee.

"Is that good?" Cherry asked.

I slid my Lumberjack Special toward her. She looked at the burnt eggs, fatty steak and barely thawed hash browns.

"No, thanks."

"It's bad," I said. "Not awful."

I had another bite. Hit it with more coffee.

"But if you don't like it, how do you-"

"Eat it?" I wiped my mouth with my napkin. Held my coffee cup out as the waitress came by and refilled it. I thanked her. Looked back to Cherry. "I close off my nostrils. Can't taste anything."

"How do you do that?"

"Trick I taught myself as a kid."

"You had to eat a lot of bad food as a kid?"

"Many times."

Cherry put her hand under the table, touched my leg and smiled. "Finish up. I want to get out of here."

I had made up my mind the night before that my time with Cherry would be brief for both our sakes. She leaned forward and smashed her tits into the table causing her cleavage to nearly explode.

"Where'd you learn to do all that stuff?"

"What stuff?"

"How you handled Lonny and Stefan?"

"I watched a lot of Chuck Norris movies as a kid."

"Who's he? Like Jason Statham or something?"

"Or something. Speaking of fighters, it would have been nice if you would have told me Stefan was a cross between Goldberg and Boy George. Other than his French manicure his hands looked like cinder blocks."

"Yeah, he was big and strong. You seemed to manage just fine though."

Cherry leaned back and took a sip of her lemon Coke. She was beautiful. Naturally beautiful. The kind of girl that didn't need tons of makeup. The kind of girl that didn't deserve to know how ugly this world could be.

I finished my coffee and put a few bills on the table.

A shadow appeared.

A filthy hand reached down between us and stubbed a cigarette out in the tin ashtray on our table.

Smoke was exhaled and blown my way.

I turned. It was an overweight, bearded man wrapped in denim and plaid. He had on some kind of cheap fake leather vest and his nose was flat. Actually, it looked like his head had grown in a jar. He looked at Cherry.

"Goddamm. You might be the prettiest thing I've seen in years."

Cherry smiled. "Why, I bet you say that to all the girls."

The man laughed. "Hard to say much to 'em when I've got 'em bent over. I seen you somewhere. You a porn star?"

"No," Cherry said.

"Yeah, you are. I've seen that face."

I looked at Cherry. It wouldn't surprise me if she'd been in a movie or two. Hell, anybody could be filmed with a smartphone these days. But porn star? What an absurd and antiquated term.

I looked around. The place was old. No security cameras.

"You've got the wrong girl," Cherry said taking a sip of her lemon Coke.

"Mister," I said calmly, "you need to turn around and walk away right now."

"Ha, ha. Oh yeah? Or what handsome?"

"Or you're going to be very, very sorry."

"Sorry? Shit!"

The Trucker grabbed a fry off my plate, dipped it in ketchup then popped it into his mouth. He picked up my water and washed it down.

"Buddy, I'm warning-"

"Shut up, asshole! Can't you see I'm trying to get laid?" The Trucker looked back at Cherry. "So, what's your name then 'I ain't no porn star, porn star'?"

Cherry glanced over.

A quick wink from me erased any concerns.

"Actually, why don't you tell us your name?" I said to the Trucker.

The Trucker chuckled, "You wanna know my name?"

"Sure. No wait. Let me guess. It's gotta be Dick something?"

The Trucker's face went red.

"What?"

"Your name. You've gotta be a Dick of some kind, right? Guessing a fella with a pick-up game like yours either goes by Little Dick or Limp Dick."

He was primed. I was ready.

The Trucker's fist came down hard and fast. I leaned out of the way, pulled the Trucker's arm towards me and locked it under my armpit. I picked up my dirty fork with my right hand and drove it deep into his eyeball. I twisted the fork snapping the lateral rectus then yanked with all of my might.

The man let out a horrific scream,

Cherry put both hands over her mouth.

"Ready?" I said.

Cherry slid out of the booth. I guided her out of harm's way as the man flailed around on the tiled floor with his optic nerve flapping like a wet noodle.

I looked over at our waitress - still as a mannequin - holding out a pot of coffee. I pulled out a few more twenties and tossed them on the table.

"For your discretion in this matter."

The waitress nodded.

I took Cherry's hand and led her over to the convenience store side of the building.

"You want anything for the road?" I said calmly.

"Maybe some gum?" Cherry said robotically.

"Good. Grab some," I said.

I looked down into a bin of ancient cassettes.

A woman in a cheap wig behind the counter said, "Mister. You better get out of here. Police are on their way."

"How far is the nearest town?"

"Ten minutes."

I had some time.

"Are these cassettes on sale?"

"Yes," she said. "But they're all books on tape."

I liked Van Halen, but I'd grown tired of Alex's obsessive use of the crash cymbal. I reached in, pulled out a random cassette and tossed it on the counter.

"You want anything?" Cherry asked.

I considered asking for a peanut butter Twix, then thought better of it.

I looked at the cashier.

"Hey, is that an Icee machine?"

"We call it a Slurpee roun' here."

"Ring me up for a large one please." I tossed some bills on the counter and walked over to the machine. "You want one, Cherry?"

She shook her head no.

There were four different flavors.

I went with original cola. I took a sip. It was flat.

I paid and walked back into the dining area. The Trucker was still writhing around on the dirty floor, his eyeball dangling from a fork.

I called out, "Anybody have a problem with this guy getting his?"

No one said anything.

"Good. You should ice that gaping socket, mister."

The Trucker went for my leg.

I stepped out of his reach and dumped the Icee, no sorry, Slurpee on his head.

"Take it easy, Dick."

I got to the car and immediately felt remorse.

I should have grabbed a peanut butter Twix.

17

I took back roads and rural routes for the next few hundred miles. Nothing but cotton, corn and wind farms.

Cherry was talking. "He made me do one or two scenes in things. He mostly produced the gay stuff. He had some boys. Eighteen he said, they looked younger. He'd have them dance at some of the parties he made me work."

"Hard to believe what some people do for kicks, eh?"

"Do you like what you do?" Cherry asked.

"I think anytime you can make a positive change or difference in someone's life it's a good thing."

"Wait. But, you kill people."

"Right, and sometimes the change I make in people's lives is to end theirs, which for some other people, aka my clients, is a positive."

"Who are these people that believe the death of someone else is a good thing?"

"Well, for one, you. Right?"

Cherry thought about it.

"Yeah. Okay. But who else?"

"Normally, the person with the checkbook."

"So as long as the money is right, right?"

"For the most part. Did you like your job? The uh, haircuts."

Cherry thought about it and popped her gum.

"Kinda. I mean I hated the circumstances, but it was exciting in a way. All different kinds of men coming in. It was kind of like a sexy science experiment, I guess."

"Sexy?"

"Well. Not everybody. Not all the time. What, you think killing people is more noble than getting them off?"

"Well. Not everybody. Not all the time."

Cherry tagged me with a playful punch.

"So, you have to tell me. Are you CIA or what?"

I laughed. "CIA, FBI, UPS, NWA, ROTC, does it really matter?"

"Kinda."

"Why?"

"I mean, you could just be a total psycho."

"If I were a total psycho would I go around poking people's eyes out with forks?"

"Uh. Yeah. Maybe."

"Fair point. Look, I can give you a band of bills right now and you can go wherever you want."

"Wherever I want?"

"Up to you."

"Good," Cherry said. "Because this is where I want to be."

I looked out the window as we passed a sign.

"Osceola, Arkansas?"

"No, dummy. With you."

Cherry's hot mouth went to my neck and ears.

"Fuck me," she said.

By the time I pulled off to the side of the road we were both half naked.

I ambled out of the car with Cherry's legs locked around my waist.

The moon was full.

I laid her gently down on the hood of the car and got my pants down.

She brought her hips up to meet mine every time.

Wyoming, I thought, you're getting a good one.

18

Cherry was fast asleep in the passenger seat.

There was nothing but fuzz on the radio.

I looked at the cassette I had blindly grabbed.

Self-Help.

Out-fucking-standing!

I pushed the tape in and waited for the good doctor to sock it to me.

First. Let me just start this tape by commending you for taking positive action in your own life to make changes for the better in understanding your place in the cosmos by listening to me today.

Perhaps this tape was a gift. Maybe a friend loaned it to you or you bought it. No matter how this tape came into your hands doesn't matter. What matters is you are about to change your life for the better.

What makes a person end up being the person that they are?

Past experiences? Influences? How they were raised? Perhaps a tragedy, an accident, a life changing event? Well, what if I told you...

Cherry sat up rubbing her eyes.

"What are you listening to?"

"Some Tony Robbins knock off with an internet degree."

I ejected the cassette and tossed it out the window.

"What was he saying?"

"Bumper sticker slogans mostly."

"You think those people, shrinks I mean, are for real? Do any good?"

"They're like surgeons and place kickers. Some are reliable."

"You ever seen a psychiatrist?"

I smiled. "How do you think I became the man I am today?"

"What did they tell you?"

"Well, depending on how you play your cards, life can either be a bucket of delicious fried chicken or a bucket of shit with a barbed wire handle."

"Geez. How have your cards been so far?"

"I'm at maybe a three piece of original recipe with a half-eaten biscuit and lukewarm mashed potatoes."

Cherry unwrapped a piece of bubble gum. Chewed it for a bit then popped it.

I was growing fond of the smell. The sound too.

"I want to get a tattoo."

I turned to look at her.

"Yeah? I'm surprised you don't have a bunch already."

"I wasn't allowed to get tattoos."

"Allowed?"

"Stefan hated them. Said the debutante fantasy was what his clientele preferred."

"So, he was your pimp?"

"Not quite. Pimps let their girls keep some money."

"How'd you pay for groceries."

"He gave me a gas card at the Quick Stop."

"That's it?"

"They had Top Ramen. Sometimes fresh fruit."

"What an asshole."

"Yeah." Gum pop. "Do you have any tattoos?"

"You should know."

A playful punch.

"I've seen plenty of military guys with tattoos. Just a matter of taste, I guess."

"Or prudence."

"Huh?"

"For some it may be wise to limit ways that they can be identified."

"Oh," Cherry said. She thought about it for a moment. "So, you mean you?"

I shrugged.

"I mean anybody."

"But you have scars. Can't people identify you with those?"

"Sure, but everyone in my line of work has scars. It's like how commercial fisherman have rough hands."

Cherry felt my hands.

"Your hands aren't too rough."

"No. Just deadly."

Another gum pop and playful punch.

"I'm hungry."

We swung through the drive-thru of a fast food joint I'd never heard of.

Cherry's sandwich was suspect. She lifted the bun. It looked like someone had blown their nose on the American cheese.

"Ughh."

"Don't worry about it," Cherry said.

"Bullshit," I said. "This is a step down from your Quick Stop."

I whipped back into the parking lot and took the food to the counter.

"Help you," a chubby black woman said. She looked like life had already given her a square kick in the ass. She didn't deserve my ire.

"Is there a manager here I can speak with?"

"Joey!"

A skinny kid, maybe nineteen was playing grab ass with the blonde working the drive-thru.

"What is it, Shanice?"

"This man." Shanice pointed towards me.

Joey stepped over. He was wearing a leather choker with a native fish hook pendant that looked like it came out of a gumball machine.

"Sup?"

"Joey," I said. "I'm not satisfied with the quality of this food."

I showed him Cherry's cheeseburger.

"Kay," he shrugged.

"This is the part where you say, I'm sorry sir, what was wrong with it?"

"Kay," he sighed.

I showed Joey the grease soaked bun. The translucent pickle that hung off the side attempting to jump to its death.

"Looks like you ate some of it."

"You know the whole thing with books and covers. We took the obligatory bite."

I thought of Judge Reinhold's Brad in *Fast Times at Ridgemont High*. I thought of mentioning it to Joey, but it was clear the reference wouldn't register.

Joey opened the bag.

"Almost all of the fries are gone."

"Take my word for it, Jo-easy, they were horrible."

"So, why'd you eat 'em?"

"I was hungry. Plus, I figured it was impossible to screw up a French fry. I was wrong."

Joey looked me over. "Yeah, well you don't look like the kind of guy that really needs his ten bucks back."

"Just give me five and we'll call it a day."

"Why just five?"

"Cokes taste great. Plus, I like your ice."

"No. I mean why should I give you any money back?"

"Because your food is not good."

"You think I don't know that. Our employees don't even eat here. Well, Shanice does, but the rest of us eat something before we come in for shift."

"So, do this," I said. There was a clear plastic box on the counter for donations to help cure pediatric cancer. "Give me the five bucks and I'll put it in here to join that lonely nickel."

"I can't do that. Then the drawer will be short."

"Surely, you have a loss report for unsatisfied customers."

"Yeah, maybe. I've never seen one."

I looked around. The place was loaded with security cameras. Joey's pump from the drive-thru was on her cell phone staring at me.

"Joey, I'm at a point where I'm afraid I may begin to use language unbefitting of this establishment. Can we have a discussion outside for a moment?"

The kid must have seen it in my eyes. I was going to make him eat out of the dumpster after I hooked his nose with his cutesy necklace.

"You know what?" Joey said. "Forget it." He opened the register and counted out some bills.

"Atta boy," I said. "You have the key for this box?"

I pointed to the small lock on the donation box.

"No."

"Good."

I pulled a hundred from my wallet and folded it into the slot with the bills Joey had given me.

"Have a nice night, Joey."

I walked out of the restaurant and within seconds felt like a tool.

I was tired. Frustrated. Bummed that I had wasted my time and energy on such a paltry thing as shitty fast food. Cherry deserved better.

I was sick of hiding.

Tired of avoiding places with security cameras.

Sick of truck stops.

Tired of dive motels.

I drove straight into Fayetteville and bought a brand new black label Lincoln Navigator with a twin turbocharged 3.5l engine.

Cherry ran her hands over the leather.

"Oh, my God. This is amazing. This car is more expensive than some houses in Meemaw."

"A step up from the Marquis."

I turned on the radio.

Buddy Guy boomed through the speakers.

"You know what else is amazing?"

"What?"

"Chicago."

19

I hadn't noticed the silence in the car until a future organ donor rocketed by me on a rice burner doing ninety-five in the right lane.

I considered driving up on him and giving him a kiss with my door until I heard a sniff.

I looked over to check on Cherry. She was crying.

I peered out of the windshield and saw the Chicago skyline.

Unless she had been shoved in a trunk and taken across state lines for illicit activities, Cherry had never been out of Mississippi. I reached over and patted her thigh.

"You okay?"

Cherry wiped her eyes. "Yeah."

Then she did something no one had ever done to me before. She picked my hand up and kissed it, then held it between both of hers and rested it back on her leg.

It was such a simple act, but for some reason felt significant.

"So, tell me about them."

"What?"

"The buildings. What are we looking at?"

"Ah, yes. The skyline."

I pointed and went through some of the tallest and most well-known buildings.

I told her how the Sears Tower was the eighth tallest building in the world. How it was built to withstand a three-foot sway in high winds. That you could see four states from the top on a clear day.

I told her about the ninety-fourth floor stair climb race at the John Hancock. The Observatory Deck. That Farley died there.

She hung on every word. It was nice to see something through someone else's eyes for the first time. She looked like a kid in Disneyland.

It was time to drop some coin.

We got a room at the top of the Intercontinental on Michigan Avenue.

Cherry couldn't believe it. The lush bedding, the view. I opened a beer from the mini-bar. Offered her something. She was too excited to drink. She loved the bathroom. The way glass and marble sparkled. The soft towels.

Cherry unzipped and stepped out of her skin-tight cut-offs and peeled off her tube top. She turned on the water, waited for the steam then stepped into the shower. She tilted her head back and let the water flow through her hair.

"How is it?" I said.

"Wonderful. It feels like summer rain."

I undressed.

"Room for one more?"

"Always." Cherry smiled.

I stepped under the other shower head and nearly moaned. After standing beneath the weak stream at the Sandpiper it was magnificent.

Cherry stepped forward and kissed me. It was soft and wet like the rest of her.

We took our time with the soap.

A moment later the bar slipped from my hand and landed on the glass tile near the drain.

Cherry looked at me over her shoulder with an *oh my* hand over her mouth. She bent over and guided me inside her tight ass. I grabbed her hips.

"Let's make some suds, baby," she moaned.

I took off like a high-speed steel piston in Castrol. Within minutes the shower looked like Bobby Brady had been doing laundry.

Maybe it was the mood, the shower, the moment, but we put in the work to make sure we got full use of the entire room. Floor, bed, counters, chairs.

An hour later we were in the hotel bar. I finished my second martini. Cherry was on her third beer.

"Let's go."

"Where?"

"Time to get out of these road clothes."

I threw down some bills and grabbed Cherry by the hand.

We strolled down Michigan Avenue looking in the windows of all the shops. Cherry was like a kid at Christmas.

God, it was nice to be around a smile. A genuine, happy smile. They were in short supply in the circles I kept.

Cherry chose Levi's and Rag and Bone. I hit Ralph's flagship on the corner of Michigan and Chicago.

"You look incredible," I said when I saw Cherry in her new togs.

"You look like a rich professor," Cherry joked when she saw me.

"After my beach bum ensemble, I'll take it."

We took our bags back to the hotel, had another drink in the bar then went to grab some dinner at Joe's.

"Where do people get the money to live like this?" Cherry marveled. "I mean for some people, this is their everyday."

"Some are business people, athletes, engineers, movie stars, crooks. Some deserve their success, some got lucky, some grabbed it when no one was looking."

"How did you do it?" Cherry smiled.

"A combination of all the above."

The food came. Cherry was amazed. Steak, stone crab.

"That steak could feed four people."

I looked down. It was beautifully seared. I cut into it and I forked a perfect piece of pink NY strip into her mouth.

Cherry closed her eyes and shook her head.

"Wonderful."

I heaped more slices on her plate.

The crab. Everything. Top shelf.

The next few days we put the Japanese tour busses to shame.

The Field Museum, the architecture tour, the Lincoln Park Zoo.

Millennium Park, a show at the Vic, a play at the Steppenwolf.

We had ribs at Twin Anchors, dogs from the Wiener Circle and gorged ourselves at Mr. Beef.

One afternoon we took a sailboat out on the lake.

During the sunset Cherry put her head on my shoulder

"This is the best time I've ever had," she said. "I feel like I'm living in a dream."

The poor kid had been stuck in a nightmare long enough. My bullets had killed the demons. Now, hopefully, she could replace the bad memories with good ones.

A drink here and there and soon after we found ourselves at the Redhead Piano Bar. Cherry was wearing a new pair of Chucks. In spite of the dress code I knew the bouncer, Lou.

"You kiddin' me?" Lou said. "She looks like Claudia Cardinale. She could be barefoot with dog shit between her toes and I'd let her in every time."

I laughed. Thanked Lou. He insisted on a picture with Cherry. Kissed her hand.

We found a seat at the first piano.

Of all the great instruments, none ever struck me like the piano. I loved music and bars, but a piano bar, man… a piano bar was as close as a sinner could get to a cathedral and still sin. It was magical, the ice took it's time melting in the cocktails, everyone in the room was your best friend and no matter who was singing, you'd swear to God they were an angel.

Cherry had never been to one before. Nothing like the Redhead anyway. Every time I went it seemed like my first time.

Kenny 'the Chisel' was playing that night. They called him the Chisel because of the way he could chip away at any song he heard for the first time and nail it. I know nothing of the supernatural, but on nights I heard him play, I'd believe you if you told me the man was a wizard.

I couldn't spend enough money that night. I had Cherry under my arm and the best key tickler in the world banging out my own hand selected playlist.

Some patrons were annoyed at first.

I kept having Kenny play *Angel in Blue* by the J. Geils Band, but after taking care of everyone's tab they came around.

I had the Chisel do Warren Zevon's *Desperadoes Under the Eaves,* and Queen's *Somebody to Love.* By the end of the night everyone had called out a song or two. It was official, we were all best friends, if only for two or three hours.

I've always had a solid handle on my booze, but that night I got into the cups. There was no sex. Cherry and I just fell onto the bed in one another's arms.

The Long Island Teas had been good to Cherry. The whatever the hell I was drinking had been good to me as well.

Cherry rested her head on my chest

"Tell me something, Archie. Tell me something no one knows about you."

"Like what?"

"Tell me how you got this scar."

I looked at my stomach. It was an impressive gash.

"That one?"

"The truth. Don't bullshit me, okay?"

I was too groggy to make anything up.

Hell, with it. The truth it was.

"You couldn't try out. They came to you. And you had to green or red light it right there. There were all these tests; Combat Assessment, Combat Operations, Combat Readiness. Military and Ecological Survivability, Weapon Effect, Damage Criteria. There was every kind of physical test and obstacle course you could imagine. We all came from different branches, backgrounds, specialties. Word was they were putting together a squad of some kind. They trimmed us down from one hundred to twenty.

One day the Colonel came in. He rattled off a few things about what an honor it was to still be in contention for the gig. He said a few things about the expectations of the team, the diversity of the operations, the stress tolerance, and gladiatorial acuity in theatre, but no one's ears really perked up until he gave word on the bennies and pay.

There were twenty of us, only ten spots.

They had us climb down into a pit, maybe fifteen feet deep with a thirty-foot radius. There was a cargo net fastened above that ran down one section of the dirt wall. First one out, the Colonel said, won ten thousand in cash and some kind of hot shit wristwatch.

The Colonel blew the whistle.

The first thing one of the bigger guys did was throw up the cargo net.

There was nowhere to go.

In less than ten minutes we had turned each other into hamburger.

Some were laid up longer than the others in the infirmary. Some with more severe injuries. Fortunately, all survived. Thirteen off us came out fully recovered. One more was cut. Two others dropped out.

In the end, it was ten of us.

We were told we were a family, a team, a unit. A good thing since most of us didn't have one in the first place.

You got a wife, Chavez? No.

You got kids, Rhodes? No.

Siblings, Williams? No.

Parents, Moses? No.

Anybody that gives a goddamm flying fuck about you, Vaught? No.

We were perfect. We were the ones.

The ones that no longer existed.

The ones ordered to kill and not die.

After more tests, both physical and mental they whittled us down to eight. They had us all sign wills; how we wanted to be buried and where, what songs to play at our service, who to be notified first, who got whatever shit it was we owned or had in the bank and so on.

We had, they said, the finest qualities they were looking for in an elite kill team. To me, everyone just looked mean and crazy.

Everything was classified. Taking out high value targets, hostage rescue, special recon, whatever the mission, we handled it.

This was back when Saddam was still wasting space.

There was this stronghold. Our intel was about fifty to seventy-five al-Qaeda were running a supply chain of RPG's and AK's between civvies and insurgents. Our job was simple. Kill everyone except for the innocents they were using for shields. Easy, right? What could go wrong?

The firefight lasted nine hours.

Only two of us made it out, but I'm told we did what we had to do. What in the hell did that mean? Who was we? The US military? Me and Vaught?

Sometimes I have hazy recollections of what I pray are only nightmares.

It would have been far easier to die, but I don't know, I'm guessing God nor the devil wanted Vaught or I that day.

I don't remember the helicopter evac. They said I had lost a ton of blood.

They put me in an induced coma and fed me through a tube for five weeks. I shit, pissed and breathed through three more just like it.

When I woke up, I did the rehab. The whole time all I could think about was a juicy cheeseburger and an ice-cold beer.

A few months later when they wheeled me out, it was like they had read my mind. The only problem was the burger they gave me was burnt, with no cheese. The beer was warmer than the fries. Worst of all the ketchup packets weren't even Heinz.

While I forced myself to enjoy my "dream" meal - of which ninety-five percent of the details were ignored - they spoke of my diligence, discipline and clinical accuracy in following orders.

Of my recovery, the doctors said they'd never seen anything like it. I had a few second and third-degree burns, minimal scarring, but other than that no permanent damage to any organs or senses. I was a goddamm miracle, they said. In fact, after a cognitive and emotional stress test I was an anomaly.

For our reward, Vaught and I got to hand pick our own new teams.

As soon as we did they sent us right back in.

The countries changed, as did the enemy and objective, but at the end of the day it was basic high-level cowboys and Indians.

They cut us loose after five or six years. Those of us that still had it together contracted out to private interests. Some moved into the wilderness, others disappeared or escaped into different realities.

Me? I found a new job, and when memories from the old one crept in, I just repeated the mantra: *you did what you had to do.*"

I waited for Cherry to say something.

She was fast asleep on my chest.

I closed my eyes and was pleasantly surprised.

Nothing but black.

20

I woke up the next morning around 11AM. Either I was being waterboarded or my face was being flogged with the slimy tentacles of a highly agitated squid.

"Oh, I need it, baby. Your tongue," she said. "I need your tongue."

It was the first time I'd seen Cherry with a hangover. She had read somewhere that an orgasm quelled a pounding headache after a night of heavy imbibing. Now she was rocking her pudenda up and down my face with the fervor of a pioneer woman scrubbing dirty dungarees against a washboard.

Due to the previous night's escapades my mouth and tongue were dryer than a Palm Springs saltine. Thanks to Cherry's enthusiastic writhing the problem was immediately remedied.

In the end Cherry got her prize and I got some air.

After regaining my bearings, I decided to get my ashes hauled as well. We ran through all the rudimentary positions of a seventies porn film then I shit, showered and shaved.

"You know what kills a hangover better than anything?"

"What?" Cherry said pulling on a black pair of barely there panties.

"Chiliquiles verde and warm ten-dollar beers."

"Where do we get those?"

"Cozy Corner for the first. Wrigley Field for the latter."

"Let's do it," she said.

Two hours later we were in the bleachers of the Friendly Confines soaking up the sun and the bouquet of hastily poured tall boys in plastic cups.

Cherry was breaking necks in her short shorts and tight ripped Save Ferris t-shirt.

Everyone else wanted to break my neck for being with her.

"What a beautiful day," Cherry kissed my cheek. "I love this."

I patted her thigh and kissed her back.

My God, Wrigley Field. Not a cloud in the sky. With Cherry and an early afternoon buzz.

I wasn't foolish enough to believe I'd die of old age. One day a bullet or something else equally deadly would close my curtains for good, but days like that in Wrigley. Days like that, made the realization of my possible demise acceptable.

I had just cracked open my first peanut when my phone vibrated in my pocket.

I pulled it out and looked at the number.

All the things I'd done.

The places I'd been.

Few things phased me anymore, but seeing those old numbers in that familiar sequence gave me chills.

I picked it up.

Didn't say a word. Just listened.

"You need to come back. Now."

21

Cherry was curled up in a ball on the bed crying.

"You're married, right?"

"No."

"You have a family?"

"That's not it."

"Then why can't I go with you?"

"I told you already. Look, I've got money. I can put you up here until we find you an apartment. A job. You can start over. Meet someone. Start a family of your own."

"Meet someone? I've met him already. I want you."

"You think you do. Compared to what you've known I get it, but you're young. The whole world is out there. If your life was a novel you'd barely be ten chapters in."

"I want you in my novel."

I kissed her head.

"Let me be an interesting short story."

Cherry pushed me away.

"You think you're too good for me, that it? Someone better out there for you?"

"No, but I can guarantee there is for you."

"What a cop out."

I felt pangs of guilt. Was it for her, or my own ego that I had given her the whole *Pretty Woman* treatment?

"It's not you, Cherry. It's what I do. You could get hurt, or worse killed. This new thing-"

"You shot a guy in the head who had a knife to my throat. I can handle it."

"I know. You can handle more than most, but-"

"Let me handle this."

Cherry reached down, gently cupped my balls then began a slow stroke. In moments, she was on her knees trying to suck my reason and resolve right out of me.

I hung in there like a champ.

I had been tortured, interrogated, and sliced and diced for intel. There was no way this young beauty was…

"Okay, you can come," I said.

And then I did as well.

22

I took a sip of my coffee.

Cherry popped her gum and patted my thigh.

"So, what's in Southern Illinois?"

"Soybeans. Corn. Meth. Small towns you've never heard of."

"Where you're from?"

I took a sip of coffee and nodded.

"Am I going to meet your parents?"

"No."

Cherry waited to see if I'd offer more. I didn't.

"What's the name of the town?"

"Briarfield."

"You went to high school there?"

"Yeah."

"When's the last time you went back to visit?"

"Never have. I bailed the summer after I graduated."

"You never went back once?"

"No."

"Why?" Cherry popped her gum. "College?"

"I'd hoped."

Cherry ran her fingers through my hair.

"What if we someday became an item, would you tell me all of your secrets then?"

"I don't have any secrets."

"Oh, really? Where'd the glass bead come from that you're wearing around your neck today?"

"Nowhere. A quirk of mine I guess. I wear it every now and again."

"That's it?"

"That's it."

We rolled on for a few miles. Cherry put her toes on the dash and began painting them bubble gum pink.

"I have a question for you."

"Okay, ask away," Cherry said.

"That gun you had in your drawer in your apartment. Did you ever have to use it?"

"I pulled it on a few guys that were getting a little too worked up, but I never shot it."

"It was loaded?"

"It was filled with lead or something. All the stuff Stefan made me do. You really think he'd let me have a loaded gun? I've never even held one."

"You want to?"

"What?"

"A gun. You want to learn to handle a gun?"

"Are you serious?"

I took exit 105.

"I am," I said.

23

"What are we doing here?"

I unhooked the padlock and rolled up the metal door. There was nothing in the unit except for an oiled canvas duffle.

I unzipped it.

Cash. Guns. Ammo.

"Here. Try one of the semi-autos."

I handed Cherry the Sig. She held it in her hand.

"Wow. Is this loaded?"

"Yeah. Safety's on."

Cherry pointed the gun in the corner and did her best shoot 'em up pose.

"Can we drive out to a field and set up a bunch of bottles and cans on a fence?"

"You mean like when first timers do target practice in the movies?"

Cherry's eyes lit up. "Yeah."

"No. Just hold the gun like this." I showed her. "And load the clip like this." I showed her.

"Then what?"

"Aim and relax."

"How do you relax holding a deadly weapon when someone is in front of you trying to kill you?"

"I get a song in my head. Kind of zone out."

"A song in your head? Like what? Something from Metallica?"

"No, something more chill. More relaxed. I normally go with Steely Dan's *Dirty Work*."

"You shoot people to soft rock?"

"Kid, I walked into a drug deal once, humming *Moonshadow* by Cat Stevens and left less than two minutes later with a briefcase full of cash in one hand and a dead man's donut in the other."

"Are you serious?"

"Well, I switch it up sometimes. Maybe do a little Paul Simon or James Taylor."

Cherry's shoulders fell and her head cocked sideways.

"Are you kidding?"

"Do you even know who any of those acts are?"

"I know who Tom Petty is."

"Counts for something."

"Where did this bag come from?" Cherry popped her gum.

"Someone put it here."

"Who?"

"You don't know them."

I grabbed the bag, pulled the door down and put the padlock back on.

"Why lock it? Nothing's in there now."

"There will be. Somebody has to replace the bag."

Cherry wrinkled her nose.

"Why replace the bag?"

"For next time."

"What if there isn't a next time?"

"There's always a next time."

"So, who put the bag there to begin with?"

"An anonymous associate."

"How can they be anonymous?"

"Because I don't know them."

"How can they be associates if you don't know them."

"Because they associate with one of my associates."

Cherry popped her gum.

"So why here? Why this storage unit off this highway? You just randomly knew this was here?"

"I don't randomly know anything. None of them are placed at random."

"Them?" Cherry's head backed up on her neck. "You're telling me you have go bags stashed in random storage units in every state?"

"Not every state. Nothing ever happens in Rhode Island." I slid the mag into the Glock. "You ready?"

"Uh, yeah. I guess so."

"Let's go."

I tossed the bag into the back seat of the Navigator.

"I'm nervous for some strange reason," Cherry said.

"Don't be. Just remember if you fire that at someone keep pulling the trigger until they're down."

"I thought we were going on some kind of fun road trip. You make it seem like we're gearing up for a crime spree."

"No," I said. "We're going to a funeral."

24

Interstates became highways, highways became two-lane blacktop. Buildings turned to barns. Wind farms to silos.

Traffic was no longer a log jam of commuters, but instead a dented pickup waiting to get around a tractor that was taking a shortcut down the road.

We passed double wide trailers on hills with cows grazing below them.

Beat up houses with sparkling above ground pools.

Corn ran up to the gravel shoulders of the road for a few miles.

"This isn't much different from Meemaw." Cherry popped her gum. "I think I'll fit right in."

I smiled.

"What? Oh no!" Cherry deflated. "You think people will think I'm a stripper."

"Plenty will hope."

Cherry popped her gum and gave me a playful punch.

Seeing old familiar farms brought back memories, strange feelings. I was rolling in with a grab bag of excitement and trepidation.

Cherry clapped.

"Oh my God. Is this it?"

I looked up and saw the battered sign with fresh paint.

Welcome to Briarfield – Pop. 5,200

As soon as we crossed the railroad tracks the lights blew up behind us. Moments later a siren added to the obnoxious display.

"Is he after us?" Cherry asked.

"He is."

"But what did we do?"

"We came back."

I slowed down and pulled over to the shoulder.

I adjusted the rearview mirror and nearly burst into laughter at the site.

It was Dallas Roth.

"Stay put. I'll be right back."

"But-"

I muted Cherry with a slam of the door.

I walked to the back of the car. It was a souped-up Dodge Charger with Sheriff painted over a big gold star. The man standing next to the car was average height and build. He was leaning over his open door with a toothpick hanging between his teeth. His crisp khaki uniform had been over starched.

"Well, I'll be dipped in shit. That really you, Arch?"

It was Dallas Roth all right.

"Hi Dallas. How've you been?"

"Well, well, well. The prodigal son doth returneth."

I cocked an eyebrow. "That's an impressive biblical reference for you, Dallas. You a church goin' man these days?"

"As a matter of fact, I am. Not always mind you, but as a servant of the people it doesn't hurt to keep up appearances."

"What are you doing in the Sheriff's car?"

"Whatever, I feel like. Benefits of the badge."

"Ah, so the yearbook superlatives were correct. Most Likely to Abuse Power, Dallas Roth."

Dallas spit off to the side. Pretended he didn't hear me.

"Back for the reverend's funeral?"

I nodded.

"Sad situation. Sad indeed," Dallas said. He looked back at Cherry. "Who's that sweet piece of ass you got up front with ya? I better go up and introduce myself. Wouldn't be polite otherwise."

Dallas strolled up to the passenger window. He tilted his hat back and leaned in.

"What's this about officer?" Cherry asked.

"Just a routine traffic stop, ma'am. Nothing to worry about. Actually, just welcoming Mr. Moses home."

Dallas stepped back and mouthed the word *WOW* as he walked back towards me.

"Man, she is smokin'. I'd give half my pension just to watch her pee."

I gave Dallas an odd look.

"It's just an expression," he said. "Where'd ya find her?"

"We met on a country road twenty-three years ago when my wife gave birth and I delivered her."

I watched Dallas' face turn beet red.

"She's your daughter? Now look, Archie. I didn't. I had no idea that-"

"It's okay, Dallas. Really. Relax. I think she'd be flattered to know you'd decimate your retirement savings just to watch her urinate."

"Now listen, man. Please know-"

"You don't have to say another word, Dallas. It's fine. You had no idea."

"You're darn right. No idea at all. I mean. None. Whatsoever. I am so sorry. Please forgive me."

"It's okay, Dallas. Really. Just try to clean it up a bit, huh? For the sake of the badge. Keep up appearances. You know?"

"Sure thing," Dallas said.

"Anything else you need? Want her to get out of the car and dance around for you?"

"No. No. Not at all. Just wanted to pull you over and say hello. It's been a long, long time. I'm 'sposed to tell you to get up to the courthouse as soon as you can. The Sheriff is waiting for you in his office."

"Thanks Dallas. Oh, one other thing. She's not my daughter."

Dallas' face turned beet red

"You think I didn't know that? Shit, I knew it all along."

Dallas got back in the Dodge and peeled out. It was too much car for him. He struggled to regain control behind the wheel. He nearly plunged into a ditch before getting it back in line.

I almost felt sorry for him. It had not gone the way he'd rehearsed.

25

I gave Cherry a hundred bucks and told her to explore Main Street. With eight buildings, three reaching the height of two stories, I knew it'd be a brief adventure.

I walked into the courthouse. Despite its age, it stood proud. The hallways were narrow and dimly lit. Had it not been for a large window missing a curtain at the end of the hall I might have missed the painted glass door.

I knocked and went in.

The room reeked of cigarettes, strong coffee and after shave.

Spaceman was still thin as a reed but his long blonde hair was now shaved into a high and tight. Age and time had done little work on his face, but his eyes looked like he hadn't slept in days.

I didn't know whether to expect a haymaker or a hug.

We settled on a firm handshake.

"Thanks for coming. Take a seat."

I pulled out a metal chair. The seat stuffing was brown and brittle where the pleather cover had ripped ages ago. I sat down.

Spaceman took a drag off his cigarette and studied me.

"How long's it been?"

"Twenty-eight years."

"Jesus Christ, Archibald you look like shit."

"I was wondering if you had AIDS," I said.

Silence.

We both burst into laughter, got up and this time embraced for a second or two. The first second was warm, the second awkward.

Back in our seats, Spaceman tapped his cigarette over a round glass ashtray.

"How was the drive down?"

"Fine. Tell me about Bob."

"Let's take a ride."

Robert Cole, or Colesy as we had called him back then, was an offensive lineman on our high school football team. He was one of those guys that seemed frightened by their own strength. He would brutalize guys on the field, but off it he was the one of the nicest guys in school.

"A pastor?"

"Can you believe it?"

Spaceman led me up the steps of the church, down the hall and into Bob's tiny office. The room smelled of old books, Bibles, hymnals. A print of Christ on the cross hung behind his desk.

"This is where he did it?"

"Cut him down myself," Spaceman said.

I looked up at the fan in the ceiling. It was cheap.

"How did that hold?"

"Inch and a half screws into a support beam."

"Any thoughts as to why he did it?"

"I'm guessing this."

Spaceman held up a brown plastic bottle.

I felt a jolt like I hadn't felt in ages.

"They still make that?"

"I guess."

"Where'd it come from?"

"No idea. One was dropped off in front of my office just like it a few days ago. My guess is you'd have gotten one too if anyone knew where the hell you were these days. Somebody is fucking with us, Arch. And whoever it is we need to shut them down."

"You think someone saw us?"

"Had to."

"That's impossible. Why wait until now?"

Spaceman tapped out another cigarette and lit it.

"I'm up for re-election."

"Against who?"

"Dooley Hicks."

"He wouldn't-"

"Nah, I don't think so."

"Do you have any debts? Gambling?"

"No."

"What's your rep in town?"

"Come on, Arch. I was elected by the people four straight terms."

"You must've pissed somebody off."

"I've put away a ton of scumbags. Some have bounced in and out of the system. Some have disappeared. Others moved away somewhere."

"How many busts resolved in sentences."

"Shit, I don't know. A hundred or so?"

"Damn. So, it could be anybody."

"Provided they were there that day. Which, if that were the case I'm guessing they would have tried to bargain with me when I arrested them."

"So where do you wanna start?"

"That's why I called you."

I picked up the bottle and looked at it, amazed the dumb cartoon label could evoke such unease. It was a fat white guy asleep in a hammock with a straw hat pulled over his face.

Tahiti Tom's Beach Butter. *Never burn. Always brown.*

26

It was one of those green-eyed bug shit, crazy things to do in high school. Like jumping off the trestle bridge at midnight or leaping back and forth between swerving pick-up beds blasting down a gravel road.

The spillway was different though. It took more than just a cheap beer buzz and a misplaced dose of testosterone.

The spillway took strength and athleticism.

A keen sense of awareness.

Timing.

Guts.

It also took balls.

Balls to fly the bird in the gnash-toothed face of fear.

Dug out back in the 1970's by the Army Corps of Engineers, Green Reservoir's sole purpose was to irrigate surrounding farmland in Shoal County.

This was done by constructing a spillway, a hollow cement tower that rose teen feet above the surface of the water and went thirty feet down into the belly of the reservoir. After a heavy rain, the water level would rise and rush through the flood slats of the spillway.

Once the spilled off water fell down to the bottom of the tower it rushed down a pipeline which ran beneath a large embankment out to the other side.

At the end of the pipeline was a shallow stilling basin. At the end of the basin were three tall cement blocks that broke the spilled off water into three different chutes that led to three separate stream beds.

The pipeline ran down at a ten-degree angle. It was roughly a hundred and fifty feet long and four feet in diameter, or as Tim Stoobe had discovered after two hits of acid on a hot summer day in 1977, just big enough to sit in and slide down if the water was rushing.

To do the spillway, or as some knew it, Tim's Tube, you first had to find Green Reservoir. This involved navigating numerous poorly marked county roads, some of which cut through several corners of private property. Not a big deal if you didn't mind a little buckshot Swiss cheesing your paint job.

Like all destinations of lore there were numerous ways to get to the spillway.

To ask five different people was to get five different sets of directions, each rationalizing the merits of their preferred route. No matter your choice, if you wound up in the shadow of a monstrous boulder you made it.

The boulder sat in the middle of a heavily shaded, deeply rutted dirt road. Roughly the size of a VW bus, the boulder had originally been painted a bright traffic yellow. Twelve-inch tall capital red letters ran off some spiel about *State Property, Danger, Illegal Trespass, Fines...*

Or translated through the mischief of youth, *Come on in!*

Graffiti had taken over where time and weather had chipped away at the original paint. Once parked, it was a thirty yard hike up the reservoir's access road. Ancient beer cans nested in the tall weeds. Cigarette butts, faded candy wrappers and other debris peppered the scrub.

Known as Last Chance Trail to some, the walk was just long enough to scare the uninitiated with bullshit tales of water moccasins, snapping turtles and killer catfish. Those that turned back were laughed at and ostracized by some, envied by others being peer pressured to keep going.

At the end of the trail was a large clearing. Beyond that was the steep overgrown embankment that supported the reservoir. It was a toss-up whether snakes or insects liked the place more.

At the top of the embankment was a ten-foot-tall chain link fence that wore a slinky of razor wire like a crown of thorns. *No Trespassing* signs were u-bolted every three or four galvanized panels.

The fence ran around the east end of the reservoir while the rest was protected by dense woods. Years earlier, Tim Stoobe and some of his buddies had used bolt cutters to cut away a section of fence just big enough to crawl through. The rusted jagged edges had been bent back to avoid a trip to the hospital for a tetanus shot.

At the edge of the cool, deep water, jeans and boots were tossed on the bank. Toes and feet squished into the dank mud before the water deepened enough to kick out. After a forty-yard swim to the concrete structure you had to climb up nine protruding rusted rungs to the top. On top of the tower was a large heavy steel lid which had been pried and left open.

One end of a long and thick weathered rope was tied to a rusted rung on the side of the tower. The other end of the rope ran thirty feet down to the bottom where the pipeline was. Using the rope, one would repel down to the bottom as water violently crashed on top of them through the slats.

Joined by a few friends at the bottom, a heavy, ancient, thick mossy board was lifted to block the entrance of the pipeline. Once the water rose shoulder high, the board was heaved aside and along with the rush of water, everyone blasted down the long slimy tube.

It was pitch black save for the speck of light at the end of the tunnel where another rope hung. If you were in front, it was your job to grab the rope and hold on like hell as everyone else ran into you, thus keeping everyone from pancaking into the tall cement dividers.

Once everyone dropped into the spilling basin, high fives were given and war whoops were hooted for surviving the world's most exciting and horrifying waterslide, the spillway, aka Tim's Tube.

It was perilous toil for such a brief and foolish thrill, but those that did it enjoyed watching their social status rocket from cool to kick-ass within a matter of minutes.

Crawling out of the basin and toweling off, bruises, scrapes, and cuts were all meritoriously presented as physical badges of bad-assery.

Occasionally, somebody would get a wicked case of poison ivy.

Broken bones were rare, but they happened.

No matter the physical malady, in the end, everyone walked away with a hell of a story.

Well.

Not everybody.

27

After three straight days of rain the sun finally rose.

In spite of the streets being pockmarked with puddles, everyone was anxious to get back out and enjoy what was left of summer.

The humidity was already at steam level by nine.

By ten Spaceman and I were doing the obligatory laps through town in his beat-up Monte Carlo.

We hit the park, Main Street, cut through the Dairy Queen parking lot onto Delaware Avenue.

Repeat.

Spaceman cranked up some Dokken as we went by the pool.

"Nobody'll be here yet," I said.

We crested the hill and looked down towards the pool. There in her lifeguard red one piece was Justine Lang wiping down chairs, while Emily Johnston was squeegeeing off the pool deck.

Spaceman and I both lifted a hand. The girls smiled and waved back.

"Glad we got to know them when we did."

"God bless that long bus ride back from Edwardsville," I said.

"And the heater being busted."

Back on Main Street a giant turd blew by us. On second glance it was Jarvis Koontz in his Ford Bronco. He and Emmet Turley had apparently just gone muddin' and were more than proud to leave a brown trail of wet earth in their wake for all to see.

"Choo fuckers doin'?"

"What's it look like, Jarvis? We're snowmobiling."

"Fuck you, Archie. One of these days…"

"One of these days," I chuckled.

Spaceman drove out to the empty parking lot by the fairgrounds. Long glassy puddles made it a perfect place for donuts. After about three we both felt kind of dumb and got back to cruising the main drag.

Tom Burke was wiping down the cars on his dad's car lot.

Vic Anders was moving water with a push broom in front of the bank.

We were all hot shit, freshly graduated, seniors. While the world awaited us and our contributions, some already knew their lot in life.

"I'm thinking of taking some classes at Pioneer. See if I like it, before considering a four-year school," Spaceman said.

Community college was a sound move for Spaceman. He and books were a rough and brief courtship at best.

I had applied to two four-year schools, one out of state and gotten into both. I liked history. Thought maybe I'd become a teacher.

Still, I hadn't responded to either of the acceptance letters in hopes my procrastination would somehow slow time for one last fun final summer.

I was surprised when Paige told me she was staying in state. She always seemed to be in a rush to get out of Southern Illinois. We had dated off and on for two years. In spite of our rocky patches I always felt what we had was far more than just physical. As little as I knew about love and as naïve as I was, I sometimes imagined us married with a bunch of kids. We had already come close a few times when we were too eager and skipped the rubber. Fortunately, all her late days were just that, late.

Spaceman swung a wide curve around a huge puddle.

"I'm sorry to say it, Archie, but she's gonna take those big ole titties down to Carbondale and someone else will be playing with 'em by fall break."

I knew Spaceman was right. Paige was pretty, popular too. A lot of her popularity hinged on her gift to flirt and soak up the attention of her admirers.

Paige's family had more money than most in town. Her family leased farm equipment throughout the tri-state area.

Paige's family's money allowed her to travel. Some trips more glamorous than others, but all were taken without me. There were rumors she had hooked up with a college guy on Spring Break in Cancun and with another dude on some ski trip in Taos. She had explained the hickeys on her stomach away as bruises from wiping out on a black diamond run.

She was full of shit.

I was no saint.

It didn't matter, we were just kids.

"You know why it's illegal for kids to get married?" Our health teacher, Mr. Brown used to say before every school dance. "Cause they shouldn't be. Don't waste your teen years dating just one guy or girl. Mingle. Mix-it-up. Have some fun. You've got the rest of your life to be tied down to one person."

Mr. Brown's comments seemed random and quite dubious at the time. It wasn't until my sophomore year we all discovered he was on wife number four. In fact, the great Shoal County High crab outbreak of 1987 was credited to Mr. Brown's frivolous proselytizing. Nonetheless, had it not been for his wise words, many of us would not have been inspired to have had the fun we did back then.

Still, that Paige thought I would believe her ill-gotten hickeys were bruises from a skiing accident was insulting.

But like many teens in a serious relationship staring down an impending graduation with separate futures on the horizon, we did what most do, we didn't think about it.

28

It was around noon.

Spaceman and I each had a cold beer in hand and the stereo cranked.

We swung back by the pool.

"Damn. Just moms and little kids."

"What about Nita?"

I scanned the pool deck for a woman with a huge beehive hairdo.

"Nope."

Nita was Kelly Cook's hard partying aunt. While only thirty-six, Nita's beehive hairdo was right out of the nineteen sixties. One weekend she agreed to host a party for Kelly and supply the booze if Kelly supplied the teenaged guests.

Spaceman was rolling a joint on the toilet in the bathroom when Nita barged in. She had on a pair of her niece's Umbro soccer shorts and said something about how limber she was thanks to Jazzercise. She threw her right heel up on the towel rack behind Spaceman's head then pulled the crotch of her shorts to the side to show Spaceman where babies came from.

Spaceman gave it a look. Nita asked if he liked what he saw. Spaceman told her he didn't think having two beehives was necessary, but sure why not? Nita asked if Spaceman knew what to do with it. Spaceman did. After that, Nita became Spaceman's second string hook up when things got slow.

"Where in the hell is everybody?"

I crushed my empty can and tossed it under the passenger seat.

"Ready?"

Spaceman nodded. I reached back and fished out two ice cold cans of Natty Light from a Styrofoam cooler.

We blew back down Main Street cranking *Ride the Lightning.*

"There. DQ."

In the Dairy Queen parking lot was a car full of girls. Sophomores.

Spaceman spun his tires like he was coming off pit row. We rolled into the lot.

"What are you sweet young things up to?" Spaceman said, before taking a swig of beer.

Tina Hart smiled. She was the best of the bunch and had the butt to prove it.

"Movie in Mount Vernon. What about you guys?"

"Movie?" I said. "It's gorgeous outside."

Tina wrinkled her nose. "It's hot and sticky out." She and the rest of her crew sucked on Mountain Dew through straws. "See you at the pool maybe later this week?"

"Yeah, sure. Maybe," I said.

"You believe Ross Brown is getting that?"

"That's what he says anyway."

"You think he's lyin'?"

"I don't doubt he's tryin'."

We agreed on one more lap through town before going our separate ways for the afternoon.

Spaceman and I were arguing over who was better, Judas Priest or Iron Maiden when he swung a left on Rose Street. He blasted through a puddle and sent a massive wave onto a couple of kids playing on the corner. One laughed. The oldest one, maybe twelve, shouted obscenities.

Moments later someone leaned on the horn behind us.

Spaceman stopped at the corner.

A white Suzuki Samurai rolled up next to us. It was Karen Stone and Amber Roth dressed like they were coming from a RATT album cover shoot.

Amber looked down her nose. "That was mean, Spaceman."

"Just water. You've had more dumped on you in a wet t-shirt contest."

Amber feigned outrage while Karen and I laughed.

"Still, pretty immature," Amber said.

"Immature?" Spaceman laughed. "What are you guys, moms now?"

"We're only twenty-four," Karen said, flying her middle digit.

"So, where's the party?" Amber smiled.

"Hell, if I know. Town is deader than a doornail."

"I wanna do something," Karen said. "Something really fun."

"Fun, huh?" I said. "You mean like go to the mall or hit the amusement park?"

"Maybe hit up a play or one of the local museums?" Spaceman added.

"Smartasses."

"Pool?" Spaceman said.

Karen rolled her eyes.

Spaceman polished off his beer and belched the word boring.

"Gross," Amber laughed.

"I was going more for immature," Spaceman said.

"Come on guys," Karen said. "I've spent three days inside. I want some sun."

"Rope swing?" Spaceman tossed out.

"Can't," Amber said. "All the junior high kids hang out down there now."

"Yeah, that place used to be cool," I said. "When I was twelve."

"Whatever. We'll let you ladies get on and do your thing. I'm dropping Arch off then I'm heading home for a nap, maybe watch Whitey and the Cards."

"Lame," Karen said.

"Yeah, well," Spaceman said. "What about Shively? What's he up to?"

"Workin' like always," Karen said.

"You guys still engaged?"

The question hung in the air for a moment. Amber looked at me and laughed.

"Not that engaged. Right Archie?"

"Shut up, you guys," Karen said blushing.

Spaceman revved his engine. "Alright. We'll see you guys."

Karen frowned.

Spaceman was just about to put it into gear when I heard it come from somewhere deep in my throat, "How about the spillway?"

"Huh?" Amber said.

"Tim's Tube?" I said.

"It's been raining non-stop," Amber said. "Won't it be muddy and gross?"

"Best time to go," Spaceman added. "Water'll be hummin'."

"Let's do it," Karen said. "It will be fun. We'll meet you guys on Route 5 and then get in with you."

"Cool," Spaceman said trying to sound casual. "Let's meet at two. Gives us an hour."

"Sounds good," Amber said.

The girls took off in Karen's Samurai.

Spaceman and I stayed back for a moment and high-fived.

It was going to be one of those epic days kids only dreamt about in high school.

One that never happens.

Only this time, it was.

29

Paradise City blasted through the Spaceman's speakers for the bizillionth time that summer. Karen and I yelled the words to each other in the backseat testing one another's lyrical accuracy and retention.

Spaceman drove with his left hand and air drummed with his right. Amber pulled down her vanity mirror and gave Karen and I a long and healthy stare.

"You okay?" Karen asked Amber.

"Cute couple," Amber smiled then flipped the mirror up.

The corn was high and the air smelled sweet.

Karen leaned towards me and whispered.

"Sometimes I want to call you."

"Is that right?" I said.

Karen and I had hooked up once before.

Half hooked up, I guess.

It happened at Ryker Files's pole barn bash. Ryker had some decent acreage, big equipment meant big barns. Every Memorial Day he put a pig in the ground and hired a band to kick off the summer. If four kegs didn't float that night it was considered a failure. It never was.

I had stepped outside to take a piss just in time to see Shively Barnes tear off in his shiny new Pathfinder. The cloud of dust mingled with the mosquitoes moshing beneath the glow of the lamp post.

I zipped up and walked back from a small stand of trees. Karen was sitting on the hood of Amber's beat up Camry exhaling a little homegrown.

"Why, Karen," I said feigning shock. "I didn't know you partook."

Karen laughed. "Small one. Barely a pin."

She offered me what was left. I took it.

"I don't know if I can marry him," she said.

"Who? Shively? Why not?"

"Do you think he's too old?"

It was a strange conversation to be having out of the blue. Karen was cool, but she was already out of high school before I went in. The most we had really ever talked had been the random hello.

"Shively old? Not really. He's rather strapping when his dentures are in."

Karen did one of those odd sad grins.

"Shut up. Fifteen years. Big deal. Right?"

"Hey, if you love him-"

"I don't know that I always do. I mean it all kind of came out of nowhere."

Everyone in town saw the Shively Barnes and Karen Stone engagement for exactly what it was. A wealthy older farmer locking down a younger local babe with a lifetime supply of boxed Zinfandel and a chaise lounge to drink it on.

Shively had been a bit of a hell raiser in his day, but time and farming had mellowed him. Now he just wanted a hot wife to keep him warm when he wasn't in the cab of an air-conditioned combine.

Karen didn't come from much. Having a man of means appealed to her.

"You know the day he bought me this engagement ring in Evansville, we also stopped to look at a backhoe? Our celebration dinner was at Grandy's."

"I guess you could always take a bus out to LA. See if Vince Neil is available."

Karen hopped off the hood of the car.

"Yeah."

There were voices, laughter.

Small red cigarette tips burned in the distance.

I was over Karen's pity party. I turned to go back to the barn when she grabbed my hand.

"I gotta pee. Look out for me?"

"Okay."

Karen led me over and crouched down in front of Amber's car.

"Let me hold your hand so I don't fall over."

I held my hand out. She grabbed it. I turned to give her privacy.

I'd be lying if I said I wasn't a bit turned on. I had been dancing and hanging out with Amy Rooks inside, but this was Karen Stone we were talking about. Nothing wrong with a little harmless flirt.

"Okay, you can turn around."

I did.

Karen was holding her Guess mini skirt up with her forearms and was in the process of pulling her G-string up with her hands. I could make out a small tuft of bush.

"You want me to leave these down?"

I felt a rush to my head. My body felt like one gigantic heartbeat.

"Huh?"

Karen laughed and pulled them up.

"Kidding."

She stepped forward and palmed the front of my shorts. I was at half-mast.

"What's going on here?"

Karen leaned forward and kissed my neck. She smelled good. She ran her tongue up to my ear and whispered.

"I want to suck you off."

Shively Barnes was not one you wanted to cross, but I was hard in the dark with his horny fiancée.

"What?"

"I want to blow you."

Karen pushed me back against the truck, got down, unzipped my fly then put her hot mouth around me. I had heard older guys talk about Karen's legendary oral skills, but at that moment it was clear they had sold her short.

A few minutes later a barn door opened. I heard a group of voices walk out. Karen popped up just in time.

"Archie, you bad boy." She winked and reached for my beer. "You're supposed to let me know if you're going to do that."

"The epileptic fit my legs were having wasn't a good enough sign?"

She laughed. "We should go back inside."

"Different times and doors," I said. "I'll head in in a few."

"Archie! Archie!"

I looked up from the memory. Spaceman was looking at me in the rearview.

"Beer me, will ya?"

"Anyone else?"

"Please," Amber said.

I passed up two beers.

"Fire up that fatty, Am," Karen shouted over Def Leppard.

Amber turned and held up a burning cigarette.

"I just lit this."

"Ugh," Spaceman said. He grabbed Amber's cigarette and threw it out the window.

"What the hell?" Amber said.

"Cigarettes are disgusting," Spaceman said. "This car is weed only."

"Yeah. Burn that jay," I said.

"Burn that jay, burn that jay," Karen and Spaceman joined in.

"Okay, but you owe me a Marlboro Light, you sonofabitch." Amber playfully hit Spaceman on the head.

Amber fired up a thick joint. A moment later she exhaled a chest full of skunky smoke. She passed it back to Karen who took a long hit.

"Strong?"

I immediately felt like a lightweight for asking.

"You tell me."

Karen turned my head like we were going to kiss and blew her smoke into my mouth.

She passed it up to Spaceman.

"Of what strain am I about to partake?" Spaceman asked Amber. "Dixie Ditch? Omaha Slaw?"

Amber smiled, "Try my mom's ex-boyfriend's back yard."

We laughed.

"It's not what's in it. It's how it was rolled," Karen giggled.

Amber turned back and smiled, "Shush, I was kidding when I told you that."

"What?" Spaceman asked.

"Amber has a creative way of moistening the gum on the rolling papers," Karen laughed.

Spaceman smiled, "Say no more."

He hit the jay down to the nub and tossed the roach down his throat.

"You dummy," I said. "She uses the sweat from her asshole."

We all broke up.

Amber scooted closer to Spaceman and kissed his neck.

Everything felt good. The sun, the music, the fresh air.

"Oh my God, I'm so excited." Karen clapped.

"Maybe we should do something else," Amber said.

"Are you crazy?" Spaceman said to Amber. "It's a perfect day for it. This could be our last hurrah."

Amber's eyes were wide. "You don't think the water will be running too fast?"

I finished a long pull of beer.

"I think it will be running just right. The last thing you want to do is get stuck in there with those snakes and swamp rats."

"Oh, shut up! Gross!" Karen playfully smacked my leg. "Quit trying to scare us."

"Trust me, ladies. This will be the best waterslide you've ever been down."

"Coolest anyway," I said.

"I've done it before," Karen announced.

"Tim's Tube? Bullshit, Karen." Amber laughed.

"You haven't either," Karen said.

"Yeah, we're lame," Amber copped to it. "We came out here to party a few times in high school but were too scared to go through with it."

"That's because you two were hanging out with all those pussies in your grade then," Spaceman said. "Pete Bonks, Will Letcher…"

"Pussies?" Amber said. "I woulda let Peter Bonks bonk me with his peter any day."

"Good," Karen said, "cause ya did."

"What?" Amber said. "So, did you."

"Did not," Karen grinned.

"Whatever happened to that guy?" I asked.

"I heard he graduated from college early," Amber said. "Took a job in California."

"Gay porn is what I heard," Spaceman said.

"I think it was computers," Karen said.

"Oh my God," Amber yelled. "Turn it up! I love this song!"

Spaceman cranked the volume. Rob Halford and the boys in Priest were singing about their dislike for parental guidance.

We agreed and sang along while our hormones boiled in the heat.

"Oh shit! What in the hell?!?"

"What?"

I leaned up toward the front seat.

"Is that Colesy?"

Bob Cole was standing at the side of the road with what looked like a summer's worth of fishing gear.

Spaceman pulled up.

"Dude, what are you doing out here?"

"Those idiots, Peterson and Bradley left me out here."

"Awww," the girls said.

Spaceman and I laughed.

Rob Peterson and Joe Bradley were fresh high school graduates like Spaceman and I. They were goofy, but good guys, always looking for a prank.

"Peterson pulled over and said he had a flat," Bob said. "Without checking to look first, I hopped out like a total dummy and started pulling things out of the trunk to get to the jack. That's when he hit the gas and bailed on me."

"Jerks," Amber said.

"Well, hey. Get in with us," Karen said. "You look like you're about to melt. Have a cold beer. We're gonna do Tim's Tube."

Colesy looked in the car at Spaceman and I. We shot him our best *get the fuck out of here* looks, but Karen saw us and put an elbow into my side.

"We can still have fun without you being a dick," she said and grabbed my crotch.

"Methinks the lady doth make a fine point," I said.

Spaceman popped the trunk so Colesy could load in his fishing gear. Karen slipped over onto my lap. Colesy looked at me, raised his eyebrows and smiled, then got in and grabbed a beer.

"Sorry to crash your party."

"These boys are taking us senior citizens down Tim's Tube before they split town and break our hearts forever," Karen said.

"Man, you couldn't pay me to do that," Colesy said. "I heard fishing is good on the opposite side though."

Spaceman looked up in the rearview and winked his thanks to Colesy. It was a solid move not to force in as a fifth wheel.

The mud was almost over our toes when we got out of Spaceman's Monte Carlo near the boulder covered in graffiti. The girls slipped and slid all over the trail heading up to the reservoir.

The grass was high, hot and steamy.

Amber held Spaceman's hand tightly. She looked scared and was no longer flirting.

"Look guys, we don't really have to do this."

"Are you kidding," I said. "Listen."

Everyone got quiet. Within seconds we could hear the overflow water crashing down into the spillway.

"That is fast. We shoulda brought skis."

"That's the way I like it," Spaceman said.

Amber polished off her beer.

"Screw it, let's go," she said and smacked Spaceman on the ass.

The hill was slippery and steep. By the time we made it to the top we were all wet, muddy and some had cuts from the tall grass.

Spaceman looked at Amber and pulled back the rusted chain link.

"Come on, time's a wastin'."

Karen looked at me, "I'm scared."

I laughed, "That's what the beer is for."

The four of us took turns squeezing under the fencing and made it down to the bank to the edge of the water.

Bob stayed outside the perimeter and walked around to the weeds on the far end to fish.

The water was warm and murky. The girls stepped in.

"Oooh, gross."

"Damn, I just lost a flip-flop," Karen said.

"This is cut-offs and sneaker land ladies. Not swimsuits and beach bags."

"A little warning would have been nice." Amber playfully fumed.

"What? And not get to see your hard bodies in those bikinis," Spaceman said.

"What about my bag?" Karen asked.

"Leave it on the bank," Spaceman said, casually backstroking out to the cement island.

"She's got beers in it," Amber said.

"Give it to me," I said.

Amber handed me Karen's bag. The girls waded out further.

By the time we all made it out to the concrete island and climbed up its metal bars we were all winded.

"Who wants to shotgun a beer," I said.

"We'll do that later in celebration," Spaceman said. "Come on Am, let's go."

Amber looked into the pit of the spillway. A long thick wet mossy rope ran down between four slats blasting water toward one another.

"I'm scared."

Amber was a tough athletic country girl. Stacked, corn fed and strong. When she said, she was afraid, Spaceman and I knew it was just a come on.

Spaceman grabbed the rope and slid down a few feet first.

"Now you grab the rope, Am and back down. I'm below you. Nothing can happen."

Amber turned around and did just that. Within moments, she and Spacemen were clenched onto the rope slowly descending down together into the water. Amber screamed as the rushing water knocked her top off.

Spaceman laughed. "Nothing any of us haven't seen before, right Arch?"

"You and Amber?" Karen said in shock.

"What can I tell you," I said. "It's a small town."

"When?" Karen playfully demanded.

"Whenever he wanted." Amber called out laughing from below.

"You like Amber?" Karen asked me.

"As much as the rest."

"As much as your girlfriend, Paige?"

"Not that much," I said. "About as much as you like Shively?"

"Nice," Karen said giving me the finger.

I grabbed two beers and popped them open.

"To Mr. Brown," I said holding out my beer. "Teacher, philosopher and patron of misbehavin'."

Karen laughed and hit my can with hers.

"To Mr. Brown." Karen took down half her suds then sat down Indian style with her back facing me. "Put some lotion on my back will ya?"

"Sure."

I dug around in the bag until I felt a large plastic bottle. I pulled it out and looked at it.

"Tahiti Tom's?"

"I get it in Evansville at the mall."

I looked at the sticker price.

"$7.99? Damn."

"Trust me. It's worth it. The best lotion ever. Plus, I love the little guy on the label."

I squirted some on my hand and started rubbing it into Karen's skin.

Karen left out a soft hum. She lifted her arms.

"Get my sides."

I squirted more lotion on my hands and gently massaged her hips slowly going up to the base of her breasts.

"Wait." Karen untied her top.

I sat behind her akimbo and scooted closer. My thickness throbbed against the fabric between me and her ass crack.

"Hmmmm. Is that you back there?" Karen moaned.

"More lotion?"

"Please. Rub it in good."

There wasn't a cloud in the sky. I was pleasantly pacified and had one of the best sets of tits in the county greased up and sliding between my fingers.

Karen turned her head. I bent around to meet her. We kissed for what seemed like forever. I tried to run a hand down between her legs, but she stopped it.

"Wait," she said. "We have all day."

Karen pulled her beach towel out of her bag, placed it on the concrete then laid down on her stomach. An inch of her ass crack poked out of the top of her tiny bikini bottoms.

"Will you put some lotion on my lower back too?"

I squirted more Tahiti Tom's into my hands and rubbed it on her lower back.

"Oh God, that feels so good," she said. "Get the top of my ass too will - you know what screw it - I want a full tan." Karen lifted her hips up. "Pull these off of me, will you?"

I pulled down Karen's red bikini bottoms revealing her firm round ass. For a moment, I thought my cock was going to rip right through the inseam of my cut-offs.

"Get my cheeks really good. I'd hate to burn."

I loaded up my hands with lotion then began kneading her ass cheeks like the world's finest pizza dough. I ran my hands further down her crack every time until my fingers ran over both of her openings.

Karen reached to the side, unzipped my cut-offs, pulled me out and began stroking it.

I kept my left hand on her left ass cheek and slid it down to where my fingers could enter her and my thumb could playfully be inserted into her a–

"Oh my God, we have to stop. I want our skin to be hotter, I want to be high."

"So, where's the grass?" My throbbing dick nearly shouted.

"Call down to Amber."

I hadn't seen Spacemen or Amber crest the hill coming back from the spillway. My guess was they were still at the bottom making out under the punishing waterfall or perhaps were already out of the tube and boning on the other side.

I called down. "Amber!"

A moment passed.

"Amber!"

"What?" I could barely hear through the rushing water.

"We're getting ready to move the board," Spaceman yelled up.

"Where's your weed?" I said.

"In the car," Amber yelled back. I heard her whoop and holler as she and Spaceman blasted down the tube.

"Damn!"

"Will you be a doll and go get it? Some more beers too, please," Karen said. "I'll be here wet and waiting."

I had world class diamond cutter going. I looked at Karen's naked body like a starving man would look over a roped off buffet.

"Don't you move a goddam muscle."

Karen laughed and spread her legs. "Maybe just one or two."

I slammed what was left of my beer then did a half-ass gainer off the top of the cement tower. Karen looked over the edge.

"Hurry," she smiled. "Don't make me start without you."

I swam across the reservoir like Mark Spitz with Mercury Four-Stroke outboard shoved up his ass. I made my way up the muddy bank and slid down the other side, nicks and scratches be damned.

I trotted down to Spaceman's car, grabbed Amber's bag with the weed and stuffed it full with more cold beers.

I was almost back up to the top of the hill when I looked into the bag to make sure Amber had a lighter.

That was when I heard them…

The screams.

30

I found Cherry in the place where anyone worth their salt wound up in town sooner or later, the Elks Club.

She was shooting pool with two younger guys, bent over the table giving them their fifty cents worth. She saw me and smiled.

"Thanks for the game guys."

She put her cue down on the table, walked over and gave me a tight hug and kiss on the check. Her firm breasts pressed into me. One of the players, a kid in a stained Carhartt jacket, looked at me with a thoughtful nod.

"I got some scoop on you," Cherry smiled.

"Oh?"

"You were a real stud down here in your day. Local high school hero is what I hear."

"Hardly. Who'd you get your intel from?"

"Bentley. The bartender."

I turned and looked behind the bar. It was a big burly man. Bald with a bushy moustache smiling with his huge paws on the counter.

"How the hell are you, Arch?"

"Jesus. Bentley?"

I walked over and shook his hand. Same light blue eyes blazing. He twisted off a beer and put it on the bar.

"I didn't tell her much, but as you probably already know Cherry has a way of working things out of a man."

I looked at Cherry and smiled. Took a seat.

"I was sorry to hear about Bob," Bentley said. "I had no idea he was struggling."

"Did you go to his church?"

"Maybe a Christmas or Easter here and there. This gig keeps a man late in bed on Sunday mornings."

"Busy?"

"Only watering hole in the county. You know that."

"I mean the church. Bob draw a good crowd?"

"Far as I know. He was good, I mean when I heard him preach he was good at it, you know? Lots of people in town liked him."

I nodded. Took a drink.

Bentley and I shot the shit through a few more rounds.

He had tried to make it as a stuntman in LA for a few years until he hurt his back. Low budget horror movies mostly, but it was enough for a small town kid to have fun for a while and come home with some stories.

"With all due respect to Cherry, here." Bentley winked. "I was screwing Nadine Niles for a while out there?"

"Who?"

"Nadine Niles. She starred in *Blood Forest* 2 and 3. Big tits. Had the customized pink chainsaw in part 2? Wore a patch over her eye and went topless the whole time in 3?

"Sorry to say I missed that one."

"You remember that tune? The theme song from the first one? *Split Open Heart*?"

"Even I remember that song," Cherry said. "Great video. They still play it sometimes."

"Not nearly enough," Bentley said. "Met some of the guys in the band."

"Oh, shit. What were they called?" Cherry asked.

"Leo's Feel," Bentley smiled.

He and Cherry clinked their bottles together.

"Speaking of feel. I feel gross. Where is the nearest hotel?" Cherry asked. "I need a shower."

"Try three towns away," Bentley said

Cherry deflated. "Really?"

"Small town. Nothing doing here. Can't build a hotel if people don't come."

"Sad but true," I said.

"So where are we going to stay?" Cherry asked.

"Spaceman said he'd put us up while we're here. In fact, we're late for dinner. What do we owe you, Bent?"

"Nothing. On me."

I tossed a few bills on the counter.

"You're really staying out at Spaceman's?" Bentley said, eyebrows raised.

"Yeah. Why?"

"Nothing," Bentley said scooping up the cash. "Tell the good Sheriff I said hello."

31

Spaceman's daddy, Red Bendix, had been the sheriff of Shoal County for as long as most could remember. Prior to that, Red ran his parent's grocery and produce business. They weren't rich by any means, but their modest home was neat and clean. Spaceman had a Honda three-wheeler and some go-karts with land to ride them on as a kid. Red was always generous with his time to show and teach.

I turned off Enterprise road and drove between the familiar stand of towering evergreens.

The driveway which used to be nothing more than a straight trail of dust was now neatly blacktopped and redirected into a scenic S curve.

The property now boasted a manmade pond with a long dock and sandy beach. Red's original home had been torn down and replaced with a log cabin worthy of Aspen.

"Whoa," Cherry said.

Spaceman stood in front sipping out of a rocks glass in front of a fountain.

"Glad you made it. Dinner is almost ready. Come on in. I'll get you guys something to drink."

"Beautiful place," Cherry said.

Spaceman smiled. "A little different than you remember it, eh Arch?"

"Can't say I blame you for breaking up the concrete slab where I used to school you at hoops."

"Shee-yitt," Spaceman said through a shit-eating grin.

The front door opened into a great room surrounded by a large balcony. The obligatory antler chandelier hung over stylishly aged leather furniture arranged around a bear skin rug.

"All this place is missing is a roaring fireplace," Cherry said.

"And a ski lift," I added.

"Yeah well, just because one lives in a small town doesn't mean his home has to be."

We followed Spaceman down a few stairs to a wet bar.

"Arch?"

"Whatever you're having."

Spaceman poured and handed me a bourbon neat.

"Cherry?"

"Any kind of beer is fine, thanks."

Spaceman grabbed a bottle out of the fridge.

"I'm afraid it's nothing too exciting."

Spaceman held up a bottle of Miller Lite.

"Perfect," Cherry said.

"Glass?"

"Already in one," Cherry winked.

"You a vegetarian, Cherry?"

"Depends on what's for dinner."

Spaceman laughed.

"We're having venison tonight. Killed it myself."

Cherry didn't miss a beat. "Nice. Bow? Gun?"

"Bow. Forty yards or so," Spaceman said. "Tracked it about half a mile. You still hunt, Arch?"

"Not since Red last took us."

"That's a shame," Spaceman said. He looked at Cherry. "Your man, Arch here, was always a better shot than me." Spaceman looked at me. "You've really never shot a bow since?"

I was doing a job for V a few years ago in Khimki Forest in the Soviet Union. I iced two Russian mobsters and a KGB informant using a Mathews Halon and razor rip broadheads.

"Can't say I have," I said.

Spaceman looked at me like I was crazy.

"Damn. Well, I'm glad you guys could make it." Spaceman raised a toast. "To new and old friends."

The three of us clinked our drinks together. Spaceman took a sip, sat his glass down and fired up a cigarette.

To the left was a big open kitchen.

From a walk-in cupboard came, "Dammit, Ted. No smoking in the house."

"One isn't gonna hurt anything. Place smells like chemicals anyway."

"Those are called household cleaners. Sylvia came today."

An elegant woman wearing tight jeans and an oxford shirt stepped around the corner.

She was beautiful. Familiar.

It was Paige, my old girlfriend.

Paige, Spaceman's wife.

"Archie!"

"Paige."

We did the brief hug thing. I introduced Cherry.

The women were cordial, polite, but immediately zoned in on one another looking for flaws.

"So nice to have you both," Paige said. "Let's eat."

Spaceman's venison was perfect. We caught up as much as we could without completely ostracizing Cherry.

After Red retired and moved to Arizona, Spaceman ran for Sheriff and by the grace of the populace wound up filling his dad's shoes.

"People love Red," I said.

Spaceman looked up from his plate, "Everyone loved Red."

"I bet he's tightened up his golf game out there."

"He's dead, Arch."

"What?"

"Heart attack."

"When?"

Spaceman tossed his napkin on his plate.

"Hmmmm, let's see. We got married, what babe? When we were twenty-five? Twenty-six? Had an invitation for you Arch, but no address to send it to. Red died, what? Four, five years after that?"

"Sounds about right," Paige said.

"I'm truly sorry to hear that. I had no idea."

"You were probably busy running your car dealership," Spaceman said.

"Excuse me?"

"That's a hell of a car you rolled into town with."

I glanced over at Cherry.

"Oh, that. Yeah, that's not mine. Company car."

"Fancy," Paige said. "What do you do?"

"Nothing exciting. Sales."

"I thought you went military for some reason," she said.

"Briefly. Nothing too exciting. Coast Guard."

"Damn Arch," Spaceman said. "I figured you would've led the charge to get Saddam."

"I was in Iraq for a bit, but had my head under a hood most of the time."

"Combat?"

"Avionics technician."

"What's that?" Paige asked.

"Mechanic," Spaceman said. "Engine geek."

"Well, it's wonderful to see you again and to make a new friend," Paige said.

"Thank you for having us," Cherry smiled.

"Care for another beer?" Spaceman asked.

Cherry drained the last bit of hers. "Yes, please."

Spaceman got up, grabbed one. Twisted it off, handed it to Cherry.

"Thank you."

Paige smiled at me then looked over her wine glass at Cherry.

"So where did you two meet one another?"

Cherry hesitated.

"Business trip," I said. "She was at a haircut convention. Met in the bar."

"Hair? Exciting," Paige said.

"Just men," Cherry shrugged. "Never got into the whole color highlight thing."

"Oh?" Paige nodded. "Chemistry thing slow you down?"

"Not at all. Some women can just be cunts to deal with," Cherry said.

Spaceman nearly choked on his drink.

"I don't see a ring. Dating?" Paige asked.

"Just hot sex for now," Cherry smiled. "We're still getting to know one another,"

There was an awkward moment of silence followed by a loud pop of laughter.

"Good on you, kid," Spaceman said to Cherry. "You can handle a grillin' from the best of them. I always think I'm pretty tough until I come home to this one."

Paige smiled at Spaceman. Zeroed in again. "Is Cherry a family name?"

"I got it from the book *The Outsiders* by S.E. Hinton," Cherry said. "I liked it better than Teri."

"I loved that movie," Paige said. "What a cast!"

"Was that the one about the bond of friendship and kicking commie ass?" Spaceman asked.

"That was *Red Dawn*," I said. "*The Outsiders* was a cautionary tale about choosing Patrick Swayze to be the guardian of your orphaned children."

"So, how'd you get the nickname, Spaceman?" Cherry asked.

"Oh, gawd," Paige said.

"You tell her, Arch," Spaceman said.

"Nah."

"C'mon. Sounds like I'm bragging if I tell it," Spaceman said.

"Alright" I said. "Ted, is obsessed with Neil Armstrong."

Spaceman chuckled. "Obsessed."

"Truthfully, Ted loved the band KISS," I said.

"Mostly from when I was a kid, mind you. Their stuff in the late eighties was so-so."

"Anyway," I said. "We were getting crushed by our rival Boone County. Nobody could hit the broad side of a barn. Coach is beyond pissed. He's cussing and spitting at us so much the ref calls a technical."

"The ref called a technical on your coach for yelling at his own team?" Cherry laughed.

"You might say his language was, colorful." Paige added.

"Coach pulls all the starters-"

"That included your boy Archibald, here," Spaceman said.

I went on, "and puts in the second team. First play in, Ted, steals an inbounds pass and takes off down the court. It looks like it's going to be your standard uncontested lay-up, but somehow their tallest player is already down there. We're all expecting Ted to pull up for a jumper or wait until somebody can come down to help him, but instead he keeps going right at the guy. Just when you think Ted is going to be force fed a big orange, he jumps up in the air. I can still see it now in slow motion. He floats and continues to elevate until his elbow is above the rim. On his way down he dunks it!"

"Oh my God, you dunked it?" Cherry said, eyes wide open.

"I did," Spaceman said.

"The guy is five-ten in a thick soled shoe," I said.

"Five-eleven," Spaceman said. "In a regular shoe."

"Babe, you know the story's more impressive the shorter they make you, right?" Paige said.

"Ah, just tell the truth. I'm five eleven. It was no big deal."

I barely got a mouthful of wine down and coughed.

"No big deal? The gym exploded. The roof came off the place. Everyone was going nuts. We were jumping up and down going crazy on the bench."

"No one had ever seen you dunk before?" Cherry asked.

"Nope," Spaceman smiled. "Kept it a secret. Wanted to wait for the right time."

"You believe that?" I said. "Saving it."

"Showboat," Paige said.

"Tell me you guys came back and won," Cherry said.

Spaceman shook his head. "No, they stretched the lead even more after that."

"But, it didn't matter," I said. "A legend was born that night. Ted Bendix, KISS fan, lover of all things Ace Frehley dunked and became the Spaceman."

"Technically," Spaceman said, "Ace Frehley was known as Space Ace in KISS, but we had a kid named Ace Atkins in our grade that got caught trying to finger his grandma's cat, so everyone went with Spaceman to avoid the whole Ace confusion."

"Seriously?" Cherry said.

"I never believed any of that," Paige said, "but she did have a lot of cats and the kid was weird."

"Interesting," Cherry said.

"Arch splashed some impressive three pointers in that game too," Spaceman said.

"Yeah, but nobody ended up calling me anything cool like Drano, or the Culligan Man."

"That's because you guys still lost by thirty," Paige laughed.

"You were there?" Cherry asked.

"Oh yeah! My darlin' was the head cheerleader," Spaceman said leaning back in his chair.

"I was actually Archie's girl back then," Paige said. "Right Arch, or were we off?"

"Who knows?" I said.

Of course, I knew. Paige did too. We were on. On like a house on fire. Paige and I had had done it twice that night. Once, after the game in the cafeteria supply room, then again at her house in the hallway by her sister's bedroom.

"It was a fun night."

Paige smiled and took a sip of her wine.

"Anyway," Spaceman said. "That was a long time ago. Nobody really-"

"They still call you Spaceman," Cherry said. "It had to be a big deal."

"Well," Spaceman grinned, "I guess it was."

"For a few games after that, he'd come out with his face painted like Ace Frehley to *2,000 Man*. Everybody got into it," I said. "Then when coach saw we were enjoying ourselves he put the kibosh on it."

"A pair of airballed free throws in a tight game was my undoing," Spaceman said. "The gimmick kind of soured after that, but the nickname stuck."

We all bullshitted a bit more.

Ran through another bottle of wine.

A drink or two.

Cherry had some beers. Helped Paige clean up.

We did the whole goodnight thing.

Our room was gorgeous. King sized bed. All white and gray linens. Private bathroom off to the side.

"You're still in love with her," Cherry said.

"What are you talking about?"

"I could see it. I could see it in your eyes when you looked at her."

"Don't be ridiculous."

"Does Spaceman know?"

"Know what? Hell, I haven't been back in town in twenty-eight years."

"It's okay," Cherry smiled. "She's beautiful. Besides, it's a turn on to see a bit of your romantic past."

"Stop."

Cherry gave me a long, slow kiss. It was nice.

"Let's fuck," she said.

I didn't know if Cherry would ever creep into what tiny piece of twisted shrapnel was left of my heart, but she was certainly improving my cardio. We hit it twice and fell asleep.

I woke up around 2AM and went downstairs.

It was a nice, clear night. The stars were putting on a show. I spied a pack of Spaceman's cigarettes on a table and stepped out on the back deck.

I hadn't smoked in ages, but found myself wanting one. I fired one up.

I looked over Spaceman's fancy swimming hole and marveled at the moon's reflection on the water.

The screen door slid open.

Spaceman stepped out, lit a cigarette.

"Sorry, Arch. I couldn't think of the right time to tell you. I mean we were looking where Colesy killed himself."

"We were kids. I'm happy for you guys."

"Really?"

"Really. Nearly everyone else left. You guys were stuck here."

"Stuck here's right. I stayed back, let you run off, do whatever it is you wanted to do. Meanwhile, I'm back here waiting every day for the wheels to come off."

"We were careful."

"Really? Cause Shively knew we were full of shit. He didn't buy a goddamm thing. And Colesy? Thank God he found the church because he was a basket case."

"So, you buy the suicide then? He was that lonely and depressed?"

Spaceman took a long drag and exhaled.

"Ask around, Arch. Bob may have been depressed, but he wasn't lonely."

"I'm going to figure this out and be gone."

"The least you can do, right?"

"Don't pull this you suffered for me. That you hung back so I could go live some dream. You were small town from day one. Look at this house. You got everything in it, but a bookshelf. You weren't going anywhere whether that day happened or not."

Spaceman smashed out his butt and tossed it into a flower pot.

"And what about you, Arch? What about you big time? Come on tell me. I'm waiting to hear all the great and amazing things you've done."

I tamped my butt out and tossed it into the same flower pot. There was too much to say and no time to tell it.

"What time do you get up?"

"Early. You eat breakfast?" Spaceman asked.

I nodded.

"Good," he said. "I'll see you in the morning."

"Wait."

"Yeah?"

"What about Karen? What happened to Amber?"

"Like I said, Arch, ask around. You'll believe others before you believe me."

I heard the screen door slide open then close behind me.

I fired up another cigarette.

And just like the tip.

Everything I saw was red.

32

I got up early before breakfast, made myself a cup of coffee and decided to check out Spaceman's spread.

The grass was neatly cut. The trails around the pond and through the woods were nicely cleared. Various types of flowers and foliage were kept up and served as nice accents. Nothing was over the top or ostentatious.

I crossed the footbridge over a small creek on the west side of the pond. I made my way around and walked out onto the dock.

I looked down into the dark water.

"Whatcha thinkin'?"

I turned and saw Paige sitting on a on a blue Adirondack chair. Pretty. Never needed makeup. She was wearing a cut-up sweatshirt that hung off one of her shoulders, thin tight gym shorts and flip-flops.

"The water is clear. Must have dug deep."

"Ted had them go twenty feet or so."

"Nice work."

"Kids like it."

"Kids? How old?"

"Joey's nineteen. Emma's twenty."

"They in town?"

"No. College. They both couldn't wait to get out of here. Emma's at Vanderbilt. Joey's at Stanford."

"Big ticket schools."

"Scholarships mostly."

"Smart kids."

Paige laughed. "We don't know where they got it?"

"Emma as pretty as you?" I asked.

Paige held her coffee cup with two hands and sipped. Her eyes looked over the brim deep into mine. It was the look. The one I hadn't seen in ages. The one where her eyes said things she'd be embarrassed to say out loud.

"Prettier," she said.

"Easily done." I smiled.

"What about you? Ever get married? Kids?"

"Nah," I lied. "I'm hogging all these amazing gifts to myself."

Paige gave a tired smile.

"It didn't sound like you were hogging it all to yourself last night."

"Oh Cherry? She's young. Has a lot of stamina."

"I'll say. Her moans are loud too."

"Loud? We used gags last night."

"You're awful."

I leaned against the railing.

"Let me ask you a question? Bob Cole. Did you see him much?"

"At church. Around town sometimes."

"Did he seem depressed to you?"

"I don't think so. Not when we saw him. It was always in brief snippets, ya know?"

I nodded.

"Thanks for your hospitality and putting us up. We'll more than likely head out after the funeral tomorrow."

"Oh? Ted said you might be here for a week or so."

"Well that depends. Would that be okay with you?"

"Of course, but you and Cherry have to make yourselves at home. Nobody's going to wait on you."

"Wouldn't have it any other way."

"She's sharp," Paige said. "I like her. She's pretty, but tough."

"She's a firecracker," I said.

"Want some coffee?"

"Sure."

"Good," Paige said. "Follow me."

I did.

I watched her ass sway as we walked back.

No panty line, no cellulite.

Just her and Spaceman with their big house on a small pond.

It was everything.

Everything I'd never wanted.

Almost.

33

I sifted through the file cabinets. Opened Colesy's desk drawers. There was nothing much. Old sermons, cough drops, loose change.

I took a seat in his chair. Scanned the office.

There were some quotes of scripture printed on posters with eagles in flight. There was a framed Norman Rockwell print of a soldier in church.

What was in your head Colesy?

I looked up at the ceiling fan. Imagined Bob standing on his desk, noose around his neck taking a final breath before stepping into the hereafter.

What'd you see Bob?

What's in the afterlife?

Anything?

Was Hell hot enough to curl your toenails?

Was Heaven bright enough you had to wear shades?

Or was everything just a big dark nothing?

The thought of Colesy giving up didn't make sense.

The lock on his bottom desk drawer had been pried open. It was empty. Was he robbed? Evidence stolen?

I went to his house. It was as sparse as his office. Neat and clean, but other than a TV and some furniture, it was short on belongings and personal effects.

I opened the door to his bedroom and went in. California King. Nice dresser.

I ran my hand along the top shelf of his closet.

I felt a thick envelope.

I brought it down, opened it. It was a manuscript of some sort.

Ultimate Forgiveness by Robert Cole.

I flipped through it. It was redlined with comments. A few notes were scribbled in the margins. Beneath it was an uncashed check for five thousand dollars from Flock Press in Lafayette, IN.

Congratulations! The note said. *We'd like to publish as soon as possible. Enclosed is an advance check and a few suggestions from our editing staff.*

Nothing added up.

34

"Don't get me wrong. He was great guy, far be it for me to judge, but as a preacher you don't expect a guy to be pulling ass the way he did."

I was talking to Jarvis Koontz in his garage on Main Street. He was working some kind of industrial cleaner into his hands.

"Colesy? A man of the cloth pulling ass? You know this how?"

"I mean, hell, Arch. You know this town is small and most people are full of shit, but you hear a rumor more than three or four times you start assuming it must be true."

"Like how you ruined Sandra Wilkens life?"

"Now goddammit, see, that's more bullshit right there."

Back in junior high some guys were already finger banging the faster girls in our class. Guys would hold out their middle finger and say the girl's name then share a whiff of her nether regions with their pals. It was classy stuff.

Jarvis was desperate to look cool and join the conversation, but wasn't much of a ladies man. Being the idiot that he was, he shoved his middle finger up his own ass then waved it around at lunch one day saying Sandra Wilkens.

Sandra was an awkward short and shy little thing in thick glasses, who years later blossomed into a beautiful sophomore babe, but thanks to Jarvis' nuclear digit blasting pollutants all over our sloppy joes that afternoon, she remained dateless until she moved away. It wasn't until Jarvis was drunk and high one night that he came clean on the story. A tale that was as hilarious as it was sad.

"Your story, not mine Jarvis."

"We were kids, man. A joke. Besides I saw on Facebook she married some rich doctor. She made out okay."

"Back to Colesy. Did you go to his church?"

"For a while. You know Victory Bunk?"

"Sounds familiar."

"Well, his cousin Tina used to sing in the choir there. We dated for a bit."

"So? She was sleeping with Bob?"

"No. But, she told Victory that Bob was damn near sleeping with all the other lady singers. Don't get me wrong. I feel creepy talking about a dead man and what he chose to do with his dick, but that was the word I heard on him." Jarvis turned around. "Hey, Kenny!"

A rail thin kid part blackhead, part grease, slid out from underneath a Dodge Caravan.

"Yeah?"

"Come here a minute."

Kenny got up, spit a loogie then walked over to Jarvis and I.

"What can you tell my friend here about Reverend Cole?"

"He was a good man. Honest. Baptized me. Loved the Lord. God rest his soul."

"Not that," Jarvis said. "The other stuff."

Kenny's eyes lit up. "Oh, you mean all the pussy he was taming? One of 'em, was Myra Tiggs. Them two was hot and heavy."

"Myra Tiggs?" I laughed "The Myra Tiggs that taught us in third grade?"

Jarvis laughed.

"The same, Archie. I'd be lyin', if I didn't say the thought of her now still puts a little lead in my pencil."

"That's crazy. She's gotta be what?"

"Sixty somethin'. Don't look it though," Jarvis said, "She kinda reminds me of that Southern gal that used to have that cooking show on TV."

Kenny happily chimed in, "Only she's a lot firmer. Fit. Great legs. Would love to see her nekkid."

Jarvis frowned. "Class it up, pervert. That's a dead preacher's mistress you're talking about."

Kenny slunk back to the garage.

Jarvis scooted closer to me, opened his eyes wide and cocked his head down.

"You know some say Bob was doing that artificial asphyxiation deal in his office and slipped on a puddle of Myra's lube. Like you know, she was in there with him or something. Isn't that awful?"

"Yes, Jarvis. It is. It is awful."

"Hey, man. I'm just tellin' you what I been told."

"Gotcha. Thanks for your time."

"You bet. Good seeing you, Arch."

"The pleasure was all mine."

Jarvis lit up with a big smile.

"Really?"

"Absolutely."

"We should drink some beer one of these days."

"We should," I said, knowing I'd be long gone or dead by then.

"Say, you need an oil change or somethin' while you're here, let me know. I'll do it for free."

"I appreciate it, Jarvis."

"Hell, if a man can't help out a friend, who can he help?"

Who can he help? Indeed.

35

I was driving down Main when I saw the Lion's Club was doing a fundraiser. They used to sell amazing corn dogs when we were kids.

I nearly leapt for joy when I pulled up and saw the bucket of batter next to a fryer.

I ordered two.

"Holy cow! Archie?"

It was Boyce something. Nice guy. A few years younger.

"Hey."

"In for the pastor's funeral?"

"Yeah."

"I was sorry to hear."

"Yeah."

"Damn, that is some kind of SUV."

I was now embarrassed I had driven such a car down.

"Loaner."

You want your lemonade with a lid?"

"I'll just take the corn dogs."

"Lemonade is good. My wife made it. The real deal too. Not Country Time."

I looked over. A woman roughly Boyce's age, held two foot long hotdogs on sticks waiting to be battered. She had nice smile.

"Sure, I'll take one. What kind of ice do you have?"

"We got that small pellet ice."

"Outstanding. Load it up with ice, please."

I tossed him a bill.

"Say, is Dooley Hicks a Lion?"

"Sure is. He manned the booth last year."

"Where does he live these days?"

Boyce gave me directions.

Hicks had a nice California craftsman on a good-sized piece of land north of town. Word was he had built it himself with his brother-in-law. Lawn was nice. No clutter other than a big tractor tire that had been converted into a planter. The tire had been turned inside out and cut up. It resembled Goober's hat from Andy Griffith.

Did I think Dooley had seen us that day? No.

Did I think Dooley would run a dirty campaign against Spaceman? No.

Did I want to turn over every stone possible before I began busting skulls? Yes.

"Shit," Dooley said. "I got no beef with the man. Just feel four terms has been long enough. He's done a good job. Wouldn't mind taking a crack at it myself."

"There's got to be more to it than that," I said.

Dooley took a seat on his porch swing. Extended his arms across the back. I took a chair across from him.

"I want this off the record, got me? I want nothing more than a fair and clean campaign with the man. In fact, I still consider him a friend."

"Won't say a word."

"You know the town. Quiet. Tired. Slow. Hell, a day here can sometimes seem like three."

"Yeah."

"Doesn't keep a bad seed from passing through from time to time though. There was this creep. A real weirdo. He was exposing himself to women around town. Peeping in windows. In fact, come to find out, he had been stalking some women. One of 'em was Ted's wife, Paige."

"Okay."

"Guy gets arrested, then disappears. Vanishes in thin air."

"You mean broke out of jail?"

"No, I mean. Gone disappears. No trial, nothing. Word from the department was he was extradited back to Ohio to answer for more serious charges."

"Not so unusual."

"Maybe, but this happens with a few other arrests. All creeps. All vanish."

"I don't follow."

"My sister, Denise, was killed by a drunk driver three years ago. Guy was twenty-five coming back from a poker game in Mill Shoals. Anyway, he plows his car into Denise who was on the side of 45N buying produce from this farmer in a truck. Fucking awful. Farmer and his friend died, too. Driver of course comes out of the whole thing with nothing more than a cracked collarbone."

"Jesus."

"Anyway, Ted pays me a visit one day before they transfer the guy. Asks if I want to see the see the drunk piece of shit. I'm like, what in the hell for? Ted's like, whatever you want."

"Not necessarily legal, but okay."

"No, Arch, I'm telling you he was gonna let me beat or worse, kill the guy."

"Did he say that?"

"Didn't have too. I could tell. There was a real heft to the question."

"What happened?"

"Told him no. Guy did sixteen months which was bullshit. We sued him, won a settlement, but of course that doesn't bring Denise back."

"That's tough."

"Guy gets killed execution style outside of a Pizza Hut three months after his release. I'm telling you, it was Ted."

"Now Dooley, that's a real-"

"Ask around. Two wrongs don't make a right. I know in his mind he thought he was looking out, but I'm telling you, I think the man is dangerous."

"Last question."

"Sure."

"In high school, did you ever go out to the spillway?"

"You mean to do Tim's Tube?"

"Yeah, right, sure, Tim's Tube."

"No. I wouldn't go near there or any other lake or pond if you paid me to."

"Why is that?"

"I have ichthyophobia."

"What's ichthyophobia."

"I'm afraid of fish."

Dooley Hicks was off the list.

36

We were sitting on the roof of the old grandstand at the fairgrounds.

Rather than facing the track we were looking into the opposite direction watching the sun go down.

Cherry was enjoying her newfound freedom from the shackles of Meemaw, but was curious about what was going on in Briarfield.

I told her about Colesy, well, nothing about Colesy other than I wondered how he had died.

"I used to think about it," Cherry said.

"What suicide?

"Somedays. Sometimes. The things I had to do for Stefan. The things he made me do at those parties."

"Wasn't your fault. You were trying to survive."

Cherry put her head on my shoulder.

"Still. I know you think less of me."

"I don't."

"Your friend, Bob. He was a preacher, right?"

"Yeah."

"So, you believe? In God, I mean."

The sunset was beautiful.

I let out a long sigh.

"I've been taught, heard a lot of things. But, I don't know. I guess the jury is still out for me. I mean you see a sunset like this one, but somewhere a hurricane is decimating a city."

"Wanna know what I think?" Cherry said.

"Sure."

"God quit."

"What?"

"I think he made us, loved us, but then saw what we were capable of and quit on us.

"We are amazing in what we can do and accomplish. Ballerinas, scientists, artists, we had to have come from something more than dust or a big bang to have the gifts we do. I think God loved us for a while, but he quit."

"Caught the last train for the coast?"

"Huh?"

"Nothing, old song."

"My uncle. Well, I used to call him that. He was one of my mom's boyfriends. The one that hung around the longest. The good one that never touched me. He was a duck hunter. Trained his dogs. They were smart. The neatest part though was they were all rescue dogs.

"Anyway, this one. I guess it was a mastiff or something. My uncle really loved. He loved them all, but the mastiff I think he felt a kinship to. The previous owner had been cruel, abusive. So, when my uncle showed this dog love, the dog's heart melted for him. That dog was so well trained. He would do anything for my uncle. Follow him anywhere. People said he was the best hunting dog they had ever seen. That is until my uncle's dog attacked them. See that dog loved my uncle so much, if anyone got near him, that dog thought they were a threat.

"His name was Zephyr. He went after mom and me. Almost killed the mailman. My uncle, he didn't know what to do. What other people saw in Zephyr's eyes was the complete opposite of what my uncle saw.

"Anyway, my uncle hunted alone because of Zephyr. One day, Zephyr sniffed out a blind full of hunters. Zephyr attacked them and they shot him. It broke my uncle's heart. Not so much that the hunters were protecting themselves. They had every right too, but that Zephyr had it in himself to be so good. To do good. To follow, except for his flaws. His deadly flaws.

"My uncle quit hunting after that. Sold all his guns, gear, what have you. I think God did the same when he saw what we were. Some people loved him so much, worshipped him so crazily it scared him. That belief saddens me. Makes me feel alone. Sometimes, it even scares me. The idea of it. Being abandoned and alone."

"There is nothing worse than abandonment."

"What about betrayal?"

"That is abandonment. A kind of abandonment anyway."

"You ever been abandoned?"

"We've all been one way or another."

"I worry about you. I mean us. I mean that I'm not good enough for you. That, you think I'm a bad person."

"You're not a bad person, Cherry. You wanted to know why I wear this bead? I got it from a woman. A woman in the Middle East.

"I was over there doing some work. The specifics don't really matter. I guess what I can tell you is that incompetence exists in every occupation and on nearly every level. US intelligence and the military is no different. Misconduct, war crimes are a big deal. Every time one is reported in the media it weakens the US position. There were these guys. This small group of soldiers. Four of them. They were successful in carrying out their objectives, but it was what they did after.

"My job was simple. Get rid of them.

"Sometimes, for the military, it makes more sense to give an undeserved medal to a dead soldier, than to have news headlines of that soldier's misconduct disgrace the entire operation.

"It was Baghdad, early on. Some snipers thought to be al-Qaeda were wreaking havoc on the streets. They had kids walking in and out of the very buildings they were operating from all day and night. They were picking off a number of our guys on patrol.

"A small unit of ours infiltrated the nests, but not before taking significant casualties.

"The shooters, it turned out, were Iraqi men with families. Cowards, who hid behind their kids and fired freely at our guys, all the while promising allegiance to our faces. Our guys, as one would understand, were out for blood. When they got up there they decided to take far more than that. They were raping a woman when we walked in.

"Myself and another guy on my team took them out.

"This old woman. This mom, or grandma had been hiding. She heard the shots and came running out with a knife. When she saw what we had done to the men attacking her daughter she dropped the knife and fell on her knees and began kissing my boots. I pulled her up. She started pulling out small amounts of currency trying to pay us.

"We wouldn't take it.

"Mick, the guy I was with was covering the front.

"I was leading her out to safety when she ran back to get something. When she stepped back into the hallway one of the original snipers that had been taken down sat up and shot her. It was her own nephew.

"She died in my arms. In her hand was this bead.

"Other than a watch I've never worn jewelry, but sometimes I wear this bead around my neck to remind me that good and bad can come sometimes come from the same side, sometimes the same person.

"Colesy was a good man. Not a perfect man, but a good man. I don't think a God he loved would send him to hell for ending his own life. Especially, if his life here on Earth felt like hell, be it of his own making or otherwise.

"Don't get down on yourself. Don't ever think you're not good enough or don't deserve to be loved. I don't really know what in the hell is going on in this town right now, or who is really who, but I know this. I know you are good."

I took the necklace off and gave it to Cherry. She put it around her neck and kissed my cheek.

We stayed on the roof until we could see the stars.

37

You've been to a funeral visitation before.

Hushed whispers in the funeral home.

Pictures of the deceased at different times in their lives.

Hugs and handshakes.

Some awkward standing around. Shifting weight from one foot to another.

That was Bob's.

A lot of people were going to the Elks afterwards for a drink.

On the way out, I saw Myra. She gave me a small wave. I walked over to her.

"How long has it been, Archie?"

"Long time. A real long time, Myra."

She stepped towards me. We hugged. She smelled nice. Not old lady nice, but actually nice. Expensive perfume, not poured on, but lightly applied. Beautiful skin. She was wearing a simple skirt and silk blouse. Pearls. A nice heel. Bob could have done much, much worse.

"I understand you two were close."

"Yes," Myra said. She dabbed a tear with a handkerchief.

"Would you say you too spent a lot of time together? I mean you knew him well?"

"We were lovers, if that's what you mean. Actually, I guess I should say I was one of many, per town gossip." Myra's eyes sparkled and stared into mine. "You're not surprised, you heard."

"Something like that. It's Briarfield, right?"

"Robert was dashing, handsome and smart. He could also be really sweet. Naturally, as choir director we worked together. I'd heard rumblings of Robert's picadilloes, if you will. Good things," Myra smiled. "I started having him over for dinner from time to time. First, he'd eat and dash, then a time or two later stay and chat over a glass of wine. At my age, those of us still able bodied, anyway, know time is fleeting so we don't waste it. One afternoon, Bob came over to help me clean the gutters. When he arrived, I was in the back yard up on a ladder in a short tennis skirt."

"I didn't know you played tennis."

"Never have. Nor do I like panties. Fortunately, for me Bob liked the view. After that we'd see each other no less than twice a week."

"How long were you together?"

"We never considered ourselves dating. It was more like an adult arrangement. Sometimes we'd have a bite. Watch PBS."

"I'm assuming you had your fair share of pillow talk. Learned things about one another."

"For the most part."

"Given what you know about Bob, do you think he was capable of-"

"I never saw anything that would make me think he could do that, but then again, how much does anyone really reveal of themselves when they're suffering?"

"Will I see you at the Elks tonight?"

"No. I'm still trying to make sense of all of this. Besides, Bentley can't make a proper martini to save his life."

"One other thing," I said. "Ever seen one of these?"

I pulled out the Tahiti Tom's bottle.

Myra looked at it.

"I remember the t-shirts. Didn't know they actually made sunscreen."

"Used to."

"Never seen one."

"Okay. Thanks, Myra. Sorry again for your loss."

Myra wiped a single tear from her eye, stepped forward and embraced me.

"I still live in the same house. If you need something, or want to talk. I'm around."

"Thanks, Myra."

I watched her walk away. Her eyes were wet with tears, but her strut dripped with confidence.

38

In theory, and perhaps even on occasion, the purpose of the Elks Club in Briarfield was to service the community socially as well as educationally. Not only did a number of smaller groups and organizations use the building for meetings and presentations, the Elks also hosted a number of entertainment functions like weddings, high school dances and the occasional gospel concert.

While the Elks Club was the social hub of Briarfield and stood as a beacon for fellowship and goodwill, the small bar on the first floor was known for drunken sweaty dancefloor kisses, ill-advised hook-ups and the occasional sucker punch.

By the time I got there after my chat with Myra, the place was packed.

"Where were all these folks at the visitation?"

"Probably here," Spaceman said. "Got ya a bourbon."

He handed it to me.

"Thanks," I took half of it down. "You come here a lot?"

"Only if I get called down here to break something up. I do most of my drinking at home. People get a little uptight when they see a badge belly up at the only watering hole in town."

"I'm sure they appreciate your thoughtfulness."

I was getting lots of looks, quick turn aways, some nods.

"How was Myra?"

"She was open. Said they were lovers."

"Figured she would."

"Why didn't you tell me that earlier?"

"What different does it make? If I told you that you didn't need to talk to her, you would've anyway."

"True."

"She's still got what it takes, huh?"

"Yes, she does."

"Look, I'm heading back to the ranch. You're going to be a popular guy here tonight. Backdoor will be unlocked whenever you and Cherry get home."

I looked up and saw Cherry laughing and talking to some backwards ballcap wearing kid.

"Nah, we'll be back before you know it."

Spaceman laughed. "There's supposed to be some hot shit band playing tonight. Overlords of the Prairie or something like that."

"Sounds like a real treat."

Spaceman finished his drink. Put it on the bar.

"Alright, see ya when we see ya."

"Adios," I said.

Once the booze started flowing through everyone, all the glances and hushed whispers in my direction turned into loud hellos and plenty of back slappin'.

Damn, thatchoo Arch?

I heard you OD'd on heroin or something.

Who's the piece of tail you're with?

You haven't changed a bit.

Where you been all these years?

Somebody told me you got shot up in Iraq.

Heard you were flying planes for one of the big airlines.

How about Spaceman marrying your old flame?

Small towns. It was funny. I could have listened to that shit all night.

But I didn't.

I did some shots with some folks.

Slugged down a few beers.

Tossed back a few bourbons.

I looked around the place. It was surreal. All that time away and nothing had changed. The décor of the Elks, the smell of the place, the busted floor tiles in the men's room.

There was a new flat screen TV and the jukebox had been swapped out with a digital unit, but for the most part it was like stepping back in time. It didn't feel warm though. More like cold and depressing. Foreign. Almost hard to believe I had once been a part of the town, the people.

"You ready?" I said to Cherry.

Cherry was loving the attention she was getting. I think seeing other women around me, talking, flirting was turning her on too. She put her hand on the front of my pants.

"Are you ready?" She smiled.

I felt awkward being with her. Not just there, but altogether. She was beautiful, but it all felt like borrowed time. Like fate had dealt us some twisted idea of a blind date. Still, it was better than being alone. No telling who I might have gone home with had Cherry not been there. Maybe no one.

I tossed some bills to Bentley and nodded. He gave one in return.

On the way out of the door, I slid my hand down the small of Cherry's back into her jeans. No underwear.

We got about five steps outside when I saw the red tip of a cherry cheroot light up. A man leaning against the wall stepped into the light.

"Well, well, well. Archie Moses."

It was Colt Boone. He stood about five-foot-six and looked like an aging rocker had discovered hair plugs, steroids and the gym.

"Colt Boone?"

"That's right, motherfucker."

Cherry and I coughed out a laugh at the intensity of the retort.

"Wow, if I didn't know any better I'd think I was looking at Dog the Bounty Hunter."

Colt smiled. You could tell it was the look he'd been going for. The spurs hanging from the back of his silver tipped cowboy boots were a bit much, but then again, to each their own.

"Still got that impressive head of hair," I said. "Those are some sharp looking muscles, too. New?"

"Shit. Just be glad I didn't have 'em when I was younger."

"Probably would've smashed the buttons on your clarinet."

"It was a bassoon, asshole."

Colt did his best Josey Wales and puffed on his cheroot. His fists were balled up.

"Something on your mind, Colt? Seems like there's a lot of animosity coming from you."

Colt stepped forward again. Cherry stepped behind me.

"Bo has a hard time getting out now and then. He wanted me to stop by and tell you hello."

"Mighty kind. Give him my best."

Colt looked nervous. He didn't expect me to be at such ease. He turned his head and shifted his shoulders.

"You better watch your ass around-"

There were a lot of things I had grown to dislike over my forty-six years of living on Earth, but false bravado and macho posturing had always been near the top of my list.

Before Colt could finish his sentence, I had stepped away from Cherry, got my right heel behind his and had his back on the ground. I lowered my knee onto Colt's chest and pinned him against the asphalt.

He attempted a few swings at me, but couldn't connect.

I grabbed Colt's lit smoke off the ground, stuck it in his left nostril then squeezed his nose shut like I was trying to clench off a leaky hose. He screamed and kicked.

I got off of him and let go of his hair.

"That's assault. I'm going to sue your ass off."

"This is assault."

I pulled back and clocked Colt right in the nose. Bones buckled and popped.

"Tell Bo I'll be around town for a few days if he wants to chat."

I grabbed Cherry's hand and walked to my truck.

Under a wiper blade on the windshield was a bottle of Tahiti Toms.

I opened Cherry's door, got her in, then grabbed the bottle of suntan lotion and walked over to Colt. I pushed him against the wall. Watched the blood run out of his nose.

"This you? This you and Bo?"

"Wha, I don't know-"

"Where'd this come from?" I pushed the bottle onto his forehead.

"What is it? I, I don't. I've never seen it before."

"Who's doing this? What did you see?"

I put more pressure on Colt's head and the brick wall.

"I don't know what you're talking about."

"Did Bo put you up to this?"

"To what?"

I pushed off. Colt smiled.

"Bo did want you to have this though..."

Colt's fist came blasting towards me wrapped in brass knuckles.

I ducked. Grabbed his arm and smashed his face into the brick wall.

Colt dropped the knucks.

I scooped them up and put them on.

We squared up again. This time Colt pulled a black jack.

"I'm gonna lay you out," he said.

I was fast. Nothing Colt could do to dodge it. I drove the brass knuckles so deep into his stomach that his lungs wished they had cancer.

He fell to one knee and gasped for air.

I held out the Tahiti Tom's.

"What do you know about this?"

"Noth, nothing."

I shoved the brass knuckles in my back pocket and grabbed the black jack.

Colt was no longer the Bounty Hunter he'd wanted to be. He was now Colt, the pathetic forty-something with a bad mullet and bad tattoos on his overworked arms.

"One more chance."

"Kiss my-"

I brought the blackjack across Colt's chin. He went night, night.

I picked up the bottle of suntan lotion and got back in my truck.

"Oh my God," Cherry said. "What was that all about?"

I wish I could tell you I told her something funny, hilarious, but I didn't.

Instead, I was burning. Burning from anger, and as much as I hated to admit it, fear.

Not of dying so much, but fear of the unknown.

Fear of what the person fucking with us wanted.

Fear I had just killed Colt Boone.

"Gum?" Cherry asked.

"Sure."

She unwrapped a piece and put it in my mouth.

It was soft, sweet and chewy.

I wondered if the canteen would offer the same kind in prison.

39

The red, white and blues lit up behind us a mile from Spaceman's place. I didn't pull over. Just drove on.

Spaceman was waiting for us at the end of his driveway. He had a highball and was smoking. Cherry and I got out of the car. Seconds later Dallas Roth screeched in behind us in his cruiser.

Spaceman looked at Cherry.

"I just whipped up a batch of Texas snow cones in the blender. Go inside and help yourself. I think Paige is gonna take a soak in the hot tub if you want to join her. Arch and I will be there shortly."

"Okay," Cherry said. She kissed my cheek and went inside.

Dallas popped out of the cruiser like a rookie cop about to make his first bust. Spaceman coolly blew out his last drag and flicked the butt skyward.

"Freeze! Archie. Turn around slow-"

"Dallas," Spaceman said. "Put the goddamm gun down and turn off your travelling disco."

Dallas exhaled and shook his head like a kid who just found out the pool was closed. He begrudgingly did as he was told. He walked towards Spaceman and I.

"You want to know what this crazy sumbitch did, Sheriff?"

Spaceman took a sip of his drink.

"Well? Do ya?"

"You're all fired up and agitated like this is some kind of emergency. Is this an emergency, Dallas? You know it's a Friday night, right?"

"Look, Sheriff, I'm sorry, but Arch just damn near ripped the jaw off Colt Boone outside the Elks Club. Burned the hell out of his left nostril too."

"His nostril?"

"Said Arch shoved his ciga-"

"Did anybody see it?"

"Colt said Archie's gal saw the whole thing."

"That true, Arch?"

"Cherry and I were walking out of the Elks. Colt comes up talking like he's John Wayne and takes a swing. I was just defending myself."

"Sounds more than reasonable," Spaceman said.

"Are you kidding, Sheriff? Come to the hospital. Guy looks like a car hit his face."

"That doesn't prove anything other than Arch throws a solid punch."

"Why the hell would Colt lie?" Dallas said.

"Why would I?" I said. "You think I came back home to jeopardize my standing as a solid citizen?"

"Archie's got a point," Spaceman said.

Dallas shook his head in disgust.

"I don't give a shit that you two are friends. If I catch you breaking the law, just one step out of line, Arch, I'm taking you in. You can write me up if you want to Sheriff, but the law is the law."

Spaceman lit another cigarette.

"Look Dallas. I admire your passion for protecting and serving and all, but if you ever roll up on my property again with your gun drawn and siren on you'll be the one with the broken jaw. Understand?"

Dallas barely nodded.

"Good then," Spaceman said. "I'll see you tomorrow."

Dallas gave me a scowl then got back in his car. We watched the red tail lights fade away.

"What in the hell, Arch?"

"Colt waited until we came out of the bar. He mentioned Bo and how he wanted to see me. He was talking like he was doing a promo for the WWE. I lost it."

"For talking tough?"

"No." I grabbed the bottle of Tahiti Tom's. "For putting this on my car."

Spaceman looked at the bottle and shook his head. He blew out a line of thin smoke, stepped on his cigarette and ground it into the driveway.

"Jesus. You think it's them?"

"Doesn't make sense. Why wait until now?"

Spaceman let out a sigh. "Let's start fresh in the morning. Right now, I need another drink."

I wanted to eradicate the problem as quickly as possible and move on, but if Spaceman wasn't too stressed, why should I be? A drink sounded good.

Paige opened the front door in a faded Aerosmith t-shirt. It was from the *Permanent Vacation* tour. The one I had taken her to. The one we-

"Why don't you men get your suits on and come join Cherry and I. The stars are beautiful tonight."

"I don't have a swimsuit."

"That didn't stop Cherry." Paige laughed.

"I got an extra one," Spaceman said.

Paige went and got it. Handed it to me.

"See you boys out there," she winked.

I watched her wet ass jiggle down the hall. I looked at the trunks. Pink seahorses on blue seersucker.

"You're okay loaning me your favorite pair?"

Spaceman laughed. "You were the prep. Not me. This is my favorite pair."

He stepped into the hallway wearing vintage Marlboro Adventure Team trunks.

"How old are those?"

"I got a couple pair. Earned 'em five miles at a time. What're you drinking?"

"Anything brown."

"On it." Spaceman walked down the hall to the bar. "See you out there."

"See you out there."

I went in the bedroom and put on the seahorses. No way they would've fit his skinny ass. They fit me perfect.

I looked in the mirror and laughed. The tag was still on.

The sonofabitch must've had Paige buy them for me.

40

The hot tub was one of the classic cedar jobs worthy of the Swiss Alps. White tiny Christmas lights hung tastefully in a hip non-pattern in the tree branches above us. The tunes of J.J. Cale played lightly in the background.

Paige's wet cleavage just cleared the water line. It was almost as impressive as Cherry's.

Spaceman walked out and handed me a drink. I did the cheers hoist thing. He did the same. Spaceman put his drink down and pulled off his long sleeve t-shirt.

"Whoa," Cherry said.

Spaceman's upper torso and arms were covered with distinct and elaborate tattoos. He looked part rock star, part coffee shop hipster.

He stepped down into the hot tub.

"Quite the epidermal tapestry," I said. "You look like you spent five years in a Russian prison."

Spaceman looked at my scars.

"You look like you got sliced up at a Mexican pig roast."

Ball busting and casual racism. It's how men gave hugs.

"Are we supposed to believe you got all those scars as a mechanic?" Paige said.

I glanced at Spaceman. "Not all of them."

I stepped down into the water.

Paige took a long drink of margarita out of her straw.

Cherry drank her beer and swayed to the tunes.

Spaceman had both arms wrapped around the top edges of the hot tub. Cigarette in one hand. Drink in the other.

Paige looked at Cherry.

"So, Cherry are you from a small town?"

"Yeah."

"So, then you know what it's like. Everybody in everybody's business."

Cherry nodded.

"Some in other's business more than their own," Spaceman said.

Paige sent a playful splash in Spaceman's direction.

"Were you guys always good friends?" Cherry asked Spaceman.

"Oh gawd," Paige said, "back then if you saw Arch, you saw Ted and vice versa. Ballfield, raisin' hell out in the country, gettin' in trouble and so on."

"Trouble?"

"Just kids being kids," Spaceman said.

Paige pulled a joint out from under her towel and fired up. She took a long hit then handed it to Cherry. Cherry looked at Spaceman.

"It's okay," he said to Cherry. "I'll put you in handcuffs later."

"Kinky," Cherry smiled. She took a hit. Handed it back to Paige.

"Dallas alright?" Paige asked.

"Well, he's never been alright," Spaceman said," But yeah, he's fine. Just doin' his job."

"That guy started it," Candy said. "He was outside waiting."

"Oh, I'm sure," Spaceman said. "I'm sure Colt got what he deserved."

"Why does he hate Arch so much?" Candy asked.

"He hates me too."

"Why?"

"It's a sad story really," I said. "Do we need to tell it?"

"The woman asked a question, I believe she deserves an answer," Spaceman said.

"Do you care?" Paige asked.

"Not at all. Not a fun one to tell though."

"Maybe not," Paige said. "But it's a doozie."

"I'm fine with it," I shrugged.

"Good," Spaceman said. "So anyway-"

"These two were a lot of fun to hang out with," Paige interrupted. "If you were a girl, this was the double date you wanted to be asked out on. Problem was, they went on a lot of double dates with other peoples' girlfriends."

"Doesn't sound accurate to me. You Arch?"

"Not in the least," I said.

"So anyway, Colt's older brother, Bo, had this girlfriend."

"I'll take it from here doll," Spaceman said to Paige. "So anyway, Colt's older brother, Bo, had this girlfriend."

"Tammy Wand," Paige laughed.

Spaceman sighed. "You want me to tell this?"

"Sorry," Paige said.

Spaceman laughed. "Hell, you weren't even there."

Paige sent a finger in Spaceman's direction.

"I'm just trying to have some fun," Paige laughed. "Go ahead."

"So, Bo was like twenty. Tammy was a freshman. You know, one of those creepy older scumbags that date girls a bunch younger?"

Spaceman smiled and winked at me.

This time Cherry shot Spaceman her middle digit.

"Anyway, Arch and I had been riding around with Tammy and her friend, this girl, Jen Jergansen."

"I still can't believe-" Paige began.

"Somebody muzzle her will ya? She was cute, Paige. Lay off. Anyway, I kind of liked Tammy and Jen was over the moon for Arch. Or was it the other way around?"

"You got it right," I said.

"Right," Spaceman said. "So, Bo finds out about it. People start telling us to look out. That we're on Bo Boone's shit list. All this nonsense. Now, keep in mind we've only ridden in a car with these two girls once. One time. Well, me maybe more than once with Tammy, but whatever.

"Arch and I are throwing the football back and forth one night at the park. Back then they cut the lights at 10PM. We're walking back home sharing slugs from a Gatorade bottle, when out of nowhere, we get tackled by four guys. They lay a pretty good beating on us, tie our hands behind us, throw bags over our heads and toss us in the back of a pick-up.

"Now, what made this funny was there were like three hundred empty beer cans in the bed of the truck, so we know it's Bo's cousin, Terry's truck, so the bags over our heads were senseless, which should let you know the sharp minds we're dealin' with here. Anyway, they're blasting Mercyful Fate or something."

"Slayer," I chimed in.

"Okay, Slayer," Spaceman said. "Every now and again one of them would punch one of us and they'd laugh. They held the tips of their lit cigs just inches from our hands and arms, burning us occasionally. Suddenly we take a hard turn and I can taste the dust from the road. We go over some railroad tracks and I know they're taking us to the trestle bridge."

"Sorry," Cherry said. "What's the trestle bridge?"

"It was this old train bridge the county was too cheap to tear down. They rerouted the railroad over a new bridge and left the old bridge to rot away. The county had a big condemned sign on it. It ran about fifty feet above Ridge River. Anyway, they get us out there and rip our hoods off. They got Spaceman and I bent over the rail. We're staring down at this black river watching the moonlight reflect off of it.

"We get spun around and get punched by some doofus, Bruce Earl. There is like a small crowd on the bridge. A bunch of Bo's buddies, loser seniors that couldn't get laid if they paid for it and some of his co-workers from the spark plug factory. Bo is standing there in front of us and goes, you motherfuckers think you can get with someone else's girlfriend and people won't find out about it? Arch and I didn't say anything which only made him madder. Bo was like, think you're tough? Too cool? We'll see.

"So, Bo looks at Tammy and says which one? Now Tammy was with me, but since my dad is the Sheriff she was worried that Bo might get in worse trouble, so she lies and says she was with Arch. Of course, Arch, being Arch, lets it slide.

"Anyway, Bo calls Tammy over. Tells her to unzip Arch's fly. She says no, Bo slaps her. Arch tries to get loose, but is held back by Bo's buddies. Tammy is crying, tells Arch she is sorry. Unzip him, Bo yells. Pull his cock out.

"Tammy was crying and was like, no I'm not going to do it, so Bo hits her again. Arch and I want to kill this guy, but like I said earlier we got our hands tied behind our backs. Bo goes, you didn't have a hard time touching it the other night. Now pull it out or I'm going to stab him."

"Oh my God," Cherry said taking the joint back from Paige.

"It gets better," Paige said. "Tell her babe."

"I'm trying to, dammit," Spaceman said. He sucked the last bit of nicotine out of a brown filter. "Bo calls for Bruce's knife. It's like a hunting knife. Big buck knife. Everybody is watching. Tammy is bawling, says sorry again to Arch. Arch shakes his head like, don't sweat it."

"Don't sweat it? No, I was shaking my head like don't pull my dick out."

"Keep goin," Paige said.

"Sweet God of thunder, I plan to dammit," Spaceman lit another cigarette.

"So, Tammy pulls out Archie's dick. Bo looks down says somethin' like that's the one you just had to have last night, huh? Don't look so big now does it. People are yelling, kick his ass, from the crowd. Someone yells, he's scared shitless. Bo laughs and is like, you're goddamm right he is.

"Bo tells Tammy to pull out Arch's ball bag."

"What?" Cherry said, taking a big pull of her beer.

"Yep," Spaceman nodded. "Your boy Arch here is taking one for the team and I'm feeling like shit about it. Arch and I are trying to break free to kick Bo's ass, but his guys got a good hold on us. Bo yells for Tammy to pull Arch's balls out. Tammy finally does. The crowd whoops, laughs.

"I tell Bo, don't. He gives me something about, he doesn't give a shit if my dad is the Sheriff. Says when he's done with Arch, he's going to cut off my fingers for driving that night. Now, you gotta imagine this. The moon is shining off this hunting blade and Bo is threatening us on top of the trestle bridge. Meanwhile, the crowd is loving it. Think you can fuck around with anyone just because you score touchdowns? Bo yells at Arch."

"You played football too?" Cherry asked.

"Small town. We played everything," I said.

Spaceman went on. "Arch is quiet the whole time. Playing it cool."

"By cool he means I'm hoping I don't become a eunuch," I said.

"Anyway," Spaceman said, "Bo goes, know what happens when a bull is castrated? It loses the urge to fuck. So, I'm going to do this town a favor and take Romeo here off the prowl for good.

"I tell Bo, it was me man, not Arch. Bullshit, Bo says. Tammy has Arch's balls out. Bo's waving his blade in the moonlight. Just then Arch tells Bo, you do this and I promise you, I'll kill you.

"The crowd oohs and aahs. Bo is taken aback by that, but can't show it, so he takes the knife and holds it up in front of Arch's face. Tough talk, Bo says. Look, I say. It was me Bo. I was with Tammy.

"Bo laughs. He's like shit, nice try. Then he goes, you know what? Her pussy ain't worth prison. Bo tosses the knife back to Terry. Just know though boys. You mess with another man's woman, especially mine and I promise next time something very, very bad will happen to you. At that point, he hauls back and knocks the wind out of Arch. Some seniors laugh, high five Bo. Terry cuts our hands loose and laughs. Everybody begins walking back to their cars.

"Arch slowly gets to his feet and spits in Bo's face. Hold up, Bo says. He looks at Arch. You dumb bastard, this was over until you did that. Now you have to decide if you want me and the boys take you two for a long ride out in the country or if you want jump off this bridge.

"Everybody kind of gasps. At this point it's like thirty-five degrees outside. River's running at a good clip.

"The thing about Ridge River was nobody swam in it. It was full of debris. Some parts of it were deep, others shallow.

"Bo goes, well, faggot, what's it gonna be? Get your ass kicked and left in the country or go night swimmin'? Arch rears back and head butts Bo square in the nose. All of Bo's buddies rush him, but Arch is now upside down, backflipping into some kind of gainer off the bridge.

"Oh my God," Cherry said.

"Right? That's exactly what I'm thinking when I jump off right after him. So now," Spaceman said taking down the last swig of his drink. "People are freaking out and screaming. Yelling at Bo. He says something like, you saw it, they jumped on their own. I didn't mean nothin'. So, Terry takes off his jacket, sayin' we gotta try to save 'em or we're going to jail. He goes over to the end of the bridge and starts sliding down the bank calling our names. Now, Arch and I are freezing our balls off as we have now swum to the other side of the bank, and are hiding under the bridge. Everybody else is looking down in the water for us.

They haven't come up.

I don't see them.

Oh my God. They're dead.

"Dammit, boys say something, Bo yells in a panic. Arch and I don't say a word.

"Terry calls back that he can't see us.

"Boys, boys, Bo yells. He's scared to death at this point, probably knows if he doesn't attempt to save us he's going to jail, so he jumps. Now Bo's a big ole farm boy, not the most athletic guy. He comes off the bridge at a weird angle. Kind of cockeyed like. He's screaming all the way down and BAM!!! There is this awful, awful sound."

"Oh my God," Cherry said. "What happened?"

"Bo's neck hits a log floating in the water. Snaps his back. Been in a wheelchair ever since."

Cherry put a hand to her magnificent rack. "That's horrible. Who saved him?"

"That's the thing," Spaceman said. "Arch did, but in Bo's mind it's still Arch's fault. His family tried suing and all that, but after Tammy's testimony and a few other guys the court threw it out. Now, every so often Bo's little brother, Colt gets drunk and tries to play tough guy."

I poured down the last sip of my drink.

"I'm getting another. Anyone else?" I said.

Cherry had beers in a cooler by the hot tub.

Spaceman and Paige handed me their glasses. We reloaded.

"Okay, so that was a fun one," I said. "Let's lighten the mood."

"Would love to," Spaceman said, "Cherry."

"Yes," Cherry smiled.

"Are your boobs real?"

"Now dammit, Ted." Paige splashed water at Spaceman.

Spaceman chuckled. "I'm kidding. Come on, I know they're real. Cherry, no offense."

"None taken," Cherry laughed.

Paige sent another splash at Spaceman.

"Say, whatever happened to that little nine-hole scrub brush golf course that used to be here?" I asked.

"Looking for a tee time tomorrow," Spaceman said, exhaling a tendril of blue smoke.

"I was trying to make polite conversation," I said. "I guess I could ask Paige some questions about her ass."

Spaceman laughed. "Golf course went from nine to eighteen holes, then got too expensive to keep up. They got rid of the employees and made it a volunteer system, but only the same people volunteered, they got sick of it and closed it."

"Small towns, man," Cherry said. "Hard for businesses. In Meemaw, unless the place fed you or got you drunk it struggled to stay open."

"How'd you make any money cutting hair?" Paige said.

Cherry smiled and stood up out of the water naked.

"Can't argue with that." Paige said. "I'd let you cut mine."

"Speaking of failed businesses in small towns," Spaceman said pointing to Paige, "This one can tell you all about it."

"Oh Lord," Paige rolled her eyes.

"Let's hear it," I said.

"Well, first she wanted to do a fancy little tea room. Which we all knew would fail."

"We were getting the space for free," Paige said. "I thought it would be so cute."

"Then, she had this, what was it? A women's-"

"It was like a Victoria's Secret, only I picked everything out. Did all the buying-"

"Yeah. All the buying," Spaceman laughed. "No selling."

"Kiss my ass," Paige sent another playful splash almost extinguishing Spaceman's cigarette. "I brought it all home and wore it for you."

Spaceman smiled, "I guess you did do that," he laughed. "What were some of the others?"

"Let's see. There was the bakery, the pet store, the retro shop."

"Retro shop?" I asked.

"Yeah, you know what's old is new again. A lot of these places, companies, whatever kept making stuff that went out of fashion. I had like a fun 80's store for a while. Then Wal-Mart started carrying the stuff. How can you compete with that?"

"Hell," Spaceman laughed, "the other problem was in this county there is no such thing as retro. People never stopped using the stuff."

Paige rolled her eyes. "Like your Marlboro swim trunks from the early nineties."

"I earned these," Spaceman smiled. "Great lookin' too."

"Speaking of great looking. I love your tattoos," Cherry said. "All original work?"

"There's a guy in Indianapolis that did all these. They're all his own drawings, but none drawn solely for me, except this one."

Spaceman pointed at the inside of his right forearm. The work was about four inches in length and maybe three inches high. It featured three skulls on spikes, there was a fourth one without a skull. The spillway was in the background and the water was blood red.

"What is that?" Cherry said.

Spaceman laughed. "Awful right. Horrible screw up."

"I never got that one either," Paige said. "When are you going to have that one covered?"

Spaceman looked at me.

"Very soon."

"Good to know," Paige said. "Stand up, babe."

Spaceman did. Paige pointed out some of her favorite tattoos. Roses, anchors, stars.

"Holy shit, is that the Hamburglar riding a unicorn?" I asked.

"No asshole," Spaceman said to me, "It's the Greek God of War Ares riding on Pegasus."

"Well, I'll be."

Spaceman flipped me the bird.

"What do your constituents think about their Sheriff having his torso and arms covered in ink?"

"That's the best part," Paige smiled. "They're just for me. No one else in town has seen them."

"Nobody?" I said.

"Nope. I wear long sleeves at all times," Spaceman said.

"Would anybody really care in this day and age?" Cherry said.

"Probably," Paige frowned. "It's a conservative town."

We stayed up another hour or two laughing, telling more stories and listening to tunes.

The more relaxed everyone seemed to get, the more tense I began to feel.

I thought about what Dooley Hicks had told me about people disappearing.

I turned to look at Spaceman. He was staring right at me. He ran the ember on his cigarette from stem to stern.

That night I had a dream I was in a dense forest being stalked by a hungry tiger. I kept calling out for Colesy, trying to warn him, but there was no answer. Suddenly, Spaceman emerged from a path. There was blood all over his face, running down his cheeks and chin.

"Did you find Bob?"

"No," Spaceman said.

I stepped closer and looked at Spaceman.

Between his teeth, dangling like a cigarette was a bloody finger wearing Colesy's Claddagh ring.

41

"Autopsy said Bob was a hundred and eighty-five pounds, but the ligature marks on his neck showed stressed bruising for nearly twice that weight."

"Jesus, Archie. We went over this." Spaceman took a drag like he was allergic to oxygen. "Look, as sad and weird and however messed up it is, Bob's suicide is an open and shut case. Whatever reason he had, was between him and God."

"Whatever reason?" I said. "He hated himself for what he did that day. You know that, right? He did it for us."

"Did it for us?"

"Come on man. The kid?"

Spaceman thought about it for a moment, nodded, then flicked some ash into an old Hudson hubcap ashtray

"I started smoking the day after it happened. It made me sick. Dizzy at first, but I still did it. Kept at it until I got used to it. Then one day found out I liked it. And then a few weeks after that it had nothing to do with liking it anymore. I just needed it. Probably gonna kill me. Strange, but I accept it in a weird way. Like maybe how Bob took to the church as penance."

"That's crazy."

"Is it? Something happens to a man and he punishes himself or looks for salvation. I know what Bob and I've done. But what about you, Arch? You ever think about that day, or did you blow it off in your mind like you blew out of here? Because I don't see you suffering much at all. I see you rolling into town with a sweet piece of ass and late model SUV."

"This about money?"

"Hell no. It's about you being gone."

"You should have called me when Red died," I said. "I would have come back. Paid my respects.

"Why should I have to? You should have stayed in touch. I had things under control, all you had to do was visit. You never did. For a while I blamed myself. That maybe you got word about Paige and me and that it was just too much, but shit man."

I let Spaceman's words soak in. I wanted to tell him about the collateral damage my soul had taken. How I tried to wash away the sin of that day with the blood of others by killing all the rotten bastards that I could. Some for a fee. Some for free. Not being afraid to die, maybe sometimes wanting to, but men don't always tell each other the truth if they tell each other anything at all.

I got up and cracked a window.

"Okay, so we know I'm an asshole, Bob's dead and you're a martyr with smoldering airways. You still haven't told me about Amber and Karen."

Spaceman smashed his cigarette in the hubcap.

"Go see for yourself."

42

The house was a two story, but small. I couldn't tell if it was meant to be white or gray. A fine line of chipped paint ran under the eaves in the dirt before the grass shrugged and reluctantly decided to grow.

Some kind of mongrel was chained in the backyard off to the side. I walked up to the cracked cement steps and rang the bell. It was broken. I knocked.

The silhouette at the screen was large, but when the door opened I nearly fell flat on my ass. It was Amber, not the hot, sexy Amber from a few thousand yesterdays, but the scary unattractive Amber presently.

She must've been a hundred pounds overweight. Her hair was a knotted mess of gray with sickly looking bald spots. She had bags under her eyes and her skin was pale and patchy.

"Archie?"

"Hey Am, that you?"

She didn't respond. Years ago, we might have done the friendly hug thing, but the smell coming from inside the home was far from pleasant. Amber knew this. She stepped outside on the porch.

"Come in for Bobby's service?"

I nodded. "Didn't see you there."

"Yeah, well. I don't go out much."

"You think Bob killed himself?"

"Course he did."

"What makes you say that?"

"Jesus, Archie. Why in the hell do you think?"

We both remembered that day.

"I had hoped he had gotten past all that," I said. "The grace of the church and all."

"Grace? Was that her name?"

"Who?"

"The women he fell in love with. Ever since she ran off on him he had his dick in damn near everyone else."

I said a silent prayer for Bob and his penis that Amber wasn't one of those people.

"What woman?"

"Some woman. From Mount Vernon or something. She was really pretty. Classy. Had a Cadillac. Nice clothes. They were together for a pretty long while. I heard he proposed, but she didn't want to marry no preacher. Guess it didn't look too good them together like that without nuptials. Heard he became a real Casanova after that."

"I heard."

"You think he was murdered?"

"No idea. I do know whatever happened, happened shortly after he received one of these."

I pulled out the bottle of Tahiti Tom's and held it up to Amber.

Amber's eyes widened. She stared at the bottle until they filled with tears.

"I got one too."

"When?"

"Just a few days ago. First thing I did was get Spaceman on the phone."

"You told Spaceman?"

"Yeah, you know my younger brother Dallas works for him at the Sheriff's office?"

"Yeah, I know. What did Spaceman say when you told him about the bottle?"

"Said he'd take care of it."

"Did he come out and see you?"

"Yeah, I gave it to him."

"Did he say anything else?"

"Just not to worry about it."

I looked at the label of the chubby man in the hammock.

"That little round sonofabitch seems to have it made in the shade, doesn't he?"

"We all thought we did back then." Amber said. She looked closer. "That's weird."

"What?"

"The one I got had the exact same tear on the label. Spaceman give you this?"

He hadn't. The one I was holding was the one that was left under my windshield. What the fuck?

"You got any bourbon?"

"Damn, it's 9AM, Archie."

"What, you just polished off the last drop?"

Amber grinned. "Shit. Come on in."

The kitchen sink was overflowing with dirty dishes. The stove, the curtains, everything was filthy.

Amber handed me a chipped glass that had once been a pickle jar. The label was faded and like Amber, was barely clinging to its former self.

"Fancy. What're we drinking?"

"Firecracker. It's all I drink nowadays. It's cinnamon flavored whiskey. Like Fireball only a bunch cheaper. You know Jesse Burls?"

"No."

"He comes by sometimes. Says it's the exact same thing as Fireball, just bottled in a different warehouse.

"Is that so?"

"Yep. Don't it just make you sick? All these people, the things they do, trying to act like something they're not?"

Amber pulled a bottle of Firecracker from her freezer and poured some in my jar. I took a drink. The stuff could strip paint. In fact, for a brief second, I thought I was being poisoned until I watched Amber take a five second hit straight from the bottle.

"Finishes nicely on the palate," I smiled.

"Yeah it does. Got all kinds of uses too," Amber said. "You get a cold, just drink a bottle of this. It'll be gone in three days. Ants in your house? Just make a little puddle with this stuff on your porch and they'll march right in it and die. You see my dog out there, Regis?"

"Beautiful animal."

"He ain't been right since the accident. Fell out the second story window. When he finally bounced back from that, he cut his leg up on a rusty plow. I had Jesse hold him down and we poured some Firecracker where he got sliced up to clean his wound. Dog howled like I've never heard. Now, he's practically as good as new."

I looked outside at the filthy mound of mange. The poor bastard didn't fall out of the window. He had willfully leapt to his death. And what did he get for his efforts when his plow attempt failed as well? Flavored whiskey poured into his wounds. Damn. Not only had Amber packed on the pounds she had clearly smoked half her brain away.

I looked at her. She was wearing a Farm-Aid t-shirt with no bra. Her nipples, the ones I had once gladly sucked on, were now pointing straight to hell. I had a feeling she was already there and had been for a while.

"You see Karen much?" I asked.

Amber looked out the window for a moment.

"No. Things got different after that day. It was like I reminded her and she reminded me of the worst day of our lives. She went on and married Shively. Lives out there on all that land. Stuck up now. Drives one of them Range Rovers. Hear she gets her hair done in Evansville. Never thought she'd become that way."

What in the hell happened to you? I felt like saying.

It wasn't until Amber started crying that I realized I had actually said it out loud.

"Three-time loser in marriage. Got kids by two of 'em. Lived in St. Louis for a few years. Got a job at the Bud plant. Mom died. I came back here to take care of things and never got out. Met another guy, got married. He was a partier, bad crowd. I got into meth. Xanax real bad. He beat me. Permanently messed up my knee. Couldn't work. Soon as I put a on a little weight, he run off. Left me with kids I didn't like and a drug habit I couldn't afford."

"Who's watching your kids?"

"They're out of school now. One's in prison. Other one works at DunRite Filter in Flora. Don't see him much."

I drained my pickle jar of Firecracker. It was horrible stuff. Poverty ruined everything. Even drinking.

Amber got up and went to the bathroom. When she came back I could tell she was high.

She had a yearbook with her. Opened it to a page of her playing Rizzo in *Grease*.

"You remember that? Whole town came. I think I could have been an actress had things been different."

"You certainly had the chops."

"I could have been like Karen, you know. Had one or two breaks gone my way." I looked at Amber's pajama pants and wondered the last time they'd been laundered. "You remember way back how we'd laugh and poke just about anywhere, anytime?

Out of respect I didn't correct her. It was more like one time and she did the knocking.

"Seems like a different lifetime, doesn't it?"

"Look at me." She pointed at her yearbook picture. "People wanted me back then. You always liked me. Even as a kid. Liked my tits anyway. I remember sometimes when you were in junior high you'd sleep over at our house. You and Spaceman would pay Dallas to let you guys peek through the keyhole at me getting ready to shower."

"How do you know that?"

"Girls know that kind of thing. That, and I could hear you guys snickering through the door."

It was true. We were horny kids and she was a smokin' hot high school babe then.

Then.

"Wanna fuck me now? I'll take it any way you want."

I was so shocked by Amber's bluntness I couldn't help but laugh out loud. Amber started to cry.

"I swore I'd never end up like my mom. I swore. Now look at me. I wish whoever sent me that bottle of suntan lotion would quit screwing around and just kill me."

"Quit talking crazy. You can turn things around."

"Archie, I tried to turn myself around so many times I'm dizzy."

"Listen," I got up. "Thanks for the drink. It was good seeing you."

Amber sniffed and wiped away her tears.

"Thanks for being kind enough to lie."

"It's no lie, Amber."

It was. Of course, it was.

Amber leapt up and gave me a hug. She held on like I was a life raft. She grabbed my right hand with both of hers and tried to put it up her shirt. I pulled it away.

"I've got to go."

I walked out on her porch and got halfway down the stairs.

"Wait," she said.

I turned around and looked at her.

Life had repeatedly kicked the shit out of Amber and no hand had offered to help her back up. Maybe Dallas had, but he had failed. Amber was broken. Gone. Ruined. Her eyes, the emptiness in them, told me she knew it.

"How about you let me suck you off? Twenty bucks."

I almost lied and said I had herpes, then guessed that wouldn't have been a deterrent, she probably already had them.

"No, uh…here."

I opened my wallet and handed Amber a hundred-dollar bill. She held it and looked at it for a moment, then held it up to the light.

"Moonlighting at the Federal Reserve these days?"

"Ha! You sure you don't want a suck?"

"Take a long hot shower and get some rest, okay Amber."

"Okay." Her eyes filled with tears again. "If you see Karen will you please tell her I said hi."

"Sure."

"Remember the old me. Okay Archie. The pretty one. The happy one."

"Only one I know. Be good to yourself. You hear me."

"I'll try."

I drove two blocks up the street and parked.

Maybe it was the chipped jar of cheap booze I'd slammed, but I had a hazy vision of a deep black vortex.

It was swirling and thrashing.

And we were all inside of it.

43

There are screams and then there are blood curdling death screams.

I dropped the bag with the beers and weed and scrambled up the hill as fast as I could.

I made it to the top of the embankment and looked across the water. A gnarl of flesh and bone was savagely punching and pumping inside of Karen.

I did a Pete Rose slide under the fence. A sharp twist of chain link unzipped my back from my shoulder blade to my kidney. I felt the blood rise on my skin. My momentum sent me sliding down the muddy bank on my stomach into the murky water.

I swam to the tower as fast as I could. The next thing I remember I was tackling the brute. He was bigger than me, stronger than me. His eyes looked yellow. Everything about him was pointy; chin, nose, knees, elbows.

He threw a haymaker that missed badly.

I got a piece of his jaw with a right. It barely fazed him.

He dove for my legs. I stepped out of the way and kicked him in the back of the head on his way down. He came up with quick right, missed and I went to work on his nose with a flurry of merciless strikes.

A powerful left got my temple then a right drove into my stomach. I leapt back and tried to catch my breath.

At that moment, Karen lunged at him with a nail file. She managed to drive it between two of his ribs. With a broad swift motion, he swung his arm and knocked Karen backwards end over end off of the tower and into the water below.

I heard more screams.

Amber.

Spaceman.

I sprung up looking for anything to grab. Nothing. For a millisecond in my peripheral I saw Colesy, sprinting toward us, fishing gear flying off his person with every step.

The man lunged at me and missed. His chest slid on the rough concrete, his head hung down just off the side. I jumped up, spread my legs and aimed for the back of his head. I came down just as he was picking himself up and drove his chin into the cement. He used my momentum to push me over the side. I caught the fourth rung and made my way back up. When I got to the top the man was wobbling back on his heels. His jaw hung to the side in a bloody mess.

I speared him into the opening of the spillway.

Somehow, he managed to grab the thick rope. Without thought, I jumped onto to him sending him thirty feet down to the wet concrete below.

I grabbed the rope at the last minute. Due to my speed and the slime, I slid down like it was a greased firepole. I heard a snap when I landed on the rapist's spine.

The water was rushing in at a fast clip. I couldn't see anything. I ducked under the waterfall and saw what was left of the rapist's brains leaking out of his cracked skull.

More screams came from the other end of the tube. I bent down and ran through the mossy tunnel as fast as I could, slipping, sliding and falling along the way.

When I made it out the other end, I saw a portly guy bleeding from his eye and nose standing over Spaceman who was on his back covered in blood. The man picked up a huge rock. When he brought it over his head he slipped in the mud and fell backwards into the stilling basin.

I jumped down and locked his head into a bulldog position. I dropped my feet out from under me taking us both under water. I squeezed and held on for dear life as the man thrashed and thrashed.

Amber jumped in with a thick branch. When the crown of the man's head broke the surface, gasping, she brought the branch down on his nose as hard as she could. He got to his feet and swung a left in my direction. I ducked and then shot up with a right under his chin. He splashed down into the water. Amber grabbed his head by the hair and held him under.

I turned to see Spaceman running up the hill towards Colesy and another man who were wrestling over a knife.

Mud and blood was everywhere. Everyone was sliding around fighting like wild animals.

"Someone is taking the car!" Karen yelled.

Spaceman got the man by the shoulders and held him down.

"Stop that car, Colesy," Spaceman yelled.

Spaceman kicked the blade to Bob. Bob grabbed it and took off down the hill towards the car.

Spaceman and the other man were dancing around. The man was taking wild swings but kept missing. I snuck up behind him and went for his legs. He drove a knee squarely into my forehead, slipped out of my grasp and took off running around the edge of the lake. Spaceman followed in frenzied pursuit.

The man had enough lead to get up the fence, but the razor wire at the top made him think better of it. He dropped and ran to the end where the woods were thick and full of briars. With a daring leap, he vanished into the trees. Moments later, Spaceman caught up and jumped in after him.

Approximately two minutes later I heard the man yell, or maybe it was Spaceman.

I struggled to get to my feet, but was too dizzy to stand.

I heard another guttural yell and tried to focus my eyes on the far end of the reservoir.

Minutes later Spaceman stepped out of the woods. Blood poured from a head wound. He cradled his right arm.

I heard more screams. This time in the opposite direction.

I made it to my feet and slid down the embankment. Amber and Karen were screaming behind the Monte Carlo hysterically. I made it around to the driver's side door. Colesy was crouched down sobbing. He had his bucket hat pulled down over his ears like he was trying to disappear.

When I stepped beyond the driver side door, I gasped.

Blood seeped out of numerous knife wounds in the abdomen of the would-be car thief. The body lay flat and kicked between coughs of blood. I followed the wounds up to the head and looked down into the wide-open eyes of a scared boy with a caterpillar of fine hair across his top lip. He held out a hand towards me.

Colesy's face was covered in a froth of mucous and tears. He sobbed uncontrollably and rocked back and forth.

The boy's hand fell as he took his last breath.

Colesy looked up at me panged.

"I had to stop him." He sobbed. "He was going to run. He was going to tell. He-"

I crouched down and put my hand on Colesy's shoulder to calm him.

"It's okay, Bob."

"Christ," Bob said choking on tears. "He was just a kid. Just a damn kid."

I looked at the boy, walked to the other side of the car and puked.

I wiped my eyes and walked back to Bob.

"You had no choice. He was taking our car."

"Right? I had to, Arch," Bob whimpered. "I had to. I had no choice. Right?"

"You had no choice, Bob."

But we did.

We had tons of choices.

And our futures would be determined by the ones we made in the next few hours.

44

Muddy, bloody and half naked, we all tried to keep our sanity from spilling from the car as Spaceman navigated the back roads with a broken arm and blood running down his forehead.

"Who were they?" Karen cried. "Where did they come from?"

"Didn't you see them come up, Colesy? You had the whole vantage of the lake."

"I was down in the bushes." He sobbed. "I was going to the bathroom."

Spaceman kept a steady foot on the gas.

"Where are you going?" Karen yelled.

"Town. Straight to the Sheriff's office. Dad will help us. We did nothing wrong. It was self-defense."

"Town?" Karen yelled. "Like hell. How do you explain us all being out there together?"

"We just say we bumped into you guys out there."

"How? We rode with you."

"We were nearly killed," I said. "Who cares if Shively finds out?"

"I do," Karen cried.

Bob was sobbing in the back.

"Jesus Christ!" Spaceman yelled. "What do we do, Arch?"

"Take me to the hospital," Amber said.

"Hospital? The hospital is as bad as going to the police station."

"How bad is everyone?" I said. "Pull over."

Spaceman slammed the brakes on the loose shoulder. We all got out and examined each other's wounds.

Karen's eyes were black and her nose was broken. She had abrasions up and down her back and legs. Blood ran down her inner thighs.

Amber's legs were all cut up. A huge bruise the size of a Frisbee was darkening on her left side. Her jaw hung slack, teeth were missing. It looked like someone tried to take her ear off.

Karen looked at my back.

"You need to see someone. That gash is really big. Skin is hanging."

"Can you tie it off with something for now?"

I tore my t-shirt into one long piece and handed it to Karen who wrapped me as best she could, given our mental states.

We turned and looked at Colesy. Though he was the only one fully dressed, complete with a fisherman's vest and boots he was shaking like a leaf. His lips were blue.

"What's the worst thing that can happen if we're honest?" Spaceman said.

"He was unarmed," Colesy whispered. "Just a scared kid, but I couldn't let him get away and tell."

"I'm supposed to get married in six weeks," Karen screamed. "What are we going to do?"

"Fuck, Fuck, Fuck!" Spaceman beat on the hood with his good hand then took a deep breath. "Okay. Okay. We have to think."

"Archie, it looks like you're losing a lot of blood," Amber cried.

Spaceman looked at me. "Let me see. It's not too bad, with the bandages. You good, Arch?"

I nodded.

Colesy squeezed my arm as hard as he could.

"Please don't let them take me to prison, Arch. Please!"

"I promise, Bob. You are not going to prison. None of us are."

"Why would we? They attacked us," Amber cried.

Spaceman gave me a look.

The girls were sobbing uncontrollably.

"This can't be happening," Karen said.

"It is," I said. "And we need a plan."

"Everybody back in the car, now," Spaceman said.

No sooner did Amber's door close, Spaceman had the pedal to the metal, blasting two high arching sprays of mud behind us. He turned back and looked over his shoulder.

"Everything is going to be okay you guys. Just listen to me."
And then he laid it out.
The story.
The story we all agreed on.
The story we swore we'd ride out until the end of our days.

45

Amber's appearance and her Firecracker whiskey had made me nauseous.

I drove to a spot called the Drip for breakfast. It was one of those homespun greasy spoons that served thick slices of bacon cooked perfect every time.

I was starving.

I saved some yolk from my fried eggs to top my hash browns with. Sometimes the biggest lifts came from the smallest things.

"Well, well, well."

With a presence as pleasant as a wet fart appearing in white shorts, Dallas Roth stood before me. His uniform was over starched and adorned with small pins and patches of dubious distinction. He looked like a scout leader, except for the toothpick that poked out of his mouth while he chewed gum.

Dallas grabbed an empty chair from a neighboring table, swung it around and plopped down in front of me. It was clear he had practiced the move many times given his shocked expression when he pulled it off. He settled back into make-believe tough guy mode.

"What are you doin' here?"

"Deconstructing the polio vaccine. What does it look like?"

Dallas furrowed his brow.

"I mean, why are you still in town? Bob Cole is six feet under and pushin' daisies."

"Not the most compassionate way of putting it, but yes."

"So, when you takin' your girl and your fancy SUV and leavin'?"

I swallowed my last bite, washed it down with coffee and threw my napkin on my plate. I stared in Dallas' eyes long enough to make him uncomfortable.

"Let's see, how do I put this so you can understand it?" I gave a long dramatic pause. "Oh yeah. It's none of your goddamm business."

Dallas poked at his gums and tipped his hat towards a pretty lady. He turned back to me with a grin.

"Yeah, well see, it kind of is."

"Oh?"

"Yeah. And I'm gonna get to the bottom of it. I heard Spaceman talking on his phone the other day. Didn't really sound himself. Seemed agitated, yelling and asking lots of questions to someone in a government office of some kind. Then I hear you been over to my sister's house for a chat. Matter a fact a little birdie told me they saw you give Amber a bunch of money. Now why's that?"

Dallas had been in the same class as Spaceman and I, but was a world class doofus from day one. He was harmless, but a pain in the ass. One of those guys that tried so hard, but in spite of themselves can't get over the hump of their own awkward personality. Dallas used to beg to hang out in high school, which only made it worse. Was it possible he had ridden out to the spillway that day?

"You see Arch, I know things. I know things about you that you don't know I know. Things that if you knew I knew you wouldn't want me to know."

I had no idea what Dallas was yammering about, but I figured I'd play along.

"I know you know you think I don't know, but I do know."

"Ha! If you knew that, I'd have already known." Dallas said.

"I know," I said with a wink.

"Wait. What?"

Dallas scratched his chin nervously.

No way Dallas was at the spillway that day. He was dumb, but not dumb enough to rub our faces in it. There was no end game for him. It didn't make sense. Why be silent this long? Had he seen anything he would have told everybody that very day.

The waitress came over and filled my coffee cup. Dallas turned his empty cup over.

"Thanks Fern," Dallas winked.

Fern rolled her eyes, poured and walked on. I dumped in some cream.

"What is it you know about me, Dallas?"

"I know things. Deep things."

"Deep things?"

"Well, dark things."

"Dark things?"

"Look, I got scoop on you. Got me?"

"Wait, you're saying you have scoop on me, but you're also asking if I have you? I'm confused."

"I know shit about you," Dallas said exasperated at full volume.

All eyes went to Dallas. I took a sip of my coffee.

"Enlighten me."

Dallas gave me a shit-eating grin. He spit his gum into a napkin then leaned in quietly.

"I know how Red found you out in Jasper County. Found you that night hiding on the roof of that foster home. Crying and shivering. You were eight. He felt sorry. Took you in as one of his own."

"Go on."

"I know about you and my sister. How you guys had a thing in high school. Well, when you were still in high school anyway. She was already out."

It wasn't a thing. Not really. One night after a football game Amber came knocking on my bedroom window. She'd gone to the Elks after the game. She was drunk and wanted a place to throw her tube top. I let her in. Then she let me in. Twice. Rumor was she was running through the whole offensive unit back then.

"Anything else?"

Dallas picked up a packet of sugar and dumped it out on the table. He took his index finger and tapped down the little pile.

"Yeah. You left town not long after that car accident you had with Bob and Spaceman that summer. After that you never, ever, ever came back. Not even for Red's funeral. Which was a real shock to some. Now Bob's dead and you zip right back home. Start pokin' around town getting in people's business. And, judging by Amber's tears, making them uncomfortable."

"So, you followed me to Amber's."

"Who else. Ain't like we got a huge police force."

"Okay. So what?"

"So. Something's going on. Something shady. Somethin' that has to do with you."

I had a sip of coffee.

"Some of what you say may or may not be true. Some is rumor. Some is pure conjecture. But one thing is for sure, Dallas, you nailed the part that something's going on."

Dallas proudly stabbed his toothpick between his teeth.

"That's how I got this job. My surmise'n skills."

"I don't doubt it for a minute. You know Dallas, we, that is everybody in town, were trying to think of what to get you as a gift for your cracker jack police work."

"Oh yeah?"

"Yeah. People threw out a bunch of different ideas, but the ultimate consensus was to get you one of those big, long, black, thick veiny dildoes to go fuck yourself with."

"Been practicin' that one, have ya?" Dallas' volume rose with his ire. "Let me tell you something smart ass, you don't want to know what I'd do with a big black dildo."

The room went silent.

"Yes," I said loudly. "You're right. I don't want to know what you'd do with a big black dildo."

There were snickers in the room.

Dallas stiffened, lowered his right hand down to his holster.

"Keep it up, Arch. Keep it up. I'm warnin' you. I'm serious now."

"Now, Dallas. I'm just kidding."

Dallas eased a bit.

"We passed on the dildo idea," I went on. "Figured you'd embarrass yourself walking around like it was an all-day sucker."

And that was it.

The anger from years of having his balls busted ignited, giving Dallas just enough propulsion to launch over the table. I hopped out of the way just in time for him to come crashing down on the vintage Formica, bringing himself and everything with it onto the floor.

Everybody, including an old timer in a back brace turned and looked.

Dallas hopped up and drew his gun.

"Freeze you sonofabitch. You're under arrest!"

"For what? Commenting on your gingivitis. You know that might even be early periodontal-"

Then it came, Dallas was going for the pistol whip.

I moved my head out of the way just as Dallas slipped on bacon grease and went down. In an effort to catch himself his finger accidentally squeezed the trigger sending a bullet into the tiled floor.

In a movie, people would scream and run out, but it was a small town full of seasoned hunters and gun owners who instead looked on rather amused.

I whipped out my phone and snapped a picture of Dallas struggling to get up.

"That's false arrest, damage to public property, and illegal discharge of a firearm in a place of business," I said. "At least let me pay for your coffee."

I pulled two twenties out of my wallet.

Dallas slowly got to his feet. Bits of breakfast mess stuck to his shirt. Dallas lifted his service weapon and stuck it in my face.

"You shoulda known better, Mr. Fancy Pants. Things have changed down here now."

I looked down the barrel.

"Do it, Dallas. Make your name."

DING, DING!

The bell chimed above the door. Spaceman walked into the Drip with a cigarette hanging out of his mouth.

"Goddammit, Dallas. Put the fucking gun down."

He hated himself for it, but Dallas had tears welling up in his eyes.

"Can't do it, Sheriff."

"You damn well better," Spaceman said.

"I'm tired of taking this man's lip. Got no respect for the badge."

Spaceman looked at Clem, the owner of the place. He had a dish towel tossed over his shoulder. Clem shook his head no.

"Unfortunately, Dallas. Being a dickhead is not against the law."

"Hey," I said.

"Bottle it, Arch."

"Here's how it's going to go, Dallas," Spaceman said. "You're going to holster your piece. Apologize for this grave misunderstanding and go home and get yourself cleaned up. After that you're going to come back here and pay Clem for whatever damages you've made. Got it?"

Dallas nodded and holstered his gun.

"My mistake folks. No harm meant," Dallas said.

He tipped his hat to an uninterested Fern and walked out the door.
Spaceman looked around for a minute then took a seat at the counter.
"Coffee and a piece of lemon meringue, please."
And with that, order was restored.

46

Following Dallas' performance at the Drip, Spaceman went back to his office after his pie. That left me to keep going around and asking questions.

I saw Peter Dean in front of the Fire Station hosing down a tanker truck. Peter was in my high school class and had been a decent left tackle.

"Already looks clean to me," I said.

Peter kept the hose going.

"It is. But what else is there to do?"

"When does meth lab fire season start?"

"Ha! I can't even tell you the last time we were called to rescue a cat. Spaceman runs a tight ship here in Shoal County."

"That's what I've heard."

Peter turned the hose off. We shook hands.

"Good lookin' rig."

"Yeah, thanks. She's new. County bought her. Sometimes I'm afraid I'm gonna wash the paint off before our guys get to break her in. Feel bad about it, but I keep hoping something catches fire. You wouldn't believe the pressure on the hose."

"What's it twenty bar?"

"Working pressure."

"Bursting pressure around eighty?"

"How in the hell did you know that?"

"I DVR *Jeopardy*."

"Well, I'll be damned."

I liked Peter. He was a straight shooter.

"We didn't get a chance to talk much at Bob's funeral."

"Yeah, I'm sorry, Arch. That was a rough one for me."

"I understand you two got to be pretty tight in the later years."

"Yeah. We'd fish. Bowl. I was really the only one Bob felt comfortable having a few drinks around. Y'know this town."

"I do. Hey, you were a deacon in Bob's church for a while, right?"

"For a while."

"Why'd you stop?"

"Melissa heard about Bob running around. Was worried the town dirt would rub off on me. We'd still hang out though. He was a good man, he really was. Good Christian, too. He had his faults. We all do. I mean we're men, right? I never judged him. I mean, without a wife he had to take it where he could get it."

"He ever mess around with married women?"

"Nah. Had an opportunity a few times. Bob joked he wanted to keep his broken commandments under three."

"So, you don't think it was murder. That someone killed him?"

"Who? Everybody liked the guy."

"So, it is possible he killed himself?"

"Bob had this thing, this dark cloud, this depressed mood that came over him every so often. I mean, whatever it was, it took him down pretty hard. He didn't have much, but what he did have he'd give away to people all over town. I mean, it was crazy. You know Kermit Lutz, owns the roller rink?"

"People still roller skate?"

"Yeah, high times in the big city. Anyway, Bob gave his Ford Focus to Kermit after Kermit's car got stolen in St. Louis."

"Didn't Bob need his car as a minister?"

"I'm sure he did, but he bought a bike instead. If you got the time, you can get around on a bike anywhere around here."

It was true.

"What else about these moods? What triggered them?"

"Anytime a kid died in an accident or was murdered, that threw him for a loop."

"How'd he get out of those funks?"

"The Bible. He knew the Bible backwards and forwards. Was always quoting scripture. He preached a lot about forgiveness."

"So, you think he did it? Killed himself?"

Pete took a deep breath and rubbed the back of his neck.

"He may have, but I don't want to believe it."

"Okay. Thanks, Pete."

"Hey, how much longer you down here for?

"Not long."

"You still live in Nebraska?"

"Nebraska?"

"I heard after you graduated from college you played arena football in Lincoln or someplace like that."

Small towns. The rumor mill never stopped. What the hell.

"Oh, yeah." I said, "Set a record for receptions until the shoulder gave out."

"Damn."

"What was the name of the team again?"

"The Lincoln Fighting Cobs. Our jerseys looked like kernels of corn."

"Pretty cheesy."

"Corny really."

"Ha! Now you're on to robbing breakfast joints I heard."

"Huh?"

"Heard Ol' Roth pulled his revolver on you at the Drip. What were you doing, selling fake gold watches on Main Street?"

"Oh, that." I laughed. "Yeah."

"Shit for brains is a step up for Dallas. Spaceman trusts him though. Been on the force for fifteen years or so."

"Really? That long."

"Yeah. Their first big bust was a pot field. Roth is the one that caught Koontz Beesbrook running a prostitution ring."

"Koontz Beesbrook was running a prostitution ring?"

"Well, kinda I guess. It was pretty genius really. You know that TV show *Survivor*?"

I never missed an episode.

"No. What's it about?"

"Well, see these contestants get put on an island for like a month with only rice and well water. They compete in little sports contests in groups and do puzzles and stuff and vote people off. Of course, all that time out there exercising with nothing to eat but rice, they wind up dropping a ton of weight.

"Well, Koontz wasn't making much on his gym so he hatched a Survivor-like idea of what if he took fat people out to his farm for a few weeks, made like a campground or something and fed 'em only rice."

"People did that? What about work?"

"I don't know all that. I'm sure he let 'em go to work then maybe they'd head straight back to the campground. Anyway, they'd go out for a week or two, sometimes a month and drop weight. He joked you didn't want to go a mile within the property carrying a sack of White Castles or you'd get eaten alive."

"That's incredible. But how'd he do it?"

"Damn internet. They got sites for every kind of fruit and nut out there. Koontz is sitting at a bar one night in Mt. Carmel and they're having Chubby Chaser Night, that's guys that love big women. Well, these gals out at Koontz's-"

"Wait, it's only women?"

"What man do you know is going to only eat rice for a month?"

"True."

"Anyway, Koontz gets to talking to all these big gals at his camp during chore time. Turns out most of 'em hadn't been laid in years. So, Koontz heads back to that bar in Mt. Carmel and posts a flyer inviting all the Chubby Chasers out to his campground for a dance with the big horny gals."

"So, he was pimping out his clients?"

"Well, I mean he said no in court. Said he just charged the men for admission to the dance. He told the ladies the men were there to help inspire them to dance and burn off the calories. If they ended up having sex, it was a bonus, more calories burned."

"That's brilliant. He got in trouble for that?"

"Well, he was also selling meth and coke to curb appetites. See, the first two pounds you lost were free. After that, they paid Koontz big bucks per each pound they peeled off."

"Wow, to think *Time* gave 'Man of the Year' to some dumb scientist."

Pete laughed. "Right?"

"Where's Koontz now?"

"I heard he's back out there after a long sentence in Statesville. Sold most of his land off in pieces. Most to farmers. He and his wife mostly keep to themselves on just a small piece of it now. They used to come in from time to time. Maybe still do. Who knows?"

"Thanks for your time, Pete. I'll let you get back to your engine."

"You got it."

We shook hands.

Pete squinted into the sun with one eye closed. The other on me.

"Hey, Arch. You never played arena football in Lincoln, did ya?"

"Never even been to Lincoln," I smiled.

"Goddamm town," Peter laughed.

"Goddamm town," I said.

I got in my car and slowly drove away.

I looked in the rearview. Peter had the scrub brush out and was back at it on the wheels.

47

With the closure of the air filter plant in recent years and the loss of other manufacturing jobs in the area, things had gotten rough for many people in Shoal County the last twenty some odd years.

Like any small town, Briarfield residents had adapted and improvised. Some tried to open legitimate shops and businesses while others went the illegal route and manufactured meth or trafficked for pill mills.

One man that went untouched no matter the county's many financial hardships was Shively Barnes. The Barnes family owned thousands of acres of land that for decades housed hundreds of oil derricks that pumped money right out of the ground. When the oil was tapped out in the late sixties, they leased the land to corporate farming. Shively maintained a couple thousand acres himself that he grew soybeans and corn on.

Shively was alright, I guess. He was a lot older. A spoiled only child. When we were kids he'd blow down the street in a *Starsky & Hutch* style, red and white Ford Gran Torino.

As Shively got older a lot of rumors spread about him. Most were cool. Things like rubbing shoulders with country music stars in Nashville, sometimes even hosting them out at his ranch for weeklong parties and benders.

Rumor had it that Shively kept a vending machine in his house that dispensed different brands of beer and had the shark image from the movie poster for *Jaws* painted on the bottom of his pool.

Word was, Shively had the best and coolest toys in town. When they were hot, he had dune buggies. When Honda came out with three-wheelers he had a barn full. In fact, if it was a gas operated recreational vehicle, Shively owned it. Jet skis, motorbikes, mopeds. It was playland out there.

Supposedly, Shively even owned a catamaran. Which, if it was true, made him the only guy in the county that sailed.

With all his land and money, Shively had his pick of women. The year he chose Karen Stone, a high school sophomore, fifteen years his junior, to start running around with, people noticed and began talking.

As it turned out, Shively wasn't so much a dirty old man as a hopeless romantic that fell hard and heavy for a nicely developed teenage girl.

Had she wanted to, Karen could have gone out to California and been one of Hugh's Playboy bunnies. Instead, she married Shively and had been Mrs. Barnes for over twenty-five years.

I'd never been out to Shively's place, but had long heard about it. When I made it down the tree-lined drive and pulled up it was more than advertised. The Ewing's of Southfork had nothing on the Barnes of Briarfield.

"Help ya mister?"

It was a kid, maybe fifteen. Jeans, Red Wings.

"Hi. I'm an old friend of the family. Thought I'd pop by for a visit."

The kid looked me over. Looked at my car.

"Well, dad isn't here."

"Is your mom home?"

"Your name sir?"

"I beg your pardon young man. Arch Moses. Yours?"

"I'm Brian. Brian Barnes."

Brian stepped forward and shook my hand. Impressive grip.

"Nice to meet you Mr. Moses."

"Likewise. Just wanted to say hi to Karen."

"Oh." He paused for a moment then turned his head back towards the house.

"Hey Mom! Mom! MOMMA! You got a visitor!"

"Tell them just a minute. I'll be right there."

"Djoo here that mister?"

"I did."

With that, Brian leapt off the porch and ran off to a neighboring barn.

Moments later Karen stepped out looking older, but still striking. An old chambray shirt with paint on it. Khaki cut-off shorts. Tan legs. Birkenstocks.

"Oh my God! Archie?!"

She came across the porch and gave me a hug like she had just won the Showcase Showdown. We stood back and looked at one another.

"How've you been?"

"Can't complain. You?"

"Good."

There was an awkward silence for a moment.

"Uh, well…you want a tour of the place?"

"What, this shithole? No thanks, but I wouldn't turn down a beer."

Karen laughed. "You haven't changed a bit. Come on in."

Karen left and a moment later returned with a glass full of suds. It was true. The sonofabitch had his own tap.

"Thanks."

The back patio was nicely shaded in sections. There were other areas where you could get some sun if you wanted to. The lawn was green and freshly cut.

We played catch-up.

Karen told me all about her marriage - *average.* The town - *falling apart.* Shively's businesses – *thriving.*

She apologized about missing Bob's funeral. Said she never spoke to Amber. Saw Spaceman once every blue moon. Then asked about me.

I stuck with my standard sales narrative. Threw in a stint in cooking school for the hell of it.

We drank some beers. Had some laughs.

"You look good," Karen said.

"Wish I could say the same." I winked.

I heard an engine whining in the distance. I looked out beyond the fence in a field and saw Brian, jumping hay bales on a motorcycle.

"Man, he really gets up there."

"A helmet would be nice. I can't even watch him anymore."

"Good manners, though."

"He does have those. No sense, but he does have those. No doubt you've seen Spaceman and Paige."

"Yeah."

"Blow your mind?"

"Nah. Slim pickens here I'm sure."

"What about how he looks?"

"Same really. Thin."

Karen frowned, "That's it?"

"You mean how he's tatted up like Nikki Sixx and smokes like Keith Richards."

"You believe those tattoos? Sexy as hell. Or at least I used to think they were."

"That's funny. Paige seems to believe no one has seen them."

"Oh," Karen said. "Sure. That's what I meant. Paige just told me about them." Karen looked at my hand then back to me. "I don't see a ring."

"Nope."

"That because you don't like wearing one or don't have one to wear?"

"I'm not married."

Karen took a long, slow sip of beer and put her glass back down.

"That does and doesn't surprise me. It does because you are quite a catch. It doesn't because well, you're also a handful."

"My dear, that is more than fair."

"Divorced?"

"No. I'm what you'd call a monkey poo romantic."

"Huh?"

"Lots of random flings."

"Makes sense with sales travel," Karen said. "Global?"

"Sometimes."

No one spoke for a moment. Had it not been for Brian flying off dirt ramps in the distance you could have called it silent.

"You know," Karen said. "For the first few years I kept my eyes peeled looking for you. Thinking maybe you'd come back for the fair or something. Homecoming maybe."

"Things were busy, crazy."

"I heard you were a U.S. Marshal or a Navy Seal. That true?"

"Not even close."

"Well, you sure look the part."

"It's only because I stay in shape for my side gig."

"You do sales and have a side gig?"

"Yeah."

"What?"

"Walmart greeter."

Karen rolled her eyes. Then looked at my arms.

"You got those scars from being a Walmart greeter?"

"I only work black Fridays."

Karen smiled. Took a sip of her beer.

"You're full of shit. Those came from that day."

"Some."

"You ever think about us?"

I didn't want to hurt her feelings. We were never a couple. I looked out over the plush green hills behind her and told the truth.

"Not really. I mean we were kids."

"I know that. I mean about that day?" Karen said.

I drained my beer.

"I put it away, you know?"

"Like this town and the people in it, huh?"

"Like this town, the people in it and many more like it."

Karen welled up. Tears rolled down her cheeks.

"I thought I had finally put it away too, you know, in my mind I mean. I'm sure I dealt with it wrong. I hated all of us for getting us in that situation, but got over it in time. Then..." Karen spun around on her chaise, put her feet on the ground, got up and came back a moment later. "Some asshole sent me this." She tossed a bottle of Tahiti Tom's in my lap.

"What did you do?"

"I screamed at the top of my lungs when I saw it."

"Where'd you find it?"

"On top of the mailbox."

"You got security cameras?"

Karen shook her head, no. "Not out here. Just guns. I'm scared, Archie. I checked around. I don't think they make that stuff anymore."

I told her about the others. That I thought it was what had triggered Bob's suicide.

"Bob showed it to me," Karen said. "Shively and I don't get into town much for church ever really, but when we did it had always been Bob's. Bob had helped counsel me through some things in the past. I went to him with that bottle the day I got it."

"What was he counseling you on?"

"Things."

I leaned forward in my chair.

"Think, Karen. Think hard. Was there anyone that could have seen us that day? Any random person, maybe someone spying on us?"

"It was so muddy and hot. Who would've wanted to go out there?"

"Maybe someone or some people for the same reasons we did."

"What sick person could have seen what happened to us out there and not tried to help us? We were beaten and raped."

"True."

"God, Archie. I'm glad you and Spaceman are working on this. Don't leave until you get to the bottom of it."

"I won't. Did you show Shively the sunscreen?"

"No. Wouldn't have meant anything to him. He came running out when I screamed, but I just said it was a wasp and hid the bottle."

Karen wiped her tears.

The sliding glass door opened.

"What's wrong mom?" It was Brian.

"She needs you to start wearing a helmet," I said. I looked at Brian. His cheeks were red. "You okay?"

"The assholes got the pole barn this time." Brian said. "That's twice this week."

I looked at Karen.

"Graffiti," she said.

"In Briarfield?"

"Nope just us. Nice, right?"

Brian showed me the picture on his phone.

Judgement day is coming!

"Maybe it's just some passionate Assembly of God-types spreading the word," I said.

"Hardly. Look what they did a few days ago." Brian swiped right. "Notice it's the same paint color."

All Sluts Must Die!

"You and your dad have guns, Brian?"

"Twenty-five or so."

"Outstanding." I looked at Karen. "You know how to use a gun."

"Uh, yeah."

"Keep a few loaded and close by," I said.

"Why?" Brian asked.

"Those may not be random tags of graffiti. They could be warnings."

"From who?" Karen said.

"I don't know," I said. "But do me a favor."

"What's that?" She and Brian said at the same time.

"Stay frosty."

48

We drank the last few beers in the car to calm our nerves.

Spaceman pulled up to Karen's Samurai.

"You guys have got to leave town, now. Don't let anyone see you. Take your credit cards, whatever you have. Drive until you can't anymore. Check into a motel and heal up. Don't come back to town until you do."

The girls hopped out.

"What do I tell Shively?" Karen cried.

"And my mom?" Amber said.

"Tell them, I don't know. Whatever. That you two got a wild hair and decided to go on a road trip. You went to a concert or something. Got banged up in the mosh pit. Anything."

"What about Colesy?" Karen said.

Colesy looked at me like a dog waiting to be put down.

"He's coming with us," I said.

"What are you guys gonna say?" Amber cried.

"Don't worry about it. You never saw us today, got me?" Spaceman said.

Amber nodded.

"What about the bodies?" Karen sniffed.

"We'll take care of it," I said.

In spite of the heat, the girls were shivering cold. I wanted to help them. Get them somewhere safe. Make sure they were going to be okay, but there was too much to do.

Spaceman swung a U-turn and hit the gas.

"Shouldn't we go to the hospital first?" Colesy asked.

"And say what, Bob?" Spaceman said. "Hey, can you guys hurry and patch us up? We have some psycho rednecks we gotta bury."

"But your arm?" Bob said. "Arch has lost a lot of blood."

"It looks worse than it is," I said.

"Think they can get out of town without being seen?" Colesy asked.

"As long as they take the backroads they should be good."

Spaceman turned, looked at me and nodded as if to thank me for the optimism.

He swung a sliding right up a muddy path that cut through a cornfield.

Bob poked his head up between us.

"Where are you going?"

"Beech Meechum's," Spaceman said. "Any luck, he's still sleeping off a bender."

49

The barn was dilapidated and sagged in on itself. If it had ever been painted red, there was no evidence.

Spaceman left the car running, hopped out and ran over to the barn. Two boards had fallen off the frame on the rear. Spaceman turned sideways and slipped inside.

One minute.

Two minutes.

"Come on, come on, come on," Colesy said under his breath.

Moments later Spaceman came running back to the car with an old rusted shovel and a wooden bucket that looked like it had survived the Civil War.

"How did you know those were there?" Colesy said.

"Arch and I may have spent a weekend here mending a fence we may have driven through one night."

The rest of the drive was quiet.

We made it to the reservoir and hustled up the hill with what energy we could muster.

"Colesy, take this bucket and fill it. Rinse off any blood you see. We'll bury the other bodies."

Colesy was pale. "What about the-"

"I'll take care of it." I said. I looked at Spaceman. "Take me to yours and we'll bury him first."

"He's already half buried down in the silt. I got it," Spaceman said.

"It will be faster if we help one another."

"No! There's a ton to do and we're running out of time."

Bob and I looked at each other and nodded.

Each of us took off with our tasks.

I made it down the rope to the bottom of the spillway. The falling water from the open slats had rinsed the rapist's brains away. His pointy nose had turned bulbous and black. His balding mullet? Still there.

The four inches of standing water allowed me to position him in front of the tube easier. I let the water rise until I could barely move the board. The dead man and I shot down the slimy canal. Out in the light I looked at the man's eyes. He was long gone, no doubt his soul had taken a first-class trip to hell.

I drug the body across the stilling basin and let the water take it through the dividing slat of its choice. The body floated through the right side then stopped on a makeshift beach of rocks and stone.

I struggled mightily to pick the man up. After a few minutes of trying different ways, I finally got him on my back and carried him over to a mound partially hidden by foliage.

The ground was soft from the days of rain, but after getting down close to four feet with the shovel, water started to slowly seep in.

I got down an inch or two further before I dumped the rapist into the hole. My whole body was numb, my muscles shot. It took everything I had to cover the body up.

I could hear Colesy crying. He had drug the dead man Amber had drowned up and over the berm, down to the bank of the reservoir. Colesy was tearing the dead man's t-shirt in long strips and tying them around the dead man's ankles. Colesy used fishing line, chain, anything of length from his tackle box and wrapped it all around a large stone.

I slid down the bank and helped Colesy slide the man into the reservoir. We both swam out with the body as far as we could without going down with it ourselves. On three, we released the corpse and let it sink to the bottom with the heavy stone. With any luck, hungry catfish would pick the bones clean by Halloween.

Back on land, Colesy and I collapsed.

"This is too big. This is too big to keep, Arch. I can't do it. I don't care if I lose my scholarship. If the girls make it, I mean, if people buy their story, then we can just come clean on our end, right? It was self-defense. We can leave the girls out of it totally. Just say the three of us were coming out here to fish and were attacked."

"But why? I mean if they beat us up or tried to rob us, sure, we'd fight back, but murder? The cops will know something more had to happen to provoke that?"

"Can't we just say self-defense?" Bob said.

"Was the kid self-defense?"

Colesy got up, walked a few steps and started puking.

"We've gone too far," I said.

Spaceman walked towards us. He was covered in mud and blood. He smelled like shit.

"What's done is done."

"Think you got him deep enough?" I asked.

"Yeah," he said. "For now."

Spaceman stepped down into the reservoir and rinsed off. He swam out a bit, went under, came back up.

"It's swampy back there. A lot of standing water. The mud was just thin and deep enough for me to get the body down and pin it with some big rocks."

I got to my feet.

"That's not good enough."

I began walking in the direction of where Spaceman had come from.

"It's good enough for now, Arch. It took me thirty minutes to brush out my tracks in the mud. We still have a lot to do."

"He's right," Colesy said.

I was too whipped to protest further.

The three of us moved as fast and best we could down the hill, falling and sliding on the way to the car. Spaceman used the shovel to steady himself.

"Give me that shovel." I pointed at the dead kid. "I'll do this quick."

"We don't have time for that," Spaceman said. Spaceman stepped over and hooked his good arm under an armpit of the body. "Get him in the trunk."

"The trunk?"

"Just do it."

I grabbed the kid by the other armpit. We got him into the trunk of Spaceman's car.

Within moments we were racing back to Beech Meechum's place.

Spaceman pulled up to the back of the barn.

"Colesy, sneak in to the house and see if the old boy is still passed out. Arch, you help me."

Spaceman popped the trunk. We lifted the body out.

"Help me with his clothes."

We undressed the kid.

Spaceman nodded toward a large hog pen.

"Just get him in there. The hogs will do the rest."

"Are you serious?"

"The ol' drunk won't even notice. Who knows if he even feeds them."

I was close to passing out. Did as I was told.

Spaceman was right. Within seconds of tossing the body over the fence of the pen, the hogs were on it. They tore and gnashed into the corpse with such a loud and furious frenzy that we nearly had to yell at them to be quiet.

Flesh, blood and viscera splashed across their mouths and snouts. The foul odor of earth and excrement filled the air.

What was left from the initial feast, we buried deep into the center beneath the filth of the pen. Tears ran from our eyes as each of us gagged and vomited. We took turns spraying one another off with a garden hose on the side of the house.

Minutes later Spaceman emerged from the barn holding a bottle of lamp oil and some rags. He poured the oil all over the trunk of his car.

"Let's go."

We got two or three miles down the road.

"We need to get to a hospital," Colesy said.

"We will," Spaceman said. "We will."

"How are we going to explain all of our wounds?" Colesy asked.

Spaceman smashed the pedal to the floor.

60mph

70mph

80 mph

"Do you guys trust me?"

Colesy and I looked at him and nodded.

"Then hold on!"

Spaceman turned off the road. The car rocketed down into a ditch, then up and over the slope of land that wrapped around a culvert.

My head smacked the dash.

Colesy slammed around in the back.

The day had started with such promise. The sun was shining and anything was possible. Now, we were falling upside down with the earth's fist on its way to meet us.

Fantasy had returned to reality.

And gone into full nightmare mode.

50

I grabbed a cup and poured some coffee.

"Good morning."

I turned around. Paige was in a white terry cloth robe.

"Morning," I said. "The good Sheriff get off okay?"

"He had a piece of toast. Poked at his eggs. Fix you something?"

"Just coffee, thanks."

"Ted says you're advising him on something."

"He did? What did he say?"

"Nothing really. Just that you two were taking care of some old business."

"Yeah. Dotting some i's and crossing some t's."

"Sounds like an excuse to keep his old high school drinkin' buddy around."

"Listen, I was running around your place the other day and noticed a manmade waterfall that runs off the back of your pond. Is that a grotto down there?"

Paige laughed.

"That was Barry. One of Emma's old boyfriends. He was taking some kind of landscaping course or something at Pioneer Community College. Thought he'd surprise us. I think he got a C minus. We use it occasionally when the pump works."

I poured some milk in my coffee.

Paige crunched on something brown.

"Bacon?"

"God no. Turkey bacon. Ted won't let anything pork related come within a mile of this house. You believe that?"

"Probably just being health conscious."

Paige's nose wrinkled. "But why? You guys loved pork burgers in high school. Baby back ribs, everything."

"I loved a lot of things in high school."

"Me too." Paige looked at me and smiled. "Hey, do you remember that time in my nephew's tree fort when I was babysitting?"

Of course, I did. Paige and I were screwing each other's brains out when her nephew woke up screaming from a bad dream. Paige got a huge splinter in her ass rushing to get up and check on the kid.

"Can't say I do."

Paige shook her head. "Whatever, Archie."

She looked at me. My body.

"Where did you get your scars? They all can't be from the wreck you had with Ted and Bob."

"I've picked up some along the way."

Paige reached out and touched the burn scar that ran down my left arm.

"I'm no dummy, Arch, and you're no salesman. What do you really do?"

"I'm tellin' ya. I'm a salesman. Just taken some shots over the years. Sadly, the stories behind them don't do justice to the scars."

"Okay," Paige said. "One other question."

"Sure."

Paige opened her robe. Naked. Nice.

"Think I still got it?"

"Still? I was unaware you had it before."

Paige smiled, flipped me the bird and closed her robe.

"Morning guys."

Cherry turned the corner mid-yawn. She had on her Save Ferris t-shirt and a pair of men's pajama pants that hung low on her hips. I regretted getting up early for coffee.

Cherry spotted Spaceman's uncleared plate.

"Oooh, can I have those eggs?"

"Help, yourself," Paige said. "I can fry up some fresh if you like."

"No thanks. I don't want to put you out. Okay, if I snag a Diet Coke, though?"

"Sure."

Cherry sheepishly reached into the fridge for a can. No dice.

"Oh no. I must have had the last one, sorry," she said to Paige.

"How much aspartame does that little frame need to run on?" I asked.

"It's not a problem. We have more in the garage," Paige said. "I'll be right back."

"No," Cherry said. "Let me get it. You're not here to serve me."

Cherry stepped past us.

Paige popped a piece of bread in the toaster and grinned.

"Do you still eat dry toast?"

"I feel like that's all I should eat. Cherry and I are eating you guys out of house and home. Is she wearing Spaceman's pajama pants?"

"Ted, pajamas? You must be talking about someone else. No, Cherry and I went shopping and she bought those at Walmart. She tried to give me money for food too, but I wouldn't take it."

"I'll give some bucks to Spaceman."

"Careful. He'll take it."

"I know he will. The man's hand is a black hole from which no cash returns."

The toast popped out. Paige offered it to me. I shook my head no.

After slathering it with butter and honey Paige had a seat at the kitchen table. A moment later Cherry returned with a Diet Coke and sat down next to Paige.

I leaned back against the counter.

"So, what do you ladies have planned for the day?"

"We want to hang out with you," Cherry said in between bites of cold breakfast.

"Hang out? I'm heading up to the courthouse in a few."

"Can't you two take a day off?" Paige said.

"No. We gotta do this, then I got to be moving on."

Cherry gave me a wounded look.

"Don't you mean, we'll be moving on?"

"Huh?" I said.

Paige looked at me.

"That's exactly what I meant. We indeed," I smiled.

"Can we help you and Ted with what you two are working on?" Paige asked.

"No. It'll be over soon."

"Well, hurry up then," Paige said. "We want to hang out with you guys before you leave. Have some fun."

We've done that, I wanted to say.

I needed to clear my head.

"Cool if I go for a run?"

"Of course," Paige said.

"You ladies want to join me for that?"

"Uh, hell no," Cherry said. She looked at Paige. "These eggs are so good."

I got dressed and went outside.

Spaceman's trails were neatly mowed. I went left.

Every one of us that had been at the spillway that day twenty-eight years ago, had received a bottle of Tahiti Tom's in the past two weeks.

Whoever was taunting us had to have been out there that day and seen everything. But why wait nearly three decades later to expose us? Money maybe? Did they want to wait until we were successful later in life and then cash in? But why gamble on time like that? We could have ended up dead or broke. Money didn't make any sense.

It was revenge. Had to be.

I needed to find them and I needed to end it and do it fast, while my resolve with Paige was solid and before Cherry got too attached.

I ran around the pond and slowly increased my speed with each lap until my lungs hurt.

After about forty-five minutes I slowed down to a jog.

I was drenched and stopped to look at the manmade waterfall. I crossed the bridge and climbed down to inspect it.

The small pool at the bottom was clear, deep and lined with natural stones. I couldn't tell if the masonry was poorly done or if the kid had intended to do it that way.

I took my shoes and socks off. Rubbed my feet.

Moments later I heard Paige and Cherry laughing. They both walked down wearing bikinis and flip-flops. Paige had a radio and a beach bag. Cherry carried a cooler filled with ice cold beer.

"Mind if we join you?"

The girls shook out their towels and put their things down.

"I'm just dipping my feet to cool off, then I've got to go."

"Bullshit," Cherry smiled and took her top off.

"No really. It's important."

"This important?" Paige dropped her top too. "Beer?"

Jesus Christ.

"Sure, why not?"

Paige tossed one over. It was a bad toss. I had to step down into the water to catch it. I didn't mind. The water was nice.

Cherry and Paige slathered lotion on themselves and one another. I caught the label on the bottle.

"What's that in your hand?"

"What, this? Sunscreen," Paige said.

"What kind?"

"Fifteen, I think. Want some?"

"No, I mean what brand?"

Paige looked. "Tahiti Tom's. Remember when this stuff used to be a big deal?"

"Let me see that."

Paige tossed it to me.

I examined it. The shape of the bottle hadn't changed. The font on the label had been updated, but the logo of the beach bum on the hammock was the same.

"I thought they quit making this stuff."

"You a lotion buff?" Paige smiled.

"No. Just hadn't seen it in ages."

"You're in sales. You know branding. Everything old is new again. Retro, remember?"

"Yeah, I remember." I tossed the lotion bottle back.

Was all this some sick joke. A prank? But who? Why?

Part of me wanted to leap out of the water and get into town. Pistol whip Spaceman until he told me everything he knew. He was holding back. Had to be. But why?

The other part of me. The part below the waist, wanted to soak up the sun and booze with the ladies. Didn't Nero play the fiddle while Rome burned?

"I apply it heavier and rub it in deeper on my nipples," Paige said, "Like this." Paige demonstrated her technique on Cherry's breasts.

Sun and booze with the ladies it was.

I leaned back and enjoyed the view. I drained my beer. Cherry tossed me another. I stood up in the water and caught it.

POP!

POP! POP!

POP!

Brick and stone exploded into clouds of powder and dust.

I leapt over to cover the girls then pulled them into the water with me.

"Keep your heads down."

I scanned the tree line where the shots were coming from. Nothing.

The girls were hysterical.

"Oh my God! Oh my God!" Paige screamed.

"When I yell go, I want you two to run like hell to the house. Got me?"

Cherry looked at me, "What about you?"

"I'll be right behind you guys. Go!".

In a millisecond, the girls were out of the water and up the small incline to the path around the pond.

"Get in the house and lock all the doors," I yelled.

I watched until the girls were out of site.

POP!

POP!

I leaned back against the rock and brought my fresh beer to my lips for a sip. The can had been torn in half by a bullet. That motherfucker.

I counted to ten then jumped out.

POP! POP!

I grabbed my go-fasters and slipped them on.

POP!

I was up the hill and to the driveway in ten seconds.

I opened my car door and pulled my Walther PPK out of the glove box. Within moments I was back at the waterfall. I slid down a hill of dirt and sparse brush.

I stayed low and zig-zagged towards the woods. I found cover behind a fallen tree. I lifted my gun and fired a death blossom, moving my hand up and down from right to left.

I reloaded and went into the woods. Ten, twenty, thirty yards.

Nothing.

I looked down at my gun.

It was warm.

It felt good to have it in my hand again.

I looked everywhere I imagined the sniper could be. There were two spots. I drained a clip into both. Whoever shot at us was either dead, or had made a break for it when I ran to get my gun.

I walked over to the general areas that I had swiss cheesed. Nothing.

When I made it back to the house Paige and Cherry were hysterical.

"What in the hell are you and Ted involved in, Archie?" Paige said. Tears streaming down her cheeks. "You better come clean with us right now."

I looked at Cherry. She was shaken up, but less than Paige.

I walked over to the bar and dropped two cubes into a glass. Spaceman was in the door before I finished pouring.

"Tell me?"

"We were in the grotto. Nine shots."

"Did you go in after?"

"Yeah."

"Anything?"

"Not even a squirrel."

Spaceman was a pro. His bedside manner with the frightened women was impressive. First, he listened, then provided calm and soothing words.

"No way this is Colt Boone or Dallas-"

"Dallas?" Paige said. "He'd never-"

"He wouldn't." Spaceman said to me. "Colt on the other hand."

"I could see it," Cherry said.

I could see Spaceman's wheels turning. He ejected the clip from his gun and inspected it then slammed it back in.

"Show me, Arch."

We walked down to the waterfall.

Spaceman sucked on a cancer stick. When we got there, he ran his hands over the bullet scars in the rock.

"What's your take?

"It was no .22," I said. "Look at those hits. Had to be a hunting rifle."

Spaceman exhaled a locomotive stream of smoke.

"Couldn't have been using a scope. This was nothing more than scare tactics."

"Scare tactics? Why?"

"How the hell would I know?"

"You must. You seem pretty certain how this whole thing went down. Anyone ever fired on your property before?"

"Hell no! I'd feed em their own balls."

"Well, there ya go."

"I'll have Dallas run a gunshot residue test on Colt."

"What else?"

"Help the girls pack up. See 'em off for me."

"Off? Off where?"

"You guys just got shot at, it's not safe for them to be here?"

"Not safe?" You just said it was no big deal. That it was all scare tactics. What are you-"

"I have a goddamm job, Arch. Let me go do it."

As calm as Spaceman wanted to look walking away, he practically sprinted for his car. I felt like following him directly, but I feared what I might find. Whatever it was, I'd know soon enough. Hopefully, before I was dead.

I got back to the house and poured another drink.

Down the hall I heard Paige talking to herself in the master, throwing things in a bag. I poked my head in.

"Can Cherry go with you?"

"If she wants. I'm not waiting around. This is insane."

"She'll go."

"What in the hell is going on? Does any of this make sense to you, Arch?"

"Nothing's made sense since I rolled into town."

I walked on down the hall into the guest room.

Cherry was already out of the shower and drying off with a towel.

"You wanna fuck her, don't you?"

"What? Who?"

"Who? Paige! I heard her ask you if she still turned you on this morning. Yeah. I heard you guys talking. Saw you checking out her tits at the grotto."

"Big deal. I told her no. She was joking anyway."

"I see the way you look at her."

"You mean with my eyes?"

"You know what I'm talking about. Did you tell her about my past?"

"No, why would I do that? I got you out of Meemaw to forget all that so you could start fresh. New. Reinvent yourself. I told you I'd give you money so you could go anywhere. Drive you to the airport, whatever."

"So that's it? You've always wanted to get rid of me? Why'd you bring me here to meet your friends if you knew-"

"Cherry. You wanted to come. Begged me even. Remember?"

"Oh, that's right. You've hated my company ever since you first shoved your dick in me."

"Now-"

"You were gonna just pack up and leave without me?"

"Did I say that?"

"Uh, pretty much. You didn't mention me in your plans this morning."

I took my drink down in one gulp. Put the glass on the counter.

"You really think we have a shot being together? I told you, I'm no good for you. My job-"

"Your job? What is it again?"

"This is insane. We just got shot at for Christ's sake and your choosing now to fly into a jealous rage?"

"Just admit you want to fuck her."

"Cherry, we almost got killed."

Cherry threw her towel down. Stood staring at me naked with her hands on her hips.

"Okay. You're so dangerous? You can't see us together? Don't want me? Well that's fine. You won't mind me moving on then?"

"That's what I've been telling you. Look, I obviously care for you but-"

"It's fine. I'll figure something out."

"Like what?"

"Maybe, I'll stay here for a bit. Seeing as how Paige is now my friend-"

"You can't."

"Oh, really? Why?"

"She's leaving. It's too dangerous."

Cherry laughed. "Are you kidding? After what I've been through, this is Disneyland."

"Listen," I peeled off a stack of bills and handed them to Cherry. "You've got to get out of town. It's not safe. You need to leave with Paige."

Cherry took the money. Her eyes clouded with tears.

"It's so easy for you to pay me off like some hooker."

"That's not it."

"Last chance," she said. "You want me to go for good, or hang back until you get this bullet thing all figured out?"

There was hope in Candy's eyes until there wasn't. I had waited too long to answer.

I took a step towards her. It was too late.

The door nearly took my nose off.

51

I hit the bell and waited. Glanced at the professionally arranged flowers in planters on the porch.

The door slowly opened.

For a millisecond, Myra's eyes flashed surprise then gave way to a devilish gaze. She cocked her hip and leaned against the door frame.

"Hi, Archie."

"Myra."

"Whatchoo up to?"

"Was out and about. Thought I'd stop by for a visit."

Myra smiled.

I followed her inside.

"Coffee?"

"Sounds good."

"Have a seat on the couch. I'll be right back. Sugar? Cream?"

"Splash of milk would be great. Thanks."

"I've got all kinds of flavored creams."

"Plain milk is fine."

Myra disappeared into the kitchen.

I looked around. Her living room looked like it was out of a magazine. A painting of her and her late husband hung above the fireplace. Leather bound books. Modern furniture mixed with antique pieces. Fresh cut tulips were in a vase on an eclectic and very expensive looking coffee table.

Myra walked in with a cup of coffee. She smiled and handed it to me.

"Thanks. None for you?"

"I just had some tea."

"Cool painting."

"Thanks, it's a Davenport. He was a few years under you. I had him do it from a photo. Henry was too sick to pose."

Myra sat down across from me and crossed her tanned and shapely legs. She was barefoot. Her toenails were painted.

"Beautiful home."

"Thanks. After Henry died I wanted to make some changes. I had an interior designer come in a few years ago from Chicago."

"Very nice."

"Very expensive. I kind of kicked everything into overdrive. Got a trainer, a therapist."

"Trainer? You look great."

"You can thank my trainer."

"How's the therapist."

"Turns out my father shouldn't have gotten me that pony."

"Funny."

"I'm serious."

"Oh."

"How much longer are you in town for?"

"Not much longer."

"Still staying with the good Sheriff?"

"Yeah, still there."

"I've seen him everywhere lately."

"It's an election year. Gotta be out and about among the people."

Myra lightly tossed her hand.

"Please, he'll win in a landslide. People love him. People don't even shoplift in this town."

"Really?"

"I'm serious. Teddy runs all the bad apples out of town. So much so that when Henry was working for the District Attorney they did an investigation. Not officially that is, but they looked into a few things."

"Like what?"

"Like why the crime rate was so low compared to neighboring counties. Meth, drugs. Either the bad guys don't come here or when they do they disappear off the map."

"Interesting."

"It's been like that since Ted's daddy, Red, was in charge. You know that. What bad things ever happened around here when you were a kid?"

I could think of one.

"Nothing, really." I said.

"Exactly. It's the only reason I've stayed put all these years. Clean town. No pawn shops, no head shops, no tattoo parlors. By the way. What did you think of the Sheriff's art work?"

"In his home? I didn't see any. Just a generic Ansel Adams here and there."

"No, I mean his skin. His tattoos."

"You've seen them?"

"It gets hot here. A man can't always keep his shirt on."

Myra crossed and uncrossed her tan legs.

"Are you satisfied with what you found out about Bob?"

"Yeah, I guess. Bummed it went that way."

"Did the Sheriff tell you about their argument?"

"Argument?"

"Ted didn't tell you about the argument he had with Bob? I always thought you two were close."

"What about this argument?"

"The Sheriff and Bob had a huge blowup. Bob wouldn't share the details with me, but he was really upset about it."

"Spaceman never mentioned anything to me."

"Maybe it was too personal."

"Maybe. I have a question you might be able to help me with. Bob had a locked lower desk drawer that had been pried open. Do you know what he kept in there?"

"Special documents? Private items, I suppose."

"Did you ever go into the drawer?"

"We didn't do much filing when I visited him in the office."

"Did you two photograph your escapades?"

Myra's eyes ran over me like she was soon going to have to draw me from memory.

"Why? You feelin' like a little show and tell?"

"I'm just wondering if he had an old desk or was there something somebody was looking for?"

"Knowing Bob, he lost the key and pried it open himself. Did you know about his book?"

"I may have heard something about it. Ultimate Forgiving, or something? A self-help book."

"No. Not a self-help book."

"Well, you know what I mean. File it under spirituality or whatever."

"Not hardly. It was a novel."

"Fiction?"

"Yeah. I was pleasantly surprised. It was pretty good."

"What was it about?"

"Oh, you know, some horny high school kids run afoul of the law. Truth be told, I only read the first few chapters. It was an early draft."

"Interesting. Did he show it to anybody else?"

Myra was getting bored.

"I don't have any idea darling. What difference does it make?"

"Not much, I guess."

"So where is home, Archie? What lucky city got you?"

"Why assume city, not town?"

"You look sophisticated. I'm guessing New York?"

"Too crowded."

"Los Angeles then? You're tan."

"San Francisco, actually."

"Pricey," Myra smiled. "Computers?"

"Components mostly."

"Wow, Arch Moses in Silicon Valley."

I took the last sip of my coffee.

"Hard to believe, right?"

"Not at all," Myra grinned. "You were a bit of a troublemaker, but one of my brightest students."

"Yeah well, we all liked you. Tried to be on our best behavior in your class."

Myra got up off the couch and stood in front of me.

"It's cliché, but true. The world really is a different place now. Used to a teacher and student might have a little fling and no one would say a thing. Now, it's a crime. Ridiculous don't you think?"

"You didn't do that. Did you?"

Myra smiled. "No, I was faithful to my loving Henry until the end, but that didn't mean I couldn't appreciate some of my students in the same ways some of them appreciated me…with impure thoughts. I remember watching you cut our grass. Shirt off. Drenched in sweat. I thought of you sometimes. Did you ever think about me?"

"You may have leapt over that fence with the sheep a time or two."

"That's nice," she said.

"Bob told me some things you boys used to say about me as you got older. I found them flattering."

"I don't think it was just the students. I'm pretty sure Mr. Brown and a few other teachers and parents thought you were quite something too."

"All this talk about dreamed and missed opportunities. Words can be so boring sometimes without action. Don't you think?"

I put my empty cup on the coffee table.

"Thanks for the coffee and chat."

"Sure." Myra smiled then looked into the dining room. "Do you want another cup or do you want to spread me over that table in there?"

Myra walked into the dining room and let her skirt fall.

No panties.

She spread her legs and bent over the table.

I followed her into the room and pulled a chair up behind her.

Too much caffeine put a strain on the heart.

And who knew how much longer mine would beat, now that my old ex-best friend wanted to kill me.

52

I pulled up and parked in the front of the courthouse.

Spaceman was leaning against a tall shade tree doing his best Marlboro man. He tapped out a cigarette and tossed it between his lips with panache Dean Martin would envy.

"You see the girls off?"

"Didn't follow them to the county line if that's what you mean."

"Why not?"

"I'm sorry. Do I work for you, or does Dallas? You don't think Paige knows how to drive out of town?"

"Did Cherry go with her?"

"That was the plan."

"How was Myra?"

"You're following me?"

"No, but your fly is down and you have lipstick on your neck."

"What makes you think it isn't Cherry's?"

"Cherry wears bright red lipstick. The stuff on your neck is lighter."

"So."

"That's the shade Myra wears."

"How do you know that?"

"Jesus Christ, Archie. I'm the fucking Sheriff. I know everything that goes on around here."

"You're shady as fuck you know that?"

Spaceman pointed at the shade tree that hung over him.

"Tell me something I don't know."

"I'm hungry."

Taco Fiesta had been a second kitchen to all of us in high school. It was like Taco Bell only in all the good ways a small town mom and pop can be. The fare was Americanized-Mexican food, but Fiesta had three homemade salsas and you got to operate the nacho cheese spout and sour cream gun yourself. More importantly, they had the rabbit turd style ice which was caviar to ice crunchers like me.

We ordered on foot from the drive-thru and had a seat outside at one of the red picnic tables.

"Whatcha think?"

"Good," I said between bites of burrito. "Really good."

"Good as you remember?"

I nodded. Wiped my mouth with a napkin.

"I still can't figure out how they season their meat."

Spaceman took a sip of his Coke. "I asked Mike once. He wouldn't tell me."

"Their mole sauce, it's like a melted Hershey's blended with habaneros. They could bottle this stuff."

"That's what I love about Mike," Spaceman said between bites. "He's just happy making a decent living. For some folks living a quiet happy life is good enough."

"Sure," I said, "but this sauce would fly off the shelves in grocery stores."

"Yeah, well. Mike and Rhonda don't feel the need to expand or spend the time to go out and find a company kitchen, packaging, distribution, all that horseshit. They'd just screw up the original, ya know?"

"Yeah. I get it. Would still be cool to take some home."

Spaceman wadded up his food wrappers and put them in the bag. He took another sip of Coke, lit his millionth cigarette and looked at me.

"And where exactly is home these days, Arch?"

"These days? Wherever, I lay my head."

"Huh, interesting."

"Interesting, how?"

"What kind of business are you in again?"

"I told you. Sales."

"Yes, but what's the product. The service?"

I had four products I chose from when faced with this question. Pharmaceuticals, sexual aids, household cleaners, and/or computer components. Maybe the ghost pepper sauce on my tostada was sparking my imagination.

"Industrial lubricants. Mostly for aerospace, some military."

"Oh yeah? That's impressive. What are the names of some of the products?"

"The contracts are with the government so there aren't names, just numbers."

"Same lubricants for space and military?"

I dug a chip in some guac.

"Depends on the application. Engine, projectile-"

"You handle the actual product?"

"No, it's all hazmat, incendiary. I just push the papers."

"That how you met Cherry. Through your work?"

Technically, I had met Cherry through *her* work. Whatever.

"You could say that."

"I *could* say that, or you *would* say that?"

I wiped my face with a napkin.

"You writing a book, Spaceman?"

He chuckled. "Would be a helluva read wouldn't it?"

"Depends on the artistic license."

"Mine or yours?"

I opened another taco.

"I'd probably get most of it right," Spaceman said. "After that summer though, I'd have to make your end up."

"Oh?"

"Sure, after our fiasco at the spillway, I stay back in town to take care of any unfinished business that might come our way and you leave never to return."

"Well, I might argue that the business was finished. Not to mention you told me to go. Said you had it. I told you to call if there was ever a problem. You did and now I'm here."

"True, and I appreciate it, but you sure are vague about a lot of stuff. Your background for instance."

"Background? I haven't seen you in over twenty-eight years. Do I know everything about you since then?"

Spaceman put his cigarette out in my nacho boat. I still had chips and cheese remaining.

"You could make a pretty good run at it."

"Why are you so concerned?"

"From a friendly standpoint, I'm curious. Occupationally, it's my job."

"To know my life story?"

"To know something."

"You don't trust me?"

"Can I trust you?"

"What do you mean?"

"I know this isn't your first time back here."

Spaceman waited to see if my expression changed. It didn't.

"Paige told me. Said it was a few years after graduation. I wasn't with her yet. Said you came tapping on her window in the middle of the night. I can't remember if she said it was raining or if you were crying. Maybe rain. You were soaked. She said you told her you were going overseas. You wanted to start a family with her. She said you begged her to go with you, but she was scared. Didn't want to be away from her family. Her dad heard her talking to you and hit the lights in hallway. When she turned back around you were gone."

"Okay."

"Okay? Is it true?"

"Why would Paige lie?"

"So, it's true?"

"Maybe. Give or take a tear."

"Hers or yours?"

"Maybe it was rain."

Spaceman blew smoke into my face.

"See then. Now that's a problem."

"Problem how?"

"Can I trust you, Arch?"

I laughed. "Trust me? Around, Paige? Why do you think you can't?"

"I didn't say I couldn't. I'm asking you if I can."

"Look man, I'm down here to take care of whoever is messing with us then I'm on my way, never to be seen again."

"So, it's a pattern then. Fix problems and leave."

We dumped our trays and got in Spaceman's cruiser. I looked at him. It looked like he hadn't slept in days. Maybe since I got into town.

"What's your problem?"

Spaceman didn't say a word. Just drove. One mile. Two. Three. We were out in the country west of town.

"I don't know if it's a problem yet, but I ran Cherry through the system. Saw some little story about a dust-up in Mississippi, some old solicitation charges."

"Big deal. She's a kid. Made a mistake or two."

"Sure, but you? You, Arch, are nowhere to be found. You're completely wiped off the grid. Even your fucking picture in the yearbook in the library is torn out."

"Groupies."

"Fuck you."

"Do I look like a social media guy to you?"

"Neither of us are, but you run me through any of the hundreds of state and federal nets and filters and I pop up tons of times. You don't. Not once. Not anywhere. You're a fucking ghost."

I looked out the window. We passed a beat-up trailer with a pristine Dodge Ram parked in front. The weed infested lawn was accented with badly chipped and poorly painted lawn sculptures. The property screamed meth dealer's house. Spaceman tipped his cap to the man in the front yard.

"You know that guy?"

"Not by name. People see the Sheriff go by they get nervous. Best to be friendly and wave."

"Friendly, or friendly reminder you're watching them."

"Bit of both."

"I guess big city or small town, the game's the same."

Spaceman nodded.

"What'd you do when you rolled out of here at the end of that summer? College? Family? Military? And please, don't give me some bullshit about Black-Ops."

We rode a bit.

"There is no Black Ops. That's Hollywood make-believe. How top-secret can an elite unit be if it has a name?"

"How would you know about it? I thought you were just a grease monkey."

"I may have seen some action."

"Oh really?"

"Maybe."

"Bad?"

"All war is bad. You get deep enough into the suck, pinned down, I've seen guys forget their names."

"Did you?"

"What?"

"Forget your name?"

"Tried to."

"Jesus. What did you do over there?"

"Over where?"

Spaceman was losing patience. He lit a cigarette.

"Fine. What were your last three home addresses?"

"Can't remember," I said.

Spaceman shook his head. "There is zero trace of your existence online. Why?"

"My ex-wife. She was crazy. I had a guy scrub me."

"You expect me to buy that? You can't scrub anything. It's the internet. Besides you told Bentley you never married."

"You're interviewing people I've talked to since I've been in town?"

"Interviewed? Shit, this is Briarfield. We call it having a conversation."

"So, stop interviewing me and let's have a conversation."

"What in the fuck do you think I'm trying to do."

"Then do it."

"I am. So, what was her name?"

"Come again?"

"Your wife, your crazy ex-wife. What was her fucking name?"

"Are you serious right now? I thought you just said you checked and I had no wife?"

"Give me a girlfriend's name then goddammit. Anyone you've been with in the past five years."

Spaceman pulled the retractable arm on the dash that held his computer.

"You're serious?"

"Fuck yeah, I am. You've managed to magically disappear from cyberspace, but she can't. So, what is it? What's her name?"

"She's foreign."

"Yeah? So."

"So, it's an exotic name."

"Okay?" Spaceman said. "Go."

"Zukmi."

"How do I spell that?"

"Like it sounds."

Spaceman clacked away.

"Okay. Her last name."

"I'll have to spell it for you," I said.

"Okay, shoot."

"It's b – u – l – z – a – k."

Spaceman typed it in. Hit enter. Nothing.

He squinted at the screen and tried to sound it out.

"Zuh, zuck mi, zuk my….Zuck My Balsak?!!"

Spaceman hit his breaks and took the cruiser sideways onto the dirt road.

We both jumped out of the car and went after each other.

We grappled trying to get the other in some kind of hold.

I forgot the prick wrestled for two years.

"Who the fuck are you, Archie?"

I had a clean shot, but didn't take it.

"You know who I am."

Spaceman's fist came around. I ducked. He brought another one. I caught it like a fastball and squeezed.

At the same moment, we both drew on one another.

Face to face.

Gun to gun.

I looked into the eyes of my old friend. He stared into mine.

"You answer all my questions first," I said. "Then I'll do the same."

Spaceman nodded and holstered his service revolver.

We took a moment to decompress.

Spaceman straightened his shirt and fired up another smoke.

"Strong bastard," he said.

I spit in the road.

Spaceman leaned over to pick up his hat. And seeing that simple action made me heavily consider raising my gun again.

53

It's true.

It was just like Dallas said earlier at the Drip. Red saved me. Took me on as one of his own.

The foster care system is not a bad idea. It's just flawed. Like humanity.

The first family I was with - that I can remember anyway - was good. They were good people. They had other foster kids too. They fed us, played with us. We went to church. Had nice clothes. One day something happened. I don't know if the guy went bankrupt or the marriage broke up or what, but one day, Social Services came and got all of us. Split us all up again like a newly shuffled deck of playing cards.

The second family I was placed with seemed nice at first. They had a pool and a big house. Lived in a nice neighborhood had nice cars.

But they were not good people. Had no business being around children.

Perhaps it's by the grace of God, or a neurological coping mechanism that I can't recall all of it, but I remember some things. Things I don't discuss.

I used to have horrible nightmares about it. In fact, I was glad when other horrors, other nightmares took their place.

Anyway, like Dallas said, Red took me in. And thank God, he did.

Red was a good man. So was his wife Arletta. They were caring. Their son, Teddy, had a heart of gold too. It wasn't long until he became my best friend. Well, at first, he was my only friend, but after a while, a year or so, we still ran tight.

I was a popular kid in grade school, but no more than Teddy. We played sports in the summer and Red and Arletta would take us on vacations and weekend trips.

We were in fourth grade when cancer knocked on our door and asked for Arletta.

It was awful. Unfair.

Red allowed us a day to cry and mourn her death. After that, he said we had to pick ourselves up and keep living. I did. Red and Ted did their best.

Red was a kind man, but losing Arletta made him harder. I asked him once if I could call him dad. He said no. He wasn't mean about it, but said that word was one of the few things he wouldn't share between Teddy and I.

It didn't bug me. Teddy was great. I couldn't believe how much he was willing and happy to share Red with me, Arletta too, for the few short years I knew and grew to love her.

I was a little bigger and stronger than Ted in sixth grade, but not by much. In sports, we were close skill wise. Maybe I was a little better at some things. Shooting. Hitting. Tackling. But it didn't matter.

About that time, I lost interest in baseball. Practice took up too much time. I'd rather read than shag pop flies or learn how to lay down bunts. The powers that be in the league always put Ted and I on different teams anyway, but it seemed like the year I decided to quit playing, Ted really got into it. I was happy for him.

Baseball soon became Ted and Red time. Which to me was cool. Ted and Red were blood. It wasn't in me to be jealous of their biological relationship. I mean how fucked up would that be? I was fortunate to have what I had. To have them in my life.

Ted's teams had always been marginal, but that summer they had the best record in the league. Even better, Ted was starting at second base, Red's old position when he was a kid. That summer Ted sported his JR Mobile Homes team hat everywhere he went.

We were in Mattoon one weekend for a tournament. The starting pitcher was hurt and Ted was excited to fill in on the mound. We stopped at a shopping mall on the way there to kill some time and grab a bite. Red wanted to stretch his legs and walk around so he gave Ted and I our allowance and set us loose upon the arcade.

Arcades were dark back then. Mysterious. Other than the lights from the games themselves, the rest came from black lights. The arcade employees were kids too, maybe just a few years older than us, that walked around and made sure quarters didn't get stuck in the machines.

I went over to watch some cute girl play Moon Patrol. When I got back to the pinball machines some older kid had Ted in the corner and was thumping him on the head.

As you can imagine, being from a small town and having a dad that is the Sheriff means learning how to hold your own at an early age. Ted was a smaller and skinnier than his tormenter, but he was scrappy and didn't take shit off of anyone.

"Give me your quarters?" The big kid said.

"Kiss my ass," Ted told him.

It wasn't until the kid started thumping Ted on the head again that I decided to get involved. I shoved the kid back. Other kids were watching now, including the Moon Patrol girl. I think my involvement embarrassed Ted, which is why he shoved me out of the way and squared up with the bully again.

I don't know if he'd seen it in a movie or what, but Ted was smart, resourceful. He held his big roll of quarters in his small fist to insure any shots he landed were going to be significant.

The bully danced around for a minute or two. Dodged a few swings from Ted, then kicked him in the balls. Ted went down screaming and his hat fell off his head. The bully ripped an Orange Julius out of some other kid's hand and dumped it on Ted.

Ted wiped his eyes and got up to take a swing, but the bully was faster and got him right in the eye.

I stepped in at that point and got shoved out of the way by someone from behind.

The bully and Ted squared up again and this time pulled a *Rocky III* and went for knockout punches at the exact same time. The result was their fists collided and Ted's roll of quarters went everywhere.

It was like a piñata had been busted open. Kids instantly dove on the ground, dreaming of all day game play, grabbing all the silver they could.

The bully kicked and fought all the kids back and started scooping up all the quarters.

Hot tears rolled down Ted's cheeks as he watched his hard-earned money get scooped up by the very prick that was trying to do him in.

I dove down on the ground and took a swing at the bully. Missed. I pushed the bully back and started grabbing as many quarters as I could for Ted. The bully got up and started stomping on everyone's hands.

The arcade happened to be one of those dumb rip-off joints where high scores earned paper tickets that could be traded in for stupid shit like Slinkys and gigantic fake plastic glasses.

When I looked up, Ted was running at the bully with one of those big novelty pencils. It was sharpened.

Ted tripped over some other quarter grabbing kid and went flying. The next thing we all knew the pencil had gone three inches deep into the center of the bully's navel.

The place was mobbed. Mall security, cops, an ambulance. It was chaos.

"It was the kid in the hat," someone said.

"Yeah, the kid in the hat," said another. Then another.

I looked over and saw Red tending to a sobbing Ted. I noticed Ted wasn't wearing his hat. I looked down and saw it underneath a Sea Hag pinball machine. For reasons, I still don't fully understand, I picked it up and put it on.

It turned out to be a far more serious deal than anyone imagined.

The bully's mom was an attorney. The kid was in critical condition for three days before making a recovery.

Ted's team had the best season they'd ever had that summer, but I didn't get to see it.

I was shipped off to a juvenile detention center just south of Chicago.

Things changed for me after that.

54

"After all I've done for you. You don't trust me."

"I could say the same thing."

"So, let's be men now and tell the truth."

"I'd like that, Arch."

"Good. Admit you killed Colesy?"

"What? How do you figure?"

"I think Bob was consumed with guilt and he finally wanted to come clean. I think he came to you first, to tell you what he was going to do and you told him not to. He said he had to, so you killed him, made it look like a suicide."

"That's crazy."

"You knew Bob's funeral would get me down here. You wanted to see where my head was at after all these years. If I was going to be a wild card with the truth. Maybe rub my face in some things. You've got a good life down here. Maybe you thought I was the loose end. Erase me, erase all risk from the past."

"So, if I'm that bad. That devious, why let you stay in my home?"

"How better to keep tabs on me while I'm in town? You yourself just asked if you could trust me on the ride out here. You had no idea I'd be down at your little swimming hole today, but you had someone in the woods watching me, knowing I'd probably go for a run."

"I had someone fire a gun at my own wife?"

"Not knowingly. You didn't know the girls would want to stay back for the day. You thought it'd just be me. While they were gone you could easily get rid of my body. When Cherry came back you'd just tell her I skipped town and knew she'd buy it."

"If that's true why did the shooter continue shooting after he saw Paige and Cherry up there? I wouldn't have given those orders."

"Maybe. Maybe not. Or maybe the guy you hired was good enough to hit me and miss them."

"But he wasn't, he missed."

"He did. And what did you say today? Scare tactics."

Spaceman smiled and lit a fresh cigarette off his spent one.

"Myra told me about the Feds coming down and investigating the county, your office. Crime statistics are basically nil here. A few meth and pill mills still happen in the boonies, but my guess is you're on the take. Control the market, hence your palatial estate and all the trappings."

"If I'm so secretive and can't trust anyone, who would I hire to shoot you?"

"Dallas. Who else?"

"Dallas is a dipshit."

"Yeah, and the perfect kind of guy to have in your pocket down here. He looks up to you, is eager to impress and I'm guessing you give him some nice kickbacks from your side businesses. Being in cahoots with you also gives Dallas a little leverage to misbehave a bit if he feels like it. Like chasing me onto your property with a gun. Jumping me at the Drip and so on. There is no threat. You've constructed this whole thing."

Spaceman chuckled. Took his hat off for a moment and scratched the back of his neck. "But I haven't seen you in twenty-eight years. Why kill you? You were there that day too?"

"I was thinking the same thing, but now that you told me about you running background checks, seeing I'm a ghost, maybe you think I'm a Fed coming down here to bust you on all your illegal shit. Maybe you think that will get me immunity."

"Why would you need immunity? Those bastards got everything they deserved."

"Maybe you think I need immunity from something else. And what about the labels on those old Tahiti Tom bottles. They don't make them anymore."

"So?"

"The bottle Amber gave you, is the same bottle you put on my windshield that night at the Elks."

"What? I didn't put shit on your windshield."

"Amber said the label on the bottle I showed her had the exact same tear."

"Oh, Amber said that? We better listen to her then. I forgot she is a forensic expert when she's not puffing on crystal."

Spaceman opened the trunk of his car.

"Look, here is the bottle she gave me. Where is the one you have?"

"It's in my truck."

"So how could they be the same? Hell, it could have been a mechanical issue at the bottling plant. Maybe hundreds got a similar rip or tear."

"Okay. But where did the bottles come from in the first place? I mean originate from. You can't find them online. I'm guessing your retro business was a good place to pick them up."

"But I told you about the retro business."

"You did. The classic hiding in plain sight move. Freely giving key info makes it look inconsequential."

"Jesus Christ, Arch. I don't know if I'm watching *The Princess Bride* or a *Law And Order* right now."

"Myra told me about Bob's novel. She told me you guys had an argument."

Spaceman hung his head. He put his hand on the front of his gun belt.

"Oh yeah?"

"Yeah. What was that about?"

"I don't know anything about a novel. But you're right about the bottle freaking him out. He did come to me saying he wanted to confess. Finally, get it off his chest. I told him he could do that with God. No one else."

"And what did he say?"

"That was the last we talked."

Spaceman adjusted his gun belt.

"Let's go for a ride."

"Bullshit. You wanna kill me? You got your chance. Do it now."

"Jesus Christ, Archie!" Spaceman's hands ran up to his buckle. He took his gun belt off and tossed it in the dirt at my feet.

I looked at it for a moment then picked it up.

I stared at Spaceman.

He stared back at me.

I picked up his gun belt and got in the car. "Where are we going?"

Spaceman swung a U-turn.

"Beech Meechum's."

55

Spaceman pulled the cruiser into a paved parking area.

Meechum's old house and barn had been torn down and replaced by a large prefabricated metal building.

Spaceman unlocked a series of gates and led me to the pig pen. Hogs were everywhere, snorting, digging, shitting.

"The only person I ever told about that day was Red."

"You told Red about the spillway?"

"Had too. He knew our car wreck was bullshit. Our wounds weren't consistent with the damage to the car. Shively Barnes filed a missing persons report for Karen before she called him a day later. Besides, those men we killed. Those bodies. Where did they come from? Someone was going to miss them. I knew dad would help us if anyone came sniffing around."

"You told him everything?"

"I didn't tell him I had my thumb up Amber's ass on the drive out, no, but damn near everything else. He was pissed, of course, shocked and scared, but he helped me. Said to put it in the rearview and never look back.

"What did you tell him about me?"

"The truth. That I told you to go. I told him about the PO Box and the answering service. That if I ever needed you, you'd be back."

I was quiet for a moment.

"I never knew he was sick. I would've come back in a heartbeat. You had my contact info."

"Yeah, I know."

"So why didn't you-"

"Paige and I had just gotten – look, it was a weird time. It wouldn't have been good. I hoped maybe you had started over somewhere. Found a wife, started a family, nailed down a great job."

I stared off into nothing. Must've done it for quite some time.

"Arch? Hey, Arch!"

I snapped out of it. "Yeah?"

"You alright?"

"Yeah." I looked at the hogs. "Meechum did this?"

"No. Red did. He bought the property from Meechum right after I told him about what happened. We waited a month or two then moved the two bodies from the spillway back here. Put 'em way down deep next to Colesy's kid."

"Don't call him that. His blood wasn't just on Colesy. It was on all of us."

"Sorry. You know what I mean."

"Wait. Two bodies? You left the one in the water? At the bottom?"

"Catfish didn't leave anything."

I looked in the pen. It was horrifying. Shameless beasts milling about in their own filth.

"Why'd you fix it up?"

"This place was falling apart. Made it easier to insure. We also needed it to be streamlined and redesigned to accommodate more hogs."

"More hogs? You and Red aren't pig farmers."

"No, but we had to ensure there were enough hogs to eat all the bodies."

"I thought you said there were. You and Red brought 'em here."

"The bodies from the spillway, yeah. But, there ended up being more."

"More bodies?"

Spaceman tilted his head, cupped his hand around a cigarette and lit up.

"Some bad seeds you can't fix. Red brought 'em here."

"And if anyone that knew about that day at the spillway came back with revenge on their mind?"

Spaceman patted the gate. "We had a place for them."

"Why didn't you tell me?"

"I figured the less you knew the better. That and when Red Bendix tells you to shut up, you do it. You had a future, Arch. With Red having my back it was no big deal for me to stay. I mean, I always knew I would anyway."

"You don't think it's weird Red jumped in to help just like that?"

"I told him what they did to us."

"What about Paige?"

"I married Paige because she's hot. Also, there was no one else left in town. We got along."

I looked at Spaceman's wedding ring. Gold with gaudy diamonds.

"We never did it to hurt you, Arch. Hell, if you want to know the truth, her parents didn't like me at first. Didn't think I was good enough. Still don't. All the money you think we have. Money, you think came from ill-gotten gains, her parents gave it to us. They gave Paige the home she wanted. The one I couldn't afford."

I stood there and soaked it all up. Ran it over in my mind.

It all made sense.

Spaceman continued. "I was sick when Bob died, but I was curious to see what had become of you. Your whole theory, all that noise you just said, I'm honored you'd think I was that smart."

I looked at the mass of hogs.

"Damn."

"You remember my little cousin, Kevin?"

"The little league wiz?"

Spaceman nodded. Flicked his butt into the pig pen.

"He didn't make it past thirteen. He was selling popcorn for scouts. Knocked on the wrong trailer. They shot him. We found the lab, but no arrests were made. Instead, Dad and I fed those murderin' bastards to the hogs. Alive."

I looked at the beasts in the muck and mire. Ugly. God awful creatures.

"Whoever is handing out the Tahiti Tom's, whoever is fucking with us, I want to turn into hog feed. But I need your help to do that."

"When was the last time you were out there?"

"The spillway? Ah man. Four, five years ago maybe."

"That long?"

"Not really a happy place to visit."

"Take me back there," I said.

56

The first two routes Spaceman tried were blocked off.

Either the land had been sold and re-zoned or the county or someone had blocked off access. Our third attempt was off a rural route down a gravel drive between two large grain bins. Further up, a dented gate was closed with rusted locks.

In Shoal County, encroaching on someone else's land without permission is a bad idea. Even a car emblazoned with Sheriff isn't safe in the backwoods. Spaceman figured even through the gate we'd still have a mile or two before we reached the spillway.

We turned around and tried to remember the fourth route, the one we rarely took in high school. It came back. Piece by piece as we circled back east. We went down two unmarked roads, one black topped, the other gravel. We were humming along at a decent clip when I saw a faint trail leading into the dense woods.

"There."

Spaceman slammed on the brakes. Years with a badge had given him practice behind the wheel. His control over the Charger was impressive.

The brush was grown over, but we could see tracks where tires had matted down the long grass and weeds.

We quietly rolled down the path with our windows down. The air was fresh. The sun dappled through the trees. I had forgotten how pretty it was back there, peaceful.

We reached the boulder. Still huge and covered with graffiti, the old bands of my youth had been covered with new ones. The likes of Motley Crue and Judas Priest had been replaced with Avenged Sevenfold and Black Veil Brides.

We parked and got out.

Spaceman shouted out hello a few times. Nothing

In spite of the long grass a narrow foot path was still visible.

I considered myself to be in good shape, but was a bit winded when I made it to the top of the embankment. Spaceman and his cigarette arrived to the summit no problem. It was like they fueled him like a vitamin or supplement.

The water was murky, almost green pea soup-like in some parts. Algae and various plant life floated on top. Bugs danced and buzzed just above the surface.

The fence was still there only now it was torn back in numerous areas.

Newer signs were bolted onto the rusty chain link.

Danger! No Trespassing! No fishing! No swimming!

I looked up at the top of the spillway. The steel trap door was still open after all those years. One end of what looked like a specialized, colorful rope for mountain climbing was tied to the rusted rungs. The other end ran up, over and down into the belly of the reservoir.

It felt good to know that despite our wired world full of safe zones, trigger warnings and over sensitivity, some kids still went the extra mile to still have fun the old-fashioned way.

We walked around then headed down the embankment where the water rushed out.

We heard giggling.

We moved slowly beyond the dividing slats.

Two women were laying out on their stomachs on a shared wet blanket. One was older, darker skin. The younger one had a bleach blonde crewcut and a large birthmark covering the back of her right knee. Each sported a tramp stamp and had their tops undone.

Spaceman with his Sheriff hat, yellow sunglasses and cigarette clenched between his teeth did his best Hunter S. Thompson.

"Howdy ladies."

Both women looked up forgetting their modesty.

"Oh Jesus!" Birthmark said covering herself.

The older one stayed up showing off a dragon tattoo that went between and around her breasts. Her areolas were huge.

"Ah gawd," Dragon Tits groaned. "We in trouble Sheriff?"

Spaceman flipped his cigarette butt over their heads into the stream.

"Not at all, ladies. Apologies for startling you. Everything okay?"

"It's hot," Dragon Tits said.

"We were thinking of getting into the water," said Birthmark.

Spaceman looked at the green sludge.

"This nasty stuff?"

"Wouldn't be if assholes like you didn't litter in it." Dragon Tits said, still on full display.

I laughed.

Spaceman fired up another cigarette.

"Trouble?" Birthmark said.

"No," Spaceman said. "Just a routine check."

"Well. It looks like people been coming out here forever, so you know, we didn't think it was any big deal."

Spaceman smiled, "Quite alright." He threw his thumb towards me. "Me and Archibald, here, may have slid down that ol' pipe a time or two back in our day." He rested his hands on the front of his gun belt. "How'd you girls get out here?"

"That ATV."

"Coming from where?"

"Away," Birthmark laughed.

"We're way up from Knox County," said Dragon Tits. "Heard about the place. Come down from there to camp."

"All the way down from Knox County on an ATV?"

Dragon Tits smirked, "Course not. We're staying with friends."

"Where are they?"

Birthmark looked uncomfortable.

"Why, you lonely looking for new friends?" Dragon Tits asked.

"No, not me," Spaceman said.

Dragon Tits shook her ink stained boobs and stuck her tongue out.

"You sure?"

Dragon Tits and Birthmark shared a toothy laugh that would have made a dentist shit his pants.

"You girls have fun," Spaceman said. "Be careful."

Dragon Tits gave a forced smile.

"You too." Birthmark said.

We made it back to the top and walked on further around the lake.

"Bet those two watch *Duck Dynasty* repeats like it's *Meet the Press.*

"Kiss my ass. I love *Duck Dynasty,*" Spaceman said.

"What was the name of that place in the woods when we were freshman? Lyle Parsons and those other senior burnouts would hang out there?"

"You mean the cave thing?"

"Yeah, something like that."

It wasn't much of a cave at all. Rather a huge hole with roots and earth hanging over it from a tree that had been uprooted decades ago in a tornado. Lyle and his buddies had hung a camouflage net over the front of it. Told people they worshipped the devil down there. Everybody knew it was bullshit. Lyle just didn't want to share his weed or his hideout with anyone but his closest pals.

"I don't know how long it takes deciduous vegetation to decompose," I said, "but my guess is, it's nothing but a pile of dirt by now."

"I can go get a dictionary and look up what in the hell you just said, or in the time it takes me to do that, we can walk over and take a look."

"Is that before or after you kiss my ass?"

We navigated our way through the dense woods until we found it. A rich green moss ran up the back of the dirt that now looked like a permanent roof.

We looked around. Someone had strung a green tarp over some towering roots and some lumber had been dragged inside to make a crude wooden floor.

We both stepped down into it.

Spaceman looked out. "Deer blind?"

"Or love shack or drug den." I pointed at a used condom and an empty pack of Zig-Zag rolling papers. "Looks like it's been all three."

Spaceman picked up an ancient shotgun shell and smelled it out of investigational habit. Tossed it.

I went around back and took a piss.

I looked at the mossy mound. Zipped up. Then hiked up the back side. I slipped once or twice and before making it to the top.

"Spaceman."

"Yeah?"

"You've got to see this."

Spaceman walked around and scaled the mound.

When he saw what I did, his Marlboro backflipped off his lip.

"Jesus H. Christ!"

There it was in all its glory and wonder.

A perfect view of the spillway.

57

We blasted down the two-lane blacktop.

"Where are we going?"

"Lyle Parson's place," Spaceman said.

"He's still alive?"

"Hard to believe, right?"

Lyle lived on the west side of town just over the tracks.

His neighborhood, if you could call it that, must've had an ordinance that all the houses had to be small, dilapidated and cloaked in peeling white paint.

Spaceman pointed his cigarette.

"That's Lyle's."

A cracked picture window had been cleverly repaired with duct tape.

Lyle's yard was brown. Surprising for a man that knew his way around a pot plant. There was a patch of scattered gravel on which a faded Big Wheel and rusty bike had been parked. The gate was locked.

"Lyle! Hey Parsons! Lyle!" Spaceman yelled.

Nothing.

"Let's head around back."

Next door, rock music blasted out of a blown speaker.

A faded and ripped above ground pool took up the majority of space in Lyle's backyard. It was filled with hundreds of empty beer cans dying to be recycled. Hovering just an inch or two over the cans were approximately three and a half million mosquitoes.

Lyle's back door was open save for a badly stretched screen door.

Spaceman turned his two pinkies inward and blew.

Moments later a portly man wearing a stained white t-shirt, and sweatpants came to the door. His gray hair was in a ponytail. He wore cheap ill-fitting sunglasses with purple lenses.

"Well shit fire, Spaceman? Zatchoo?"

"It is."

"You come to take me to jail?"

"I have Lyle. Get your hands up where I can see them."

Lyle did as was told.

Spaceman and I started laughing. Lyle put his arms down and laughed too.

"I was like, shit, all I got is four plants in the basement and that's for medical use. Hahahahahaha."

"You're using it medically now too?" Spaceman said.

"I'm using it every which way but makin' rope. Hahahahahaha."

"Let me guess," Spaceman said. "You're on disability."

"They didn't pick you as Sheriff for nothing." Lyle smiled. "Course you rode your daddy's coat tails right into office. Just kiddin', Spaceman. Just kiddin'. Hahahahahaha."

"Hiya Lyle. Been a long time."

Lyle lifted his sunglasses and squinted.

"Christ on a bike! Zatchoo Arch? What in the hell are you doing here? God it's been-" He cocked his head in an attempt to do the math. "Since high school I guess it was. You still learnin' up them yankee assholes at them Ivy League schools?"

"What?"

"I heard you were a professor or something like that?"

"Professor?"

"Shit, I don't know. Maybe a prosecutor. Can't remember. That was a hell of a spill I took off that ladder. Twenty feet in the air, cracked my skull and everything. Damn near forgot how to take a shit. Hahahahahaha I'm sure you heard about it. Made the County Press and everything."

"Congratulations," I said.

"Hey man, there ain't no such thing as bad publicity. Hahahahahaha. Was hopin' it would make it above the fold when it came out, but whatever. They save all that area for you, right Sheriff?"

Spaceman ignored Lyle.

"Saw the Big Wheel and bike out front," I said. "Never thought I'd see you settle into domestic life."

"Ah, hell, there was no settlin'. I'm divorced. Hahahahahaha. You remember Suzy Skyler, big ass, lazy eye? Wore her hair like a helmet with all that hairspray?"

I didn't.

"Sure do," I said. "How is she?"

"Dead I hope. Hahahahahaha. Just kiddin'," Lyle said. "Well, I knocked her up about eight or nine years ago at some party. Oh, wait, was it after a Def Leppard show in Evansville or something? Man, those guys did not age well. Hahahahahaha. Fuck it. Anyway, I tried to do the respectful thing and marry her. Turns out her ass got lazier than her goddamm eye. If I had a dollar for every Little Debbie she shoved in her maw I'd be rich. Hahahahahaha."

"Or at least get a new pool," Spaceman said.

"Hell, I did that on purpose. Every kid in the neighborhood and their cousins came over every damn day. Didn't even ask. Just jumped in. Half of 'em in dirty clothes. Water got disgusting. It was a pain in the ass to keep up. I finally poked a hole in it and drained it. Shoulda seen their eyes when they got airborne looked down and no water. Hahahahahaha. Now I use it for recycling."

We all stared at the mountain of cans for a moment.

"That's an impressive amount of aluminum," Spaceman said.

Lyle smiled proudly. "That's my kid Cody's college fund right there."

"So junior college then?" I said.

"For now, maybe," Lyle said. "Sonofabitch will be able to afford a Big Ten school in a few years. Hahahahahaha. Stuff goes down like nothing these days. Good for my cotton mouth on account of the wacky tobacky."

"That's putting in some serious work."

"You tellin' me you don't still drink like you did in high school, Arch? Shit, I remember you and Spaceman raising all kinds of hell out at the bonfires on Wyler Road. Hahahahahaha. Man, I remember hitting that rush, pounding Bud Lights. You remember Spuds Mackenzie? I had the t-shirt. First one in the school to have one."

"You peaked early, Lyle."

"Tell me about it."

"How is it you can remember what you wore in high school, but can't remember other things?"

"Easy, Sheriff. I only remember the happy times. Hahahahahaha."

"Whatcha up to these days?" I asked.

"All hell. Same thing. Cept a lot more Oxy. Hahahahahaha. Like I said that fall-"

"Lyle."

Lyle turned to Spaceman.

"Yeah?"

"Got some questions for you?"

"She told me she was seventeen, Sheriff, I swear it. Hahahahahaha."

"I'm serious, Lyle."

"For sure. Shoot. I mean don't shoot. Not me, anyways. Hahahahahaha."

Spaceman lit a cigarette.

"Oh man, can I bum one of those?" Lyle asked. "Had to cut back on the count of the disability check being so small and-"

"No," Spaceman said. "But how about when I'm enjoying my next one I'll think about you?"

"That works too," Lyle said. "Hahahahahaha."

"It's about the spillway, Lyle. Do you remember-"

"Spillway, hell I heard they closed that down."

"Well, it never was really open to the public, Lyle." Spaceman took a long drag. "I was wondering a long time ago back in high school, who all did you hang out with at the cave?"

"Oh, you mean the Hell Hole?" Lyle smiled. "That's what we called it back then. Everybody thought we worshipped Satan. We just said it to keep people away. Ken Felder's dumbass actually tried once though I think, but just ended up getting a staph infection where he cut his hand open for some blood oath. Hahahahahaha. Idiot."

"Okay," Spaceman said. "So, Ken Felder. Who else?"

"Damn, the Hell Hole. God, we got high back there. Hahahahahaha. You member Timmy Reynolds? He shorted Ken and I on grass once so we made up that rumor that we caught him trying to suck his own pecker in the showers at school. Hahahahahaha. You remember that? For a while everybody would bend their necks and make a sucking sound when Timmy come up to 'em. Classic! Hahahahahaha."

Spaceman shook his head and sighed.

"So, Timmy Reynolds, Ken Felder, who else hung out with you in the Hell Hole?"

"Mo Kendall would come back and drink with us. He had one of the first jam boxes that played CDs. He was always blasting Venom or Mercyful Fate. Man, he loved Southern Comfort. Ken called him Janis Joplin one time and Mo didn't cotton to it. Wanted to fight Ken. Hahahahahaha. You believe that?"

"Did you guys ever go out there after a heavy rain?"

"You mean to go down Tim's Tube?"

"Yeah?"

"Shit no. We were too scared, wouldn't admit it. Instead, we told everyone swimming was for queers? Hahahahahaha. You remember that? Pissed off Duck Benson and the rest of the swim team. We just went out there to get high."

"Why there?"

Lyle ran his hand over his gray ponytail and pondered the question.

"I don't know. It was our hangout, man. Nobody bothered us."

"Sure, but you wouldn't go out there if it had been raining to smoke weed in the mud, would you?

"Shit," Lyle laughed. "We'd smoke weed anywhere, anytime. Hahahahahaha."

"Sure, but what I mean is, not in some muddy hole way out in the country."

"Nah, it never got too muddy. We had it set up pretty nice, had a folding chair or two out there. Table. Stolen park bench. Had a tarp up."

I nodded.

"You remember Nathan Birdsong?" Lyle asked.

We didn't.

"Of course," Spaceman and I said in unison.

"He was back at a reunion once. Five year. No maybe ten. Anyway, he's an engineer - not of trains – and he said they don't make spillways like that no more. Not with wide tubes like that for the reason of what you guys did. Slide down it. Hahahahahaha. But all in good fun, right Sheriff?"

"You wouldn't be zooming on crystal right now would you, Lyle?"

Lyle froze. "What now?"

"Meth. You on it?"

"Huh?" Lyle said nervously.

"Have you been smoking methamphetamine?"

"Well, see. I'm really tight on dough right now on account of child support and all so I can't refill all of my prescriptions for the pain from my fall. Man, that was a fall, you shoulda-"

"Lyle!" Spaceman yelled.

"Okay, yes, yes. I'm on meth sometimes, but only cause they did a study on it at Ron Hopkins University and proved it's better for you than painkillers. Wild ain't it? Hahahahahaha. You believe that?"

"I do not," Spaceman said. "So those are the only three names you can think of at that time that hung out with you back there?"

"Yeah, that's it." Lyle gave his balls a vigorous scratch. "No wait. You member Crow Hart? He was that Indian looking kid. Half-breed. He come out there a few times too. He was crazy though. Dropped a lot of acid. Lit the park bench on fire once. Hahahahahaha. Crazy. It was like, dude, we sit on that. Hahahahahaha."

"Okay, thanks."

"Swhutt I'm here for, Sheriff."

"Good seeing you, Lyle," I said throwing my hand up.

"Likewise," Lyle said.

Spaceman and I looked at one another.

"One other thing, Lyle," Spaceman said turning around.

"Yeah. What's that Sheriff?"

"Clean yourself up. Put on some clean clothes. You've got kids."

"You kiddin'? Me dress up for them? They look worse than me. Hahahahahaha. Seriously, though. I tried to put a new shirt on the other day but it's hard for me to roll this shoulder after that fall-"

We closed the cruiser doors before we could hear the rest.

58

Spaceman was out of cigarettes.

He whipped into Huck's.

"You want anything?"

I considered asking for a peanut butter Twix, then shook my head no.

It was crazy. The guy was a celebrity. Every door he walked through, or person he passed, acknowledged him either with a smile, handshake or pat on the back.

A new Chevy Silverado pulled up in front. An older gentleman got out in work clothes. His jacket was Orvis. In spite of heavy wear, his boots looked expensive. I looked closer. It was Shively Barnes.

He gave a polite wave to Spaceman. The two walked toward one another, shook hands and began talking. I guessed it was election talk or what I had heard from his son Brian about the graffiti.

I swung the arm holding Spaceman's workbook around and typed in the first of the three names Lyle had given us. I typed in every iteration of the name I could think of then hit prospective age range.

Ken Felder. Kenny Felder. Kenneth Felder. K. Felder.

The computer did its thing.

Five Ken Felders came up within my search parameters.

Two were doctors.

One was a florist.

One lived in Boca Raton and raised show dogs.

I went the one from Midland, TX.

Jackpot.

Ken was clean.

No arrests or warrants.

Per social media he was a roughneck.

His highest level of education was Briarfield High School.

His most recent post on social media had been two weeks ago at a car show in Houston.

According to the photo he had a cute wife and son.

Next, I typed in Timmy Reynolds.

I narrowed it down by age group and last known residence.

He popped up in seconds for the simple reason that most men named Tim or Timothy don't go by Timmy once they get a little fur on their hang low.

Sadly, the poor bastard still went by Timmy.

A few minor arrests for drunkenness in his twenties.

And then…

DECEASED.

Motorcycle accident.

I went on to Mo Kendall.

Almost had his whole name in when I heard a tap on the glass.

I looked over my right shoulder.

The tip of Spaceman's nose was practically touching the passenger side window.

I rolled it down.

Spaceman sucked the fire through his cigarette.

"He's dead too, Arch."

"Do you want to tell me what in the hell we're doing then jumping through these hoops?"

"Yeah," he said exhaling. "I at least owe you that."

59

I didn't say another word until we rolled into the Elks and Bentley poured two healthy bourbons.

I threw mine down and asked for another.

"Mo Kendall. How?"

"Heart attack," Spaceman said. "Young. Thirty-three."

"You just know this randomly?"

"I dug out some old yearbooks of everyone I could think of that may have been out there that day, or any day back then really."

"What made you do that? We hadn't even talked to-"

"The same thing that made me study every face that ever went into and out of every county jail in the state. Made me pour over every mugshot."

"You said you and Red did that twenty-five years ago. Found nothing."

"And I've been doing it every day since."

"What are you saying? That Crow Hart is our man? But why? We didn't even-"

"Crow Hart is the head litigator for Native American Affairs in the ACLU."

"So, what in the hell is going on?"

"I wanted to double check with Lyle. Maybe there was another person."

"Double check? What in the hell does that mean, double check? You've talked with him before?"

Spaceman took a long drink then a long draw on his cigarette.

"Well?" I said.

Silence.

I pulled out my Desert Eagle and shoved it into Spaceman's thigh. He was shocked for a second then played it cool. I leaned in.

"I'm tired Ted. You need tell me what in the hell is going on now or a .50 caliber round is going to shatter your femur like Waterford crystal. Up to you. Bleed out before an ambo gets here or quit wasting my time."

Spaceman lit a fresh cigarette off the end of his spent one. He put his hat on the bar and ran both hands over his head. He tapped his glass for another drink. Bentley poured. Spaceman drank it down.

"I never killed him, Arch. The motherfucker got away. I had him pinned, but he caved in my elbow. Got me down in the mud. I got in a shot right above his eye, but he got away."

I didn't hear the rest. Instead, there was a ringing in my ears.

All this time. All these years.

Spaceman didn't stay in town for some noble reason. He stayed in town because he fucked up. He fucked up and was waiting for the day the guy that got away came back.

"Why didn't you tell me? I could have gone after him. We could have got him."

"I figured he couldn't report us without giving himself up. I mean it was justifiable what we did. They deserved everything they got. Who could he go to?"

"Any of his friends? Family?"

"Why do you think I insisted on staying?"

"You made me feel like shit for leaving."

"We were kids. I was mixed up. Jealous maybe. Furious at myself. Scared to death what was coming our way. I may have made you feel bad, but you were going to live. I was staying in town in case he ever came back. I didn't know what was going to happen. Did the guy get picked up somewhere? Move to a foreign country? Die in a war? Get shanked in prison? It's been twenty-eight years. What are the chances he'd come back now?"

"I need you to make me a list."

"What?"

"Whoever got away, whoever it is. He's got to be in town, right? Or just outside of it?"

"Yeah."

"So, he's got to be holed up somewhere either with someone he knows, or someplace we haven't been."

"Yeah?"

"I need a list from you of every shady character, scumbag and shithole in the county?"

"A shit list?"

"Yep."

"Got it right here." Spaceman pulled it up on his phone. "Problem is we need warrants."

I looked over his list.

"Not for this."

60

There was no blacktop, no gravel, just two parallel tire tracks pounded out over time through the scrub brush.

Spaceman parked under an old oak tree fifty yards away.

The trailer was old and beat-up. Forgotten beer cans in country ditches had more to be proud of.

Faded bandanas and shop rags stood in as curtains making the light that emitted a sickly kind of pink.

Godawful electronic music blasted out of the windows.

I pulled on a pair of leather gloves and grabbed a lead pipe out of the trunk.

No flashlight. The moon was enough.

Spaceman walked up the cinderblock steps first. There was the faint hint of sweetness in the air. Meth.

The residents were believed to be nickel and dime dealers. In the past, the gas to drive out to this shithole wasn't worth the county's money, but now, given what we were looking for it was worth turning over every stone.

Spaceman looked back at me, nodded and turned the door knob.

In my line of work, I had seen it all. White collar, blue collar, dog collar.

Still, when we got inside, we both gasped.

A toddler with dark sweaty hair stuck to his forehead was locked in a cage. He was lying on a pile of filthy rags. A crudely cut open can of Spaghetti O's was next to him. Dried orange crust from the sauce was all over his hands and mouth where he had attempted to feed himself. In some parts there was red, where he had cut his hands on the sharp edges of the can. Dirty Sponge Bob pajama pants covered most of his overflowing diaper. His tiny stomach rose and fell with his breathing.

I twirled the lead pipe like a clean-up batter waiting on deck.

We stepped quietly past the kid and made our way down the hallway.

The filth in the bathroom defied description.

Spaceman slowly pulled back the cracked plastic accordion style bedroom door.

The bedroom reeked of sweat and body odor.

A waifish woman with dirty blond hair was passed out naked on a stained mattress. She was in her thirties. The meth made her look sixty. Lying next to her, also passed out, was a huge mess of a woman wearing nothing but moles, pimples and skin tags. She had her hand between the skinny woman's legs.

In the far corner of the room, sitting at a makeshift desk of greasy cardboard boxes, was a tweaker. A large plastic cup of cigarette butts was to his right. The man was covered in a sheen of sweat. His jeans were bunched on top of his ankles. His right arm pumped furiously. In front of him was a magazine opened to a page with a photo of …

Spaceman gasped, "Jesus H. Chri-"

The sick twist turned his head. I brought the lead pipe down on his nasal bone and watched his eyes looney tune out of his skull.

"Let's take him in, Arch! Ask him some questions." Spaceman said.

"Are you out of your mind? Look at this shit." I pointed at the books and magazines. "Get him up."

Spaceman lifted the pedophile up against the wall.

The man's mouth was covered in blood from his broken nose.

"Please mister," he spat, "you can have-"

I swung the pipe again. Skin, hair and scalp splashed onto the paneling. The man screamed. Spaceman held him up.

"Please. I-"

"We're looking for a man," I said. "Maybe a stranger, or a friend of a friend staying with you."

"My wife and sister are the only ones that live here with me."

"What about the kid?" I said. "Yours?"

"Oh, oh the kid. No, we, we found him."

"Found him?"

Two swings of the pipe. Nobody was putting Humpty Dumpty back together again.

Between the two women on the bed was the same type of filth. The big one lifted her head, one eye struggling to open, the other still shut. She was so out of it she didn't see us. She had a creepy half smile.

"Les git 'im back in here," she giggled. "Whaddya say, Marn-"

I sent her rotten teeth flying like turd brown Chiclets. Her screams woke the thin one.

"I get him fir-"

Skinny got it worse.

I tossed the dripping pipe on the bed.

Back in the living room Spaceman pulled the stereo cord out of the wall.

I bent down and opened the cage.

I reached in and pulled the toddler out with the utmost care. I wrapped the little boy in an afghan, carried him out to the car and gently laid him in the back seat.

I popped the trunk and took out two full cans of gas.

Back in the trailer I handed one to Spaceman.

We splashed the place. Furniture. Curtains. The walls.

I poured the gasoline over the bodies.

"They're not dead yet, Arch."

"They will be."

"Ever worry about Hell?" Spaceman asked.

I tossed the can to the side.

"I worry there isn't one."

I grabbed the unconscious man's Bic and spun the wheel.

We didn't turn on our headlights. Like the moon before, the blaze illuminated our way back down the road.

Ten minutes later I carried the toddler into the ER. The doctors ran up and took the kid.

"What happened?"

"He's dehydrated, malnourished, most likely abducted."

"Where did you find him?"

I didn't say a word.

"Who are you? We need you to fill out some paperwork."

The bill of my cap was down far enough that the cameras couldn't make me.

Nor could the staff see my face.

Or my tears.

61

Though it billed itself as a members only hunting club, the Pelt, as it was called, was really a biker bar that catered to a garden variety of scumbags, ex-felons and cast-offs.

Every now and then some poseur in a new leather vest from the nearest Harley dealer would roll up on his shiny new bike and get the shit kicked out of him.

Though the Pelt was on the other side of the county line, the Shoal County Press and local radio station still reported on the shootings and mayhem that spilled out of its doors for those citizens titillated by such a thing.

It was around two in the afternoon when Spaceman and I pulled up in my Navigator. There were a handful of bikes parked out front that looked like they were from the movie, *The Road Warrior*. Most had been modified with spare parts. Not out of aesthetic purposes, but rather financial necessity.

There was another bike. One that looked like it came from one of those customized chopper shows.

"You know that's stolen," Spaceman said. He grabbed the door handle. "You ready?"

"Can't wait."

Spaceman opened the door. The blast of sunlight illuminated the dust and smoke that hung in the air. The bar was dimly lit by blinking neon and a pair of low watt bulbs that hung over a pool table. There was a threadbare couch. Some tables, chairs.

I counted five men if you included the sun ripened bartender with the Gandalf beard. The ole boy spit in an empty beer bottle and looked at Spaceman.

"Little early for you isn't it, Sheriff?"

"Not here to drink."

"Well, you're out of your jurisdiction then."

"I'm not here on official business."

"Well, that's a shame because I don't recall you being a member."

"I'm not," Spaceman said. "My buddy here is thinking about joining though."

The bartender released another mouth full of tobacco juice. Wiped his lip with his hand.

"Hi," I said. "I was hoping to get a brochure with a list of the club's amenities, fee structure and calendar of events."

Laughter came from a corner in the back. I squinted. Too dark.

"Well," Gandalf said. "For you and the Sheriff here, the membership is a million bucks."

"Would that give us use of the resort full time?" I smiled.

More loud laughter from the corner.

"I have a better question," Spaceman said. "Who's riding the stolen chopper?"

"That would be me," came a voice from the dark corner.

"You got registration?" Spaceman said.

"I do."

The man stepped into the dim light.

"Bring it here," Spaceman said.

Fuck me.

It was Gleason.

We were all ex-military. V had three of us in her employ. Gleason was a clean-cut Navy SEAL who specialized in unconventional warfare. When he finished doing his time for Uncle Sam, he went all Captain Caveman and got a bike. His hits for V were like mine, varying between brutal and efficient, depending on the time, place and target.

Gleason looked at Spaceman. "Let me go outside and get it."

"I got it," I told Spaceman. "Order me a cup of the lobster bisque I'll be right back."

I followed Gleason out the door and down the porch steps.

"What in the hell?"

"Just happened to be in the neighborhood."

"Bullshit."

"I had a job in Indy. Headed to the Sunshine State. V asked me to poke my head in."

"Unreal. What am I five?"

"Wouldn't take it personally. You're a valued asset."

"She ever checked up on you?"

"No. I'm not a pussy."

I laughed.

"I got something for you."

I walked over to my truck and grabbed one of the biker jackets I picked up in Mississippi. I tossed it to Gleason.

"What's this?"

"Put it on. It legitimizes your look."

"I could get killed for wearing another man's cut."

"Could, but you won't."

Gleason held it up.

"The Demon Seeds. Holy shit is that a devil jerking off?"

"Clever, eh?"

"Hilarious. How'd you get it?"

"Found it."

"Bullshit. You aced a one percenter?"

I nodded.

"Dude. Put it in your man cave at your lake house."

"I got two more,"

"Jesus. What'd you do, hit 'em with your truck?"

"Nah."

"Contract, or a pro bono beat down?"

"Freebie. They came at me first. Biggest one begged for his life."

"Always do. Pathetic."

"The other two tried that MMA shit on me."

Gleason laughed. "Hilarious. Where were you?"

"On a beach."

"You didn't tell 'em you spent four years in the sandbox?"

"I don't think they would have been impressed."

"Bet they were afterwards. You do the Achilles thing?"

"Jugulars."

"Damn, Archie."

"They got me at a bad time. I took their colors and left them on the beach with AFFA written in the sand beneath them."

AFFA, Angels Forever, Forever Angels.

"Nice. Nothing like starting a turf war."

"Give 'em something to do. Speaking of which, time for you to get out of here."

"You got this?"

"Of course. Tell V she wasted your time. This is just a personal errand. I'll see her next week."

Gleason kicked his V124 to life. The roar was impressive

"You don't have to tell me twice. I'm off to tame some Tampa poontang."

"Get that beard wet."

"You know it, asshole. See you in Hell."

"See you in Hell," I said

Gleason made it twenty yards down the road before turning around and rocketing a fully extended middle finger skyward.

Good dude.

I walked back into the Pelt.

"Told you boys," Spaceman said laughing. "They thought you were a dead man, Arch."

"Registration was legit. Nice guy. He was showing me pictures of his place on Fire Island. Where were we?"

"You both were about the get the fuck out of my bar," Gandalf spat.

"You haven't even given us the official tour yet," I said.

Gandalf turned. "Need you out here, LB."

Two swinging doors burst open behind the bar.

A freakishly large man ducked into the room. His forehead was enormous. The bone structure of his face looked as though it had been rushed by an amateur sculptor. He pointed a finger towards the door.

"Get the fuck out."

I looked at Spaceman.

"Arch, this is Little Bobby," Spaceman said.

"Ironic nicknames," I smiled. "They never get old."

"Get your asses out," said Little Bobby.

"Dammit, LB," Spaceman said lighting a cigarette. "We just want to have a drink and ask a few friendly questions."

"Like what?"

"Do you have a pre-Prohibition cocktail menu I could take a peek at?" I said.

"Listen asshole," Little Bobby said to me. "Two things walk out that front door every day. Drunk friends and bloody strangers."

"That and we don't serve fag drinks," Gandalf spat.

"Wait," I said. "You don't serve fag drinks? Or you don't serve fags drinks?"

"Both," Gandalf said.

"So how come that guy over there is drinking?" I pointed to a mean looking guy with droopy mustache and a GG Allin patch on his jacket.

"What you'd say motherfucker?" Mustache said.

"Pipe down, handsome," I said.

"I don't think anyone likes your friend, Sheriff," Gandalf said.

Spaceman nodded. "He takes some getting used to."

"Yeah, well. You got three seconds to clear out unless you got a warrant." Gandalf said. "One..."

I looked around the room. The mixed bag of muscles, fat, bad tattoos and bandanas all stood up where they had been sitting.

"Two..."

They all stepped closer.

I looked out of the corner of my eye at Spaceman.

"Lookout," he said.

I turned around just in time to see a baseball bat festooned with long rusty nails come flying towards my head. I stepped out of the way at the last second and watched as it dug into the wooden bar.

Little Bobby struggled to free the bat.

Gandalf pulled a gun and aimed it at my head.

"Mister, you better leave or I'll paint that post with your brains."

Spaceman brought his piece up. "Drop it!"

"Bullshit, Sheriff. I got the right to refuse service to anyone."

"Maybe. But your employee just tried to kill my friend."

"Yeah? And I'm damn sorry he mis-"

I brought my right hand up and grabbed the gun while pushing in Gandalf's elbow. The old man let out a less than manly squeal.

Little Bobby freed the bat from the bar. He looked at me and laughed.

"Gun ain't loaded dipshit!"

"Really?" I pointed the gun at him and gave the trigger three rapid squeezes. "Damn!"

Little Bobby laughed and threw one huge leg over the bar.

"Hold up!" I said.

Little Bobby furrowed his brow and paused for a moment.

I drew back and unloaded a ninety mile an hour heater into LB's forehead. The pistol bounced off his granite melon like a racquetball. The spiked bat he was holding fell from his shoulder and impaled Gandalf's hand that was resting on the bar.

Little Bobby stood still as blood began to pour from his right ear.

I felt a tap on my right shoulder.

I turned opposite. A barrel-chested biker's fist just missed me. I caught him with a chop to the throat and a lightning quick knee to the baby maker.

To my left, Spaceman had just caught a swinging pool cue from Mustache and was working the stocky assailant over with some powerful shots to the ribs.

A skinny kid with piercings all over his face foolishly announced his lunge at me with an obnoxious roar. I turned just in time to feel a broken bottle tear into my shirt and flesh. Unfortunately for the kid, he had gotten nothing but scar tissue. Recognizing his blow was weak, the kid's eyes immediately had the look of apology. I poked a thumb into each one of his oversized ear gauges and pulled. His earlobes snapped like calamari rings.

Little Bobby had just worked the bat out of Gandalf's bleeding hand.

Mustache was back up and coming at me with a knife. Spaceman raised his gun and fired a warning shot right over the brute's shoulder into the jukebox.

"Hold up," Spaceman said.

Everyone complied. Little Bobby pulled a piece of ice out of the well and held it on the grapefruit sized bump on his forehead.

"Enough playing grab-ass. We're looking for a guy. An out-of-towner," Spaceman said. "Anyone notice a stranger coming around? Somebody who's not a regular?"

"Yeah. The motherfucker that was just in here," Little Bobby said.

"Naw. Wasn't him. We're looking for someone else," I said.

"I ain't tellin' you assholes shit," Gandalf said wrapping a bar towel around his bleeding mitt. "Come in here tearin' up our-"

Spaceman sent two shots through the TV.

"Goddamit!" Gandalf yelled. "What gives you the right?"

"How do you cheap bastards not have a single air conditioner in this shit hole?" Spaceman said. "Honestly, it has to be like a hundred and fifty degrees in here."

"Kiss my ass, Sheriff," Gandalf said.

"Easy Pops," I said. "I'd answer his questions before he dries his balls off with your beard."

"What's this stranger look like?" Ear Lobes moaned.

"Well see, that's the rub." I said. "We don't know, but seeing as how this is a private club, we figured if a non-member came in you'd probably notice and have a description for us."

Barrel Chested chimed in, "Who's the guy that came in a few days ago?"

"Shut your hole," Gandalf said.

"He had a crewcut. Wore camo."

"Shut up, Kenny!" Gandalf yelled.

Spaceman aimed his gun at Gandalf's forehead.

"He a friend of yours?"

"Fuck you. This is bullshit."

"Did he say why he was here? Throw his weight around or anything?"

Little Bobby shook his head. "Nobody gets away with anything in here unless we allow it."

"Damn straight," said Ear Lobes.

"Well thanks for taking it easy on us," I said.

I zoned in on a picture taped behind the bar.

"Let me see that."

Gandalf begrudgingly pulled it off the wall and handed it to me. I looked at it. A few of the guys in the bar were posing in front of their motorcycles, beers in hand. Behind them were two grown adults in hockey jerseys featuring a cartoon silhouette of a person running with a hatchet. One had black and white clown paint on.

I handed the picture to Spaceman.

"Look familiar?"

Spaceman took the picture from me.

"Never seen 'em before. Who are the clowns?"

Little Bobby shrugged. No one said anything.

"These clowns run with the camo man?" I said. "They buddies?"

Again silence.

Spaceman walked behind the bar and grabbed a bottle of Everclear.

"If you boys don't start talking, your panty wall is going to go up in smoke."

"You can't do that," Gandalf said.

"No," Spaceman said. He tossed me the bottle. "But, he sure as hell can."

I grabbed a greasy bandana off Mustache's head and stuffed one end into the bottle of high octane booze.

Spaceman tossed me his lighter. I lit the bandana.

"Now goddammit, you can't do that. That's arson," Gandalf said.

"It's an act of kindness," I said. "Those panties look like they belonged to incontinent hoboes."

"Hey, some of those are my ole lady's." Little Bobby yelled.

"My condolences," I said. "You boys got a fire exit picked out?"

The flame was almost to the lip of the bottle. I cocked my arm back.

"Wait," Gandalf said. "Wait just a goddamm minute."

62

The field had never been properly cleared for farming.

Stumps peppered the uneven land.

Over time it had become a graveyard for burned out cars and rusted farm equipment.

Had a picture been taken of the metal carcasses, the combination of beauty and sadness would have expertly conveyed the state of the local economy.

"Well, I'll be damned. Right here in my own county."

Spaceman sent his cigarette butt skyward with a finger flick that must have taken years to master.

"Who owns this land?"

"Used to be a family long gone. Bank owns it now."

It was a brilliant place to cook. If used to its fullest potential it could make a ton of money. More than likely it already had.

The school bus had been gutted and lowered into a deep trench. Various pipes and ventilation tubes poked out of the packed dirt that covered its yellow roof. Above ground, an intake for clean air was camouflaged by an old tractor's exhaust stack. The noxious fumes were pumped out of another series of PVC which were filtered by what looked like a rotting hay bale.

"You believe this?" Spaceman said in disbelief.

"Criminal ingenuity never fails to surprise."

An old refrigerator door led down crudely dug out stairs topped with grimy cardboard.

Little Bobby had given us the knock, but for reasons of forgetfulness or perhaps not giving a shit, I kicked the door in.

Two rednecks with infantile tattoos looked up from the money they were counting. One was far larger than the other and looked twice as stupid. The skinny one with a milky-eye was stoned off his ass.

"You two bet-bet-better be goddamm San-San-Santa Claus comin' in he-he-here like that," Milky-Eye said.

It was hotter than hell in that bus. Moisture beaded off of the metal ceiling. I prayed whatever Spaceman and I were breathing in was just b.o.

"Damn! You guys fuckin' each other down here?" Spaceman said.

"S'my sub," Stupid said with a mouth full of food.

"What's the protein?" I asked. "Rhino taint?"

"Tha' fucks it to ya?" Stupid said. A huge piece of sandwich flew out of his mouth.

Brutal, it was white bread with a big hunk of mayonnaise hanging off of it.

I didn't think twice.

I raised my hand canon and sent him to the great beyond.

"Jesus!" Milky-Eye screamed.

"You really need to get that safety looked at, Arch." Spaceman said.

I looked at Milky-Eye. "Got some questions for you."

"J-J-J-Jesus Christ, man! You, you, you let me walk, walk, walk out of here alive and I'll tell you ev-ev-everything you want to know."

Spaceman looked at me. "That sound like a good deal to you?"

"So far."

"Okay," Spaceman said to Milky-Eye. "You seen a military looking guy in these parts recently, talked to him or anything, maybe know where he's holed up?"

"N-n-no." Milky-Eye stammered. He glanced down at his dead friend. "I-I-I can't be-be-be-believe you killed, M-M-Monte. Fat moth-moth-moth-motherfucker owes me three-hun-hun-hundred bu-bu-bucks."

"How about I shoot you and you two can work it out in purgatory."

"O-O-kay-kay-kay. Look, we seen a guy-guy earlier drinkin' at the Pelt. But he did-did-didn't say much. I don't know hi-him. He was askin' around for suppli-pli-plies. Where to buy things and st-st-stuff."

I nodded to Spaceman. "I got this." I looked at Milky. "What'd you tell him?"

"Didn't tell him sh-sh-shit. Pelt is the only place I know-know be-be-besides here and the Walmart."

"Did he give a name?"

"Nobody giv-gives names at the Pelt."

"Did he say why he was in town?"

"Just asked where he could-could get some guns, cheap."

"What did you tell him?"

"Told him if anybody had 'em, it'd-it'd be the Pelt."

"So, he bought some?"

"I'm guessin'."

Spaceman took over.

"Who do you work for?"

"It's a group of guys. They got-got a group of us cook-cooks. We move around to different sites in different coun-counties. They just let us get-get back on. We was doing too much of our-"

The kid had whistling snot. I couldn't deal with the heat and smell any longer.

My bullet sent his brains into the wall.

Spaceman turned and looked at me like I had forgotten to bring beer on a fishing trip.

"What in the hell, Arch?"

"He didn't know anything else."

"How do you know?"

"It's a gift."

I walked over and stuffed the piles of cash into a beat-up duffle.

"What are you going to do with that?" Spaceman said.

"Save the whales."

63

I walked into the Elks Club hoping to find Cherry

My plan was to give her the duffle stuffed with cash and tell her to get out of town.

It was still up in the air if I was going to give her a secure phone number in case she needed me, or just apologize for being an asshole and wish her luck on life's mysterious journey.

I ordered a beer and pondered the consequences of both options.

Giving Cherry a contact number would be cruel. It'd give her the false hope of reconnecting down the line. Of course, ghosting her would possibly lay a foundation of anger and resentment towards me that would springboard her into moving on with her life.

"Where's the girl?" Bentley asked.

"I was getting ready to ask you the same thing. She been around today?"

"No. She was in last night. Hanging around that Suggin's kid, plays baseball for Indiana State."

"Good for her. Movin' up in the world. Who doesn't love a Sycamore man?"

"Your winter summer romance has come to an end, huh?"

"She's a beautiful, intelligent, fun young lady. Deserves better than me."

"Damn right, she does," Bentley laughed. "Damn shame she's not into bald bartenders."

"Trust me. One day she'll meet Mr. Right and be glad she it ended it when she did."

"So, you broke her heart?"

"I prefer to think of it as saving her life."

Bentley looked over my shoulder.

"Oh shit. Incoming."

Bentley walked away just as I felt a hand on my shoulder.

"Archie."

I turned around on my barstool, "Yes?"

"It's Maria."

"I'm sorry, who?"

"Maria. Maria Stowers. 'Shake Your Foundations' Evansville?

"Well, I'll be damned."

"I've put on a few pounds since then."

"Haven't we all."

Maria Stowers' dad, Glen, was the principal when we were in high school. She was the classic overachieving nerd. She and Paige were friends their junior year when she tutored Paige in trigonometry.

It was nineteen eighty-eight. White Lion was opening for AC/DC at Robert's Stadium in Evansville. Maria and her boyfriend had an extra pair of tickets. They asked if Paige and I wanted to join them. Of course, we said yes. I was a huge Angus fan and the girls were totally into White Lion's brand of hair metal pop.

Maria's boyfriend played golf. They made sectionals that year and he had to miss the concert. Paige offered to buy Maria's two tickets and ask another couple to go with us, but Maria still wanted to go. She had a guy lined up from her church, but he bailed a few days before the gig when someone put it in his ear that AC/DC was evil and White Lion supported anarchy. We had a good laugh.

Two days before the show, Paige's sister called from New York to say she had tickets for *Saturday Night Live* that weekend. She said it was the chance of a lifetime. Dana Carvey was all the rage as the Church Lady.

Paige said she would go to NYC on one condition, that I take Maria to the concert.

It was AC/DC, I would've taken a corpse.

"If I have to," I said.

"Any other girl, I'd probably say no and be jealous of," Paige said. "But Maria. I have a feeling she doesn't get out much."

Maria gave the remaining two tickets to her aunt and uncle. They were older and said they'd drive.

It was General Admission. I was a floor guy.

I grabbed Maria's hand and worked and wedged our way up as far as we could go. We got about twenty feet from the stage when we hit a wall of hardcore fans who refused to move.

While we had room, Maria couldn't see over the people in front of us.

"Let me get on your shoulders," she said.

I looked down and noticed her denim mini.

"Don't worry," she said.

Maria tied my jacket around her waist, pulled her skirt up over her hips and climbed on top of my shoulders. I was shocked when instead of feeling cotton panties, I could feel her steamy Brillo pad on the back of my neck.

For the next hour and a half, Maria rode my first vertebrae like Debra Winger on a mechanical bull.

Maria matched her rhythmic undulations with the beat. Between her orgasms and Angus' guitar solos, the tip of my erection was about to burst like the ends of a Ball Park frank.

As soon as the last spotlight dropped from the encore, we made a bee line for the parking lot. Knowing we couldn't climb in the back of her aunt and uncle's car and make out, we found a stand of pine trees just inside the parking lots fencing.

We crawled under the long branches then got down to business on a bed of soft pine needles. Other than the sap and pinecones stuck in Maria's hair and the fact my neck smelled like Lady Godiva's saddle, I didn't think her aunt and uncle had a clue what we'd been up to.

The next morning, I could barely get out of bed. It was impossible to turn my neck.

When Paige got back from NYC I told her I had pulled a muscle at football practice.

She told me the hickey on her neck was a bruise.

We were made for each other.

I took a sip of my drink and laughed at the memory.

"Can I get you something?" I asked Maria.

"No, thank you."

She put her hand on my arm. Here it came, I thought. She had tickets to a Bonnaroo and wanted me to go. Although she had gained weight, she could see I had gained muscle. My guess was by her estimation, I looked strong enough to hold her on my shoulders through at least one of Widespread Panic's marathon sets, the result of which would put me in a thoracic halo for the next six months. I prepared to say no.

"My husband needs to talk to you."

I looked at Maria. She was nervous. Panicked.

"Husband?"

"He's in trouble."

"Okay, and-"

"You're in trouble, too."

"Me?"

I was getting ready to ask if any of this was related to our rock-n-roll giraffe ride nearly thirty years ago, when she blurted, "Somebody wants to kill you."

"Excuse me?"

"Someone wants to kill you, Archie."

"Who?"

Maria grabbed a napkin off the bar and wrote down a location and time with a pen. She was out the door before the ink dried.

Thirty minutes later we met where all great top-secret conversations take place in a small town, the Walmart parking lot. I parked in the far corner as directed.

I was trying to find a decent radio station when a blue Ford Festiva whipped up next to me. Maria was behind the wheel. She motioned for me to follow her. When we got to the back by the dumpsters, her passenger hopped out and got in my truck. Maria tore off.

"Arch," it was Koontz Beesbrook. "I've got bad news."

"Let's hear it."

"It's best if I start from the beginning."

Koontz met Maria when he was running the fat camp/prostitution/coke ring on his campground. While Maria dropped twenty pounds and avoided prosecution, Koontz got fifteen years. Koontz proposed to Maria while incarcerated and they got married. Maria was a dutiful wife and made all the visits. Things were tolerable on the inside for a while until one day when Koontz got a new cellie.

"This guy comes in. Not only does he look mean, he looks crazy like one of those pro wrestlers with the cheesy backstory about being institutionalized."

"Okay."

"A week or two goes by. Guy doesn't say a word. He takes my top bunk. Eats all my food. In spite of my size, I get tired of his shit and tell him. I barely get a swing in before he has me up in the air and is choking me. He slams me down and drives my head under the sink. I swing my arms out trying to push off the wall, and that's when he sees it, up my left sleeve, my Briarfield Mules tattoo.

"Guy drops me and for the next three days asks me non-stop questions about Briarfield. About Green Reservoir, the spillway. If I had ever heard any talk about some kids and an assault. I told the guy I didn't know what he was talking about.

"Anyway, this crazy bastard decides to shiv a screw one day. The guards come in all bats and hats and drag him off to solitary, maybe a diesel transfer. Anyway, I never saw him again. Then three weeks ago he shows up at my door. Tells me he's going to camp on my land. Has some business to take care of. Just as I'm about to say no, he steps into my house and shoves a gun barrel into my mouth. Tells me if I tell anyone about him, he'll burn down our house down with Maria and I in it."

"What's his name?"

"Sacks. Vernon Sacks."

"Sacks?"

"That's what the tag on his peels said anyway."

"How do you know he's here for me?"

Koontz pulled a newspaper clipping out of his shirt pocket. Unfolded it.

"He saw this in the Shoal County Press. Wouldn't stop asking me questions about it."

I looked at the clipping. It was a picture of me, Spaceman and the other pallbearers from Colesy's funeral.

"What did you tell him?"

"Nothing. I mean all I know. I told him you didn't live here and that I don't associate with the Sheriff on account that I'm a felon."

I nodded.

"Look, Arch. I'm sorry I didn't tell you about this earlier, but it's nearly impossible to get off our property. Maria and I are practically hostages. He's evil. Last night he bangs on our door covered in what looked like mud or blood. Tells me to turn the hose on. Maria is scared to death. We don't know what to do."

"Do you have a picture of this guy?"

"No. He took our phones."

I looked at Koontz. Instead of looking relieved from telling me, he looked petrified.

I thanked him for the info.

"What should we do?"

"Don't go home. Head straight out of town with Maria."

"But we didn't pack anything."

"Not worth it. If he sees you two with suitcases-"

"He'll kill us."

"Just go. Get Maria and go."

"What are you going to do?"

"You said he wants to kill me, right?"

"Yeah."

"Looks like I better kill him first."

"Listen, Arch. You don't understand. This guy, Sacks, is insane. Brutal."

"I'll handle it. Get out of town."

I dropped Koontz off with Maria.

I looked at the gas station across the street from the Walmart and considered going in to see if they had a peanut butter Twix.

I made the parking lot then changed my mind.

64

It was small, but Spaceman's body gave an involuntary shake when the picture came up.

"I'll be damned. That's him! That's the sonofabitch right there." Spaceman clacked away on his computer. "Look at this."

I looked over Spaceman's shoulder.

Sack's rap sheet read like a maniac's dream resume. Misdemeanors started as a teen gave way to more serious crimes and felonies. He was last popped for armed robbery and murder. Mistrial, mishandled evidence.

"This guy has done multiple year stretches in three different prisons."

Spaceman rattled some more keys.

Sacks booking photos.

Court docs.

And then.

An academic paper. A grad thesis written and published decades ago, now scanned and featured on some kind of liberal blog.

Spaceman hit the link

The Hard Work of Rehabilitation: Betting on the Future, Forgiving the Past.

Spaceman skimmed it.

Nothing.

Then the bombshell.

The picture was of a handful of delinquents in county jumpsuits holding various farm implements. The photo wasn't of the best quality, but could still be made out.

On the far right was a guard, an officer of some kind. Next to him stood the first man I had ever killed. The one who had attacked and raped

Karen that day at the spillway. His face, his eyes brought back emotions I hadn't felt since that day.

Standing two over was another man. Taller.

"That's him." Spaceman pointed.

I glanced down. Sure enough, V. Sacks was printed in the caption.

And then…

"No!"

"What?"

Spaceman leaned forward and squinted.

"Look!" he pointed to the far left of the picture.

Leaning up against a shiny new combine with a piece of straw hanging out of his mouth was a young, cocky Shively Barnes.

65

We were only half a lap through town when we saw Shively's truck parked in front of the National Bank.

Spaceman swung a hard left and skidded into the lot.

The decals on National Bank's front glass doors said no guns and no smoking. Spaceman should have been wearing a hat that said *who gives a shit?*

I followed Spaceman into the lobby. He had his hand on his gun and sucked his cigarette down like a crayon being pressed on a radiator. When he finally exhaled the savings and loan was as hazy as a backroom poker game.

Shively was sitting across the table from the bank manager who had a zipper-lock canvas bag in front of him.

"Have a word, Shively?"

"Not now, Sheriff."

"A word?" Spaceman said.

"Leave me alone."

"What can you tell me about this?"

Spaceman laid down a printout of the photo with Sacks. Shively looked at it. Didn't say a word. He signed a few documents on the bank manager's desk, took the bag then got up to leave.

Spaceman nodded to me.

I got Shively in a full nelson and began dragging him out of the bank.

"Call the police," Shively yelled to the bank manager.

The bank manager looked at Spaceman and shrugged.

"Hi Fred," Spaceman said to the old man in the brown suit and blue tie.

We got Shively outside the bank. He kicked and screamed like a lunatic. I spun him around and hit him with a right. I picked him back up and Spaceman got him with a left.

"You gonna talk to us about that picture, or do we need to take you out in the country for some fresh air?"

"Please," Shively pleaded. "You've got to let me get home to my family. He's coming."

"Who? Sacks?"

Shively didn't say a word.

Spaceman cuffed him and got him in the back seat. I hammered the gas.

"Goddammit, Shively," Spaceman said lighting another cigarette. "Say something."

Shively didn't say a word.

"Shively, you need to start talking now."

Shively kept his head down and mouth closed.

Twin serpentine tendrils of smoke rolled out of Spaceman's nostrils.

Spaceman said, "Shively, you better start talking or you'll forever wish you did. I can promise you that."

"This is illegal. You can't do this. Take me to my family."

"Just answer his questions, Shively."

"Fuck you, Arch and the horse you rode in on."

I looked at Spaceman. "Time to teach 'im with Meechum?"

"Yep."

The sounds that came from the hogs was the thing of nightmares.

Despite the depth of the mud and shit, one young boar rose above the rest. His eyes focused on every swing and shake Shively made dangling from the jib crane.

Spaceman smiled.

"You remember the kids rhyme, Shively? The one that went Jack Sprat could eat no fat, his wife could eat no lean?"

"Let me down goddammit, I'll have your badge."

Spaceman nodded towards me. I hit the button on the electric hoist. Shively went down further.

"Well this big ol' hog is Jack Splat," Spaceman said. "And unlike the nursery rhyme, Jack Splat eats it all. Red, white, black, yellow, brown, murderer, thief, rapist, drug dealer…doesn't matter. Ol' Jack doesn't care.

Hell, I saw him nearly bite an abusive husband in half once. Now start talking."

"That picture. I don't know what you want it to mean. All I did was help those men out. You gotta believe me. I only know them from that summer program. Honest."

"You remember their names?" Spaceman said.

"No, no I don't," Shively stammered.

"Liar." I hit the switch again.

Jack Splat leaned back on his hocks. Mud, goo and saliva hung from his jowls. He snapped at Shively, once, then twice.

"Damn he's hungry," Spaceman said.

"No. No. No please," Shively sniffed.

Spaceman nodded.

I lowered Shively down an inch or two.

Jack Splat snapped his jowls. Mucous shot out of his nose.

"Wow," Spaceman said. "You're lucky that mud's deep and that he's a heavy boy. Ol' Jack just about Jordan-ed out of there for your face."

Shively was between panic and rage.

"You can't do this. It's murder. I have my rights."

I looked over at Spaceman. He nodded.

I hit the switch and let Shively's head drop two inches into the muck then the hoisted him back up before Jack Splat knew what had happened.

Shively screamed. Tears were falling now. Hanging upside down his head looked like a throbbing grape.

"His name is Vernon Sacks. He's, he's harassing my family. Wants money."

"Money?" Spaceman said. "What's he got on you?"

"He just got out of Statesville. Thinks I owe him money."

"For what?" I said.

"He used to work for me. We had a falling out."

"Is he the one vandalizing your barns?" I said.

"I don't know," Shively cried. "I think so."

Jack Splat was locked in on Shively now. Another boar and big sow in the pen started walking over to the dangling snack.

"C' c' c'mon, man. Please. PLEASE!"

I lowered Shively. Jack Splat's snout was just an inch away.

"Okay, okay. Christ! I'll tell you, okay? Let me up. Let me up."

Spaceman lit another cigarette and shook his head no.

"How about you tell us now," I said. "While you still can."

Jack Splat was joined by the other two. It was only a matter of seconds before they went hog wild.

Shively wept.

"He's back to kill us all. I'm trying to pay him off, but he wants blood."

Jack Splat opened his gaping maw. I pulled Shively up just in time. Jack Splat's teeth smacked into one another with a loud crack.

"Who?"

"Sacks," Shively said.

"Why?" Spaceman asked.

"Your dad," Shively cried.

"Red?" Spaceman said.

"Yes," Shively answered. "There was a subsidy or something. An exploratory deal, a humanitarian program the state came up with. It was a new thing. Red said I could help some incarcerated men get some fresh air and in turn get free labor. Red said he'd fill out the paperwork and file it. If he got the green light, we'd split the subsidy money from the state."

"So why is Sacks back if you helped him?"

"He thinks I cost him. Thinks I hurt him."

"How? On the job?" I asked.

Shively screamed. "I'm not saying another word until you can guarantee safety for my family and immunity for me."

"Immunity?" Spaceman said. "For what?"

"I want my lawyer," Shively yelled.

Spaceman nodded.

I lowered Shively deeper into the pen until the mud and shit rose over his nose and mouth. Shively couldn't breathe. He thrashed and shook. Jack Splat saw his dinner dangle and began walking over. I hit the hoist.

"Okay. I sent 'em. I sent 'em, but you gotta believe me. It was just to spy on you guys. Maybe scare you a little bit."

"You sent them?" Spaceman yelled.

"I heard the rumors about Karen running around on me."

"They raped her, you asshole. They tried to kill us," I spat.

"I never thought they'd do that. Never." Shively cried.

His face looked like a blueberry dipped in dark chocolate.

"You know how many lives you've ruined? People you killed?" I said.

"Me? It was you two running around that caused it."

"Give it to me. Now!" Spaceman yelled.

Spaceman ripped the controls from my hands. He swung Shively two inches from Jack Splat's mouth. Spaceman moved Shively's dangling height up and down until the other hogs honed in.

Shively began crying.

"How did you know we were going to be out there that day?" I demanded. "Did you have Sacks trail us?"

"I never saw anyone following us," Spaceman said.

"Me either," I said. "Which means someone must have tipped them off. But how?"

"Guys," Shively cried. "Honestly. I was working. You know me. That's all I do."

"You sonofabitch. I should kill you now," Spaceman said.

Spaceman dropped Shively. Jack Splat got a mouthful of Shively's hair and partial scalp.

Shively screamed.

"My God, help me, help me. Please!"

"How did you know we were going to be out there?" I demanded. "How?"

Tears, blood and mucous dripped from Shively's head.

Two hogs lunged past Jack Splat towards Shively.

"Amber told me."

66

We got Shively off the crane.

Spaceman hit him with the hose then threw him a towel.

"I should gut you right now, watch you bleed out instead of helping you."

"Please, Ted. You've got to let me get home and protect my family. You don't understand how brutal this man is."

"WE don't understand how brutal this man is?" Spaceman said. He flicked his cigarette into the hog pen and grabbed Shively by his shirt.

I was shocked to see hot tears of rage fall from Spaceman's eyes. He brought his head back then whipped it forward and headbutted Shively. Shively dropped to the ground.

"You sonofabitch," Spaceman cried. He sent his right boot into Shively's ribs.

Shively puked and gagged.

"I wanna string this guy up, too," I said. "But we can only cover so much ground. We gotta let him get home. Let him take care of Karen and the kid."

"Please," Shively cried.

Spaceman pulled his piece and pointed it at Shively. He cocked the hammer.

"You have no idea what you let loose that day."

"Please! For the love of God." Shively cried.

"Let him go," I said. "We've gotta find this guy."

We dropped Shively off at his truck in front of the bank.

Spaceman hit the gas before the rich farmer was barely out of the car.

Back at Spaceman's office he whipped open a closet door in the corner. He started pulling down random ammo boxes from high shelves. At first, he put the boxes back, then let the rest fall to the ground. Suddenly he spotted what he was searching for on the floor. A carton of cigarettes. He tore it open and grabbed two packs.

"Let's go!"

Spaceman's phone rang. It was Pete Barnes from the fire department.

"Yeah, Pete. How long ago?

Spaceman pointed out the window. I could see dark smoke in the distance.

"We'll see you out there." Spaceman slammed down the phone.

We turned off the rural route and blew down the gravel drive to the Beesbrook place. A hundred yards away we could see the blaze. Koontz and Maria Beesbrook's two-bedroom ranch was engulfed in flames.

"You don't think?"

"Their car's gone," I said.

We both sprinted towards the house and called out. In spite of the fire hoses the heat was overwhelming.

The sound was faint at first, but then we heard it.

Screams. Screams like war.

Koontz burst out the front door bathed in flame. His whole body was blackened. A small patch of hair from his smoldering head was illuminated. His nose had melted. An eye was gone.

There was no saving him.

Spaceman mercifully lifted his gun and fired a single shot.

We circled the house and called out for Maria.

There was no way to get in or look for her. It was too hot.

Pete and his group of firefighters were blasting the blaze with high powered streams of water.

"There," Spaceman pointed.

It was a soft trail, hard to see unless you looked close where the grass had been rolled over slowly by tires. But it was there, starting at the clothesline in the backyard of the burning house.

A quarter mile in, we made it to a stand of trees in the north corner of the Beesbrook's property. Behind some brush was an old van loosely covered in camo netting.

Spaceman stopped his cruiser about twenty yards away.

We got out, pulled our guns. Scanned the area.

Nothing.

We slowly approached the van from opposite directions.

The ash in the makeshift fire pit was cold.

"Sacks, you in there?!" I yelled. "You can come out with your hands up or we can honeycomb this piece of shit and you can die like a coward. Up to you."

No response.

All the doors to the van were open. Save for fast food wrappers and piles of trash, the vehicle was empty of any personal effects.

Spaceman walked over and used a pen to pick through the mess. There was a shoe box of notebook pages stapled together.

"What the hell?"

I picked up the documents.

There was some blathering on about justice. Our yearbook pictures were taped on some pages with clippings, sketches and writings. There was a cancelled check from Shively Barnes for ten thousand dollars. Bible verses that looked like they had been written down by Colesy.

"It's some kind of manifesto," I said.

"Why leave it behind for us?"

"Maybe he thought someone else would find it."

"But why, what's the purpose?"

"Expose us. What happened that day."

"But he'd only expose himself."

"He doesn't care."

"Jesus." Spaceman lifted a bandana to his mouth and nose. "It smells like a whore's hemorrhoids in here."

Spaceman used his pen to lift an old magazine off of a cardboard box. The magazine slipped and fell. The box beneath it read, Tahiti Tom's Beach Butter, twelve 12 oz. bottles. Spaceman carefully pulled back the cardboard flaps of the box.

And there it was.

A jar. Some kind of crude bomb.

I dove and tackled Spaceman.

We went elbows and knees then got up and sprinted.

We got maybe fifty feet away and turned around.

"Was that his shit jar? Some kind of a bomb decoy?"

"More like redneck incompetence," I said. "I doubt he has the capac-"

BOOM!

Sacks van blew up like a shaken beer dropped from ten stories.

I looked at Spaceman and shrugged.

"Then again with the internet these days..."

67

Like the fire department, Spaceman and I had been too late.

Maria and Koontz Beesbrook were dead and Vernon Sacks was in the wind.

Spaceman put out an APB for the Beesbrook's blue Ford Festiva.

His next call was to Dallas on the cruiser's handsfree system over the car speakers.

"You seen your sister today, Dallas?"

"Saw her yesterday. Somebody put a brick through her window that said slut."

Spaceman and I gave each other a look.

"Run over to her place and check on her will ya?"

"What for? She in trouble?"

"Didn't you just say someone put a brick through her window?"

"Yeah. I'm going to question the little kids on the block later today."

"Don't. Go get Amber and get her ass to the station."

"What for?"

"Now!"

Spaceman called Paige. It seemed like an eternity until she answered.

"Where are you?" Spaceman said.

"At the Doubletree in Evansville. Okay to come home?"

"Hardly. Stay put."

"Paige," I said to the speakers in Spaceman's cruiser. "Is Cherry with you?"

"No."

"You left without her?"

“She said you guys had a fight and stormed out of the house with her bag. A few minutes later a Ford Mustang pulled up with an Indiana State sticker on it.”

“Shit!”

We were halfway down Delaware Avenue when the call came in. A 10-33 from the Elks Club.

Spaceman swung a hard left leaving half the rubber from his rear tires steaming on the road.

When we got to the Elks two women were hysterical. They led us to the patio outside.

Bentley had suffered a blow to the head. He was on the ground holding a bar towel over the gash to stem the bleeding.

“Guy walked in. Seemed normal. He saw Cherry and said something to her. The kid she was with walked up and the guy went nuts. I ran over and took a swing, but the prick got me with some ninja pool cue bullshit.”

“Where’s the kid?”

“Over there,” Bentley pointed.

Sitting on the floor, leaning up against the jukebox was the college boy, Cherry’s pool pal. He was his holding his arm. His nose was bloody and his left eye was nearly swollen shut.

“What happened?”

“We just came in for a burger and to shoot some pool. Guy came in and asked Cherry if she knew you. I walked up to him and asked if there was a problem. The guy went nuts, hit me in the eye with the cue ball, grabbed Cherry and took off.”

I looked at Bentley. Bentley nodded.

“Bent and I went after him,” the kid said. “Then the dude pulled a gun and put it to Cherry’s head.”

“Did he say where he was going? A message? Anything?”

“He just hit her,” the kid said. “Hit her and laughed.”

I bent down and held out my hand. “Give me your keys.”

68

I admired the kids that came up from nothing, took various jobs, whatever they needed to do to put themselves through school. But, if you ever have to commandeer a car always go with a spoiled frat boy's.

I had barely touched the gas before the 435 horses of the Ford Mustang came to life and dug in.

I had speed, but I didn't have a clue.

I had a gun, but no immediate target.

Where in the hell was Sacks? Where would he take a beautiful girl like Cherry? Somewhere private. Somewhere where they could be alone. The thought made me sick.

My God, all that poor girl had been through. Ninety-eight percent of what she had ever seen or experienced from a male was cruelty.

I'd seen what happened to women and children that suffered abuse. The way their eyes lost their spark. Their heart hardened. The warmth of their souls cooled. It was heartbreaking to watch the joy of life be snuffed out by the hatred of it.

Cherry still had that spark. That verve. That smile.

But, how much more did she have in the tank?

I wasn't going to let a scumbag like Sacks take another drop.

But I knew he would. Right away if he could.

Cherry was a wildcat though. As tough and beautiful as they came. I hoped the fight in her didn't get her killed.

Where?

Where dammit?

The Duck Blind?!

Shady Ridge Park had a stand of trees at the top of a hill that overlooked the duck pond. The tree branches were low, but looking out you could see over the pond.

Decades ago it had been named the Duck Blind by some horny teenagers in need of a place to park. Sacks didn't grow up in Briarfield, but per Koontz, Sacks had been in town for a while. My guess was Sacks had been here long enough to get the lay of the land and plot his revenge.

I blasted over the railroad tracks and felt the tires leave the asphalt. I'd like to say I flew like Vin Diesel in *The Fast and the Furious*, but the truth is there are no Hollywood stunt landings in real life.

The front end of the Mustang came down first and nearly bucked me through the windshield. Fortunately, the airbags worked and I had a knife. I sliced the driver's side airbag open and kept the gas down.

The car had taken a solid punch, but after the blow still handled well.

I had just straightened out my line when I heard the siren. I looked up in the rearview. The Charger came up on me.

The driver, Dallas Roth, was yelling something out of his window.

Time was critical, but I couldn't hear him.

I pulled over.

Dallas whipped around so we could talk from our cars.

"Amber's gone."

"What?"

"A break-in, but it doesn't make any sense. She had nothing to rob."

"Did her neighbors see anything?"

"Mrs. Myersky said two women came to her door asking about Amber. She said one had a huge tattoo on her chest barely covered up with a dirty tank top."

"Let me guess. A dragon?"

"How'd you know?"

Sacks wasn't just back to get me and Spaceman.

He was back with a small army.

A small army to get us all.

"Where's Spaceman?"

"On his way out to Shively's place."

"Gimme your shotgun. Your walkie too."

Dallas handed them to me through the window.

"What do I do?"

"Go back to the station and get another one. Keep it on."

"Then what?"

Dallas looked at me like some scared kid. A look I had inadvertently helped carve out long ago. He needed confidence, encouragement."

"Are you a good cop, Dallas?"

"Hell yes."

"Go with your instincts."

"What in the hell did you and Spaceman do, Arch? Why is this happening?"

"It's the law of unintended consequences, Dallas."

I hit the gas and choke slammed some Goodyear onto the pavement.

When I glanced up in the rearview mirror, Dallas' Charger was disappearing in the opposite direction.

69

I was never much at poker, but my read on Sacks was good.

I could see the back of the Beesbrook's blue Ford Festiva poking just out from under the pines of the Duck Blind.

I put the spurs in frat boy's Mustang and made it up the hill in seconds.

I got out of the car, pumped a shell into the chamber and walked in like John Wayne.

"Get off her scumbag. Let her go and I promise I'll only cripple you and kill your immediate family."

Two shots whizzed by me.

I dove on my stomach and crawled behind a thick pine.

I poked my head out and looked.

Save for a ripped open blouse, Cherry's clothes were on. Her limbs were duct taped to the four corners of a picnic table. There was a dirty rag shoved in her mouth and tears streamed down her cheeks.

I moved quickly on my stomach and made it to the table.

I gently pulled the rag out of her mouth.

"Where?"

Cherry shook her head. She didn't know.

"I'm so sorry, Ar-"

"Stop. I'm sorry."

I cut her hands free with my Ka-Bar knife then handed it to her.

"Stay low. Get to the car if you can."

Three shots splintered the leg of the picnic table.

I returned fire covering Cherry.

I dove onto my stomach. I crawled frantically looking for a boot, a shoe, anything that might belong to Sacks.

Two more shots cracked the base of the tree next to me.

I was moving too slow. I got up and stepped quickly to the next tree then the next.

Nothing.

"Lookout Arch!"

I turned and caught the butt of Sacks' rifle in the nose. I took it like a boxer. Stunned, but stayed with it. Didn't go down. I blinked a few times, shook my head.

The man slowly came into view. It wasn't Sacks. It was a kid. Guessing mid-twenties, head shaved, wife-beater, camo pants. He had his arm wrapped tight around Cherry's throat.

"Where's Sacks?" I said.

"I'm right here."

"You're not Vernon."

"No, I'm his nephew, Denny."

"Sweet. You folks have spawned."

"Uncle Vernon is going to make you all pay."

"Tell you what, kid. You let her go and I promise I'll only kill you."

"Ha! You pull the trigger on that shotgun, you'll kill her and me both."

Denny shoved the nose of a Smith Wesson revolver into Cherry's right breast. He pulled back the hammer.

"Take it easy, kid."

"Call me kid again and I'll splatter her milk cans all over the trees."

I sighted him up through watery eyes.

"Let her go."

The kid squeezed Cherry's neck tighter.

"I said let her go. She's not part of this."

"Oh, but she is. Just like my cousin was. Along for the ride."

The heat and humidity hung like thick wet sheets.

The trees kept any kind of breeze from blowing.

Dust had mixed with the sweat on our faces.

We stared at each other like dogs.

"One of them men you killed that day was my daddy. You know what it's like to grow up without a daddy?"

I did.

"Your daddy was a rapist."

"Mister, I'm not going to tell you again. Drop it."

I dropped the shotgun and put my hands in the air.

"Let her go. Kill me, but let her go."

The kid laughed.

"Let her go? Are you crazy. This one's a prized peach."

He looked down at Cherry's dusty tears.

"Look. You made her cry. Aww, you're upset because he interrupted us before we could get it on, aren't you darlin?"

Denny's teeth were yellow, brown and black like Indian corn. A USMC tattoo was on his left bicep.

"You go over?"

"Three times. And you know what?"

"What?"

"Oooooh-rahhhhhh! I loved it."

"Look. I've got money. Cash. Lots of it. Let the girl go. Let her go and you can have anything you want."

"Money," he spat. "You think money'll buy back what my family lost that day? I don't have nothin'. Never have, but this. This is somethin'. She… she is really somethin'."

"Your family, those men. Whoever they were, they were scum. They attacked us. We didn't have a choice."

I saw Cherry's arm in the corner of my eye. She still had the knife I had given her. I moved a little. Distracted Denny as she brought the knife up over her head and down into the meat on top of his thigh.

Denny let out a howl of pain and fired a shot between my feet before I could grab the shotgun.

Cherry pulled the knife out and took a wild swing with the blade. Denny stepped out of the way, caught Cherry's wrist and twisted the knife out of her grasp.

I lunged toward Denny again, but this time he fired wildly and sent one right over my head.

Denny brought his shoulder down in front of Cherry then elbowed her in the throat. Cherry went down.

I went at him again still dazed

Denny was primed.

His Chuck Norris roundhouse kick was textbook. By the time I got up, Cherry, Denny and the shotgun were gone. So was the Mustang.

I looked at the beat-up blue Ford Festiva.

Right next to the keys on the hood a single finger had written…

CU Soon Asshole!

70

Without the police radio, I had no idea what was going on or where to go.

What I did know was that I needed another gun. A gun and a car with a lot more juice than the Beesbrook's beater.

I made it to the courthouse just in time to find the Sheriff's department in full shit show.

The hall was packed with a mixed bag of town officials, business owners and concerned citizens regarding word of a crime spree.

I bulldozed my way through the throng and elbowed my way into Spaceman's office.

"They got Cherry," I said.

"Sparks?" Spaceman said loading rounds.

"One of his."

"They've got Karen, too," Spaceman said. "Unless she was in the fire."

"Fire?"

"They lit up the Barnes' place."

"Shively?"

"Gone or burnt up. Fire department was still putting it out when I got there."

"What about their kid?"

"No idea. Look, I'm bringing in two part-time deputies to stay in town and monitor things." Spaceman skinned a cigarette from his pack and fired it up. "Rumors have spread outside the county to other fire departments and jurisdictions. I'm doing my best to hold 'em back. We may have two hours before the State Police get wind of this and come in. We gotta finish it now, Arch."

I walked over to my greased duffle and pulled out two guns. One was a Beretta PX4 the other an HK 9mm. Both loaded and ready to kill.

Dallas was playing *Whack-A-Mole* with the flashing phone lines. Exasperated, he picked up the whole phone system and slammed it onto the floor.

"I'm coming with you guys."

"Bullshit," Spaceman said. "You wanna be Sheriff someday? You will be. I'll campaign for you. Right now, you need to stay in town and hold it down. Any questions, I'm in pursuit of suspects. Got it?"

"But they have my sister," Dallas pleaded.

"We don't know that for sure," Spaceman said.

"It looks that way," I said. "The girls from the other day."

"The white-trashettes?"

I nodded. "They paid Amber a visit."

"Girls from the other day?" Dallas said. "What did you two do? Who are these people?"

"Dallas, stay put. That's an order," Spaceman said.

Fuzz popped on Spaceman's walkie.

"Anybody out there? Ground control to Major Tom. No wait, I think that jackass goes by Spaceman."

There was laughter, the voice had a backwoods twang.

"You've got Sheriff Ted Bendix here. This you, Sacks?"

"You got him," Sacks said. "Been enjoyin' my few days in town. Got a real kick out of your re-election signs. The Spaceman? What kind of cocky bullshit is that?"

"Listen, whoever you've got. Let them go. We'll-"

"No, you listen to me, Captain Astro. You listen to me."

"Give me back my sister," Dallas screamed.

Sacks laughed, "She the nasty thing my girls plucked from that dump of a home? Time's done that one wrong. Hard to believe I slid into that one that day. Really let herself go, no?"

"What day? What are you talking about?" Dallas said.

"Ha, you must be Dopey. I mean the deputy. They been keepin' you in the dark all this time?"

Dallas glared at Spaceman and I.

"You know your friend the preacher? The man of God, the murderer? Right now, while I have you I thought I'd tell you about the good preacher."

"Sacks, this is Arch Moses."

"Arch Moses? Oh, the runner. Yeah, the preacher talked about you. He didn't think much of you runnin' off."

"You killed him?"

"I did. The best part is I was at his funeral. Matter of fact, I walked up and shook your hand. Had a wig on of course. Some glasses from the Dollar Store. You were standing around like you were the biggest piece of chicken in the bucket. Fuck man, I've been waiting for this for so long."

"Let the girls go and whoever else," I said.

"Nope. Not gonna happen. How about you come out and see us where it all began. You know the way."

"This some kind of sick joke to you, Sacks?"

"Does it look like I've been jokin', Sheriff? You two come out and see us. Bring anybody else with you and everybody dies."

"Who do you have?" Spaceman said.

"Come see. We'll have fun waitin'. Oh, one other thing. Bring some sunscreen will ya? Maybe some Tahiti Tom's. Looks like it's going to be a beautiful afternoon."

Sacks let out a sickening laugh.

The walkie sounded like an industrial band.

"What the hell," Spaceman said.

"He threw it in the reservoir," I said. "We gotta move."

"I'm comin' with you guys," Dallas demanded.

"Not with us," Spaceman said. "You need to hang back for a bit. Let things play out. We get in a bind, we're gonna need you."

"On it," Dallas said.

"You're going to head up alone. On the other side. Be quiet, careful. Be ready for anything."

"Okay." Dallas said, getting amped up. "Then what?"

"Get close." Spaceman said.

"Okay?" Dallas said. "And?"

"Kill the bad guys before they kill you," I said.

"How do I know which ones are bad?"

"If you don't recognize 'em," I said sliding another Ka-Bar knife into my boot. "Take 'em out."

"Don't they have to engage me first with like force?"

"Dallas," Spaceman said. "They are wanted for murder, rape, kidnapping and arson. You see 'em, have a clean shot, kill them."

"10-4, Sheriff."

Dallas went to the gun closet and grabbed another shotgun and a few boxes of rounds.

"You go quietly. Up old Loomis road," Spaceman said. "Be smart. Stay low. Got me?"

"I got you," Dallas said.

"Wait for an hour or so before coming out. Be smart."

"On it." Dallas said. "I won't mess this up. Quick question."

"Yeah?" Spaceman frowned.

"If we make it out of this alive will you do me a favor?"

"What's that?"

"Tell me the truth?"

"About what?" I said.

"About everything. What in the hell you guys did?"

"Let's focus on getting everyone out of this alive first," Spaceman said.

I screwed the Osprey silencer onto my Beretta.

Dallas looked at me.

"You're not a salesman are you, Archie?"

"No, Dallas. I'm not. I'm a delivery man."

Dallas' face pinched up. "What do you deliver?"

"Death."

Dallas looked at Spaceman.

"Is he serious?"

Spaceman blew out his first puff from a fresh cigarette.

"That's about the size of it."

71

Spaceman skidded to a stop next to the stolen Mustang.

Two trucks, both beaters, were parked further apart in the woods. One had a shotgun rack. The other had a rusty cab with the back glass broken out.

Someone had painted over the graffiti on the boulder with white paint. On top of that in dripping red letters was the phrase *vingents is mine.* It would have been a laugher but-

"Jesus, is that blood?" Spaceman said.

I stepped forward. "Looks like it."

"Let's hope it's a deer."

"If it is, then the deer is a bad speller."

Spaceman went to his shirt for a cigarette.

"Don't," I said. "No need to announce our location." Although, I knew they probably had eyes on us.

We moved stealthily down the shaded trail then went elbows and knees up the embankment to the top just overlooking the reservoir.

We heard faint screams. Laughter, whooping.

Spaceman lifted his binoculars.

"Sonofabitch. They got 'em strung up half-"

An arrow sent Spaceman's Stratton campaign hat skiing across the water. Spaceman rolled on his back and lifted his gun to fire in the believed location of the archer.

Moments later there was a soft chuckling. A twenty-something, goateed wonder with a long hair and knock off Jordan's walked up and spit.

"Damn, if that shot don't freeze a man in his tracks every time. After firin' on you and them babes at that fancy swimmin' hole the other day,

you gotta be wonderin' am I that bad of a shot to miss, or that good of a shot to get so close?"

"Why didn't you kill us?" I said.

"Not 'sposed too. Uncle Vern just wanted us to fuck with you. Gotta tell you though, you came down that hill a firin'. If I hadn't had a vest on you'd a gotten me right in the chest."

"You got that vest on now?" I asked.

The kid lifted his sleeveless sweatshirt.

"Shit yeah!"

"Good to know."

I lifted my gun and sent a hollow point into his left eye. He fell back like tall timber.

"Search him for a walkie."

Spaceman did.

"Nothing."

It was good news. Long Hair wouldn't be missed. Not right away, anyway. We drug him down the hill and covered him with loose brush in the woods.

We made it back up the embankment and looked out.

Cherry, Amber and Karen's clothes were dirty and torn. Their hands were tied together and strung above on a taught line tied between two trees.

Denny from the Duck Blind was taking mouthfuls of beer and spitting it on the women. Karen and Amber were a mess. Cherry was somehow holding it together.

Sacks sat on a stump with his back to me. It looked like he was filming the whole thing on his phone. With a rifle, it would've been a clean shot, but with the girls tied up, they didn't stand a running chance.

We moved closer.

About twenty yards away were two other men with the group.

One was wearing mirrored sunglasses and a backwards ball cap. He had the classic county lock-up build: skinny chicken legs, big arms.

The other man was older, way older. Like Henry Fonda in *On Golden Pond* older. He didn't seem to be as excited about the fun Sacks and the others were having with Karen, Amber and Cherry.

Spaceman peered through his Eagle Optics.

"Sick bastards have 'em strung up like-"

Lightning zapped us in the middle of our backs. Cattle prods.

I rolled over into the shadow of Dragon Tits standing over me.

"Hiya, gorgeous!"

Her middle finger rose above the rest.

"That is an impressive amount of dirt you have behind that nail," I said.

Spaceman turned and looked up at Birthmark.

"What did you guys do with Guthrie?" She asked.

"Who?" I said.

"Long hair, bow. He should be out here."

"Friend of yours?" I asked.

"Try boyfriend," Birthmark said.

"Looks like you're back on the market," I said.

Birthmark turned her head sideways. "Huh?"

I jumped up and tackled Dragon Tits.

As soon as Birthmark looked over, Spaceman tripped her and grabbed her prod. He gave her a generous dose of voltage.

Dragon Tits and I struggled for the prod. She gave me a zap, but only grazed my neck. I grabbed the stick with one hand and twisted. She did the same thing to my balls.

I abhorred violence against women of any kind, but given the fact that this wolverine was attempting to crush my testicles, I had no choice. I brought my fist back and brought it down hard. She crumbled.

Spaceman and I were up and had the prods in hand. Dragon Tits and Birthmark writhed around on the ground in pain.

"How many?" I said, "and where?"

"Kiss my ass," Dragon Tits coughed.

I walked over and gave her enough juice to pick up radio stations with her nipple piercings.

In my periphery, I saw Spaceman fall to his knees then onto his stomach. The back of his head looked like he had been shot or stabbed. I ducked and turned.

Something incredibly sharp and heavy smashed into my forehead.

72

When I came to, Spaceman and I were side by side on our knees. Our hands and feet were secured behind us with what felt like zip ties.

We were on the far side of the reservoir at the bottom of the embankment. The area was shaded and looked like it had been personally cleared for the event.

My head was pounding and my vision was blurred. I could feel the dried blood on my face and neck where I had been hit.

Judging from his voice, Spaceman was faring better than me. He was talking to Birthmark, whose hairy, dirty legs were right in front of us.

"So," Spaceman said. "You don't wear deodorant because you like to stink or dislike the way it clumps up your armpit hair?"

Birthmark swung a haymaker and raked Spaceman's cheek with her nails. It looked like a tiger got him.

"Whoa! Speaking of hair, looks like you cut yourself shaving, Sheriff." Dragon Tits chuckled. "...with a machete."

"I've had worse mosquito bites," Spaceman said spitting out a mouthful of blood.

"Sure you have Sheriff," Dragon Tits said. "How about another?"

Dragon Tits brought her arm back and got Spaceman again. This time on the other cheek.

"There's a tetanus shot," Spaceman said.

I shook my head trying to get my vision to straighten out. The only two people I could see in front of us were Dragon Tits and Birthmark.

I blinked. Things were less blurry. I closed my eyes tight then opened them.

"The other's awake now, daddy." Birthmark said.

Sacks walked into the clearing. He was a bear of a man, strong. His beer gut looked to have been generously supplemented with fried dough and pork rinds. He was bald. The pockmarks on his face made his head resemble the lunar surface.

Sacks buckled up his pants and winked at me.

"Boy did that ever feel good," he said.

"I hope you're walking out of those woods after taking a taking a piss and nothing else," I said.

Sacks laughed. "How about I let you smell my dick and you can tell me."

"After tolerating you daughter's body odor it would be a breath of fresh air."

Sacks nodded to Birthmark. She gave me a hefty helping of electricity.

"Jesus darlin'," Spaceman said. "You wanna go roll around in some cow shit for a few minutes. Improve your scent."

"Fuck you," Birthmark said.

She put the juice right under Spaceman's balls. It zinged him so badly he couldn't even scream.

"You assholes want to do anymore talkin' go right ahead," Sacks said. "We'll be here when you get done."

Nobody said a word.

"Good," Sacks smiled. "First off, thanks for all of these great guns. Beautiful hardware."

"Keep 'em. I got more," I said.

Sacks smiled. "Let's get rollin'. Bring 'em out."

Denny from the Duck Blind and a strong looking teen in a Tank Top led the girls out. Cherry, Karen and Amber were tied together. Their tops had been ripped open. The pieces from which were used to gag them. Their pants and shorts were torn like someone had tried to pull them off and pull them back on. Their makeup ran from perspiration and tears.

I looked at Tank Top. The sonofabitch had a heavy wooden table leg resting on his shoulder, the end of which was wrapped in razor wire.

Sacks noticed me taking in the makeshift weapon.

"Nasty little thing isn't it?"

Tank Top laughed. "Did a real number on them skulls of yours."

Sacks smiled and ran his hand over his stubble like he was in deep thought. He had fashioned an earring out of a spent shotgun shell. It swung back and forth as he crunched on an apple. He tossed the core.

"Put 'em on the fence," Sacks said.

Denny and Tank Top took the women up the hill. Tank Top held them against the fence while Denny zip tied them against the chain link. Cherry and Karen struggled with the men but stopped when Tank Top lifted his do-it-yourself death stick.

"You get loose?" I whispered out of the side of my mouth to Spaceman.

"Workin' on it."

"Now, the other two," Sacks said.

Sunglasses led out Shively and Brian Barnes. They were zip tied like the rest of us. Shively was crying and walking on shaking legs. Quiet tears rolled out of Brian's scared eyes.

"Drop on your knees," Sunglasses ordered.

Shively and Brian did. Shively's head bobbed up and down to the quiet beat of his sobbing.

Karen spit out her gag.

"Why is my husband here? He didn't have anything to do with this."

Sacks laughed. "Oh baby, are you ever in for a surprise."

Sacks signaled to Denny. He walked over to the fence and put the gag back in Karen's mouth.

"Kill us and let the women go," Spaceman said. "You want money?"

"Nah, money doesn't interest me. Ol' Mr. Barnes already tried that."

"That's a shame," I said. "One of your top-notch team here could buy some spelling lessons."

Fonda came out of nowhere to my right.

"That was me wrote on the rock you sonofabitch."

He lifted his rifle and drove the butt down into my ribs. The old fart broke two, maybe three.

"Man, is it going to be fun killing all of you," Sacks said.

"Let's do it then," Fonda said. "What the hell we waitin' on?"

"Patience," Sacks said.

The zip ties Sack's had used were not law enforcement grade. They were tight, but could be broken in time. Time unfortunately that we didn't have.

I looked up at Cherry bound against the fence. In spite of the tears that ran down her face, her eyes were resolute. It was unclear if she had been sexually assaulted. Either way every scumbag there was going to pay. Cherry's eyes met mine. Our silent conversation was brief.

We're getting out of here alive.

I ran through various scenarios in my head. None of which looked good for our captors. Or us. There would be casualties.

"Now for the introductions," Sacks said walking up to the fence. "First, the visitin' team. Sacks turned like Ed Sullivan presenting the Beatles.

"Up top we got, Fatty."

Amber struggled against the fence. She turned her head back and forth until her gag fell out of her mouth.

"It's Amber you piece of shit."

Sacks laughed.

"Okay, then." Sacks said. "Well, Amber. I've heard of letting yourself go, but it looks like you done smacked the pavement. Sad. You sure used to be a real piece. What a shame."

Sacks walked on to Karen. He grabbed her by the ass and laughed.

"Whew, Jed must've had fun with you. Fore he was killed that is. Be honest now, did it feel good?"

Karen squirmed against the fence.

I struggled against the ties. Tried to get to my knife out of my boot.

Sacks turned and fired a bullet that just missed my ear.

"Everybody. Pay attention." Sacks looked back at Karen and pointed to Shively. "Her husband." Sacks then pointed to Amber. "Her best friend. Ya'll remember that."

Sacks stepped on down the line to Cherry

"And finally, this generously scooped dream bar of a young lady. Would you all believe this beauty is this asshole's girlfriend." Sacks pointed at me. "You lucky sonofabitch. Don't seem fair she being with an old bastard like you. She must be blind. Glad I'm not."

Sacks ran his hands over Cherry's breasts. She fought against the fence. I wrestled with my ties.

Some of the men hooted and hollered.

"Sacks let the women go," I said. "You and the rest can jump rope with me and the Sherrif's intestines, but let the women go."

"Ha!" Sacks laughed. "That be alright with you then, Sheriff? I let the ladies leave, walk on out of here, you let us take you and tough guy apart."

"If that's what it takes," Spaceman said.

Sacks thought about it for a moment.

"Nah. No deal. This here is a story best told with, dare I say it…a captive audience."

Some of Sacks crew chuckled.

"Nice pun, daddy." Birthmark said.

"Yeah, fun when they come along natural like that," Sacks said.

I shook my head.

Sacks looked at me. "Got something to say tough guy."

"I do. You're like a German sausage."

Sacks spit. "Oh yeah, how's that?"

"You're the wurst," Spaceman said.

"You stole my punchline," I said to Spaceman.

"Sorry," Spaceman said. "Fun when they come along natural like that."

Sacks looked at Birthmark and Dragon Tits.

"Juice 'em," he said.

Stink 1 and Stink 2 put the prods on us.

"You smartasses done?" Sacks said.

We didn't say a thing.

"Good," Sacks, said. "So, for you playing at home. It was these two that day hooking up with these two that day." Sacks pointed at Amber and Karen then me and Spaceman. "This pretty one here," he smiled at Cherry, "is just along for the ride today. Like my son was. My dead son. Which reminds me…First things first."

Sacks lifted his gun, turned and shot Brian Barnes dead in the head. Brian fell over in front of Shively. Gagged gasps and muffled screams echoed across the reservoir.

Shively was now wide awake. His cheeks flooded with tears.

The women on the fence were in a mix of hysterics and shock. Karen looked on is disbelief.

Shively Barnes was beside himself.

"Tough loss ain't it," Sacks said. "Now you know how it feels."

I struggled against my ties.

"Okay, moving along. Now for the home team." Sacks pointed to Sunglasses, "This is Lester. His sister," Sacks pointed to Dragon Tits, "is Darla. Their daddy, Jed, my brother, was the one you killed." Sacks looked at me. "Say hello kids."

Sunglasses walked down the hill.

Amber somehow managed to wrangle the bandana out of her mouth again.

"Your daddy was a rapist," Amber cried.

Sunglasses turned and went up the hill after her. Sacks cut him off.

"You can finish her later. Take care of the men now."

Sunglasses nodded and walked back down the hill.

Sunglasses stood in front of me, drew back and introduced his fist to my jaw. Dragon Tits got me with the prod again.

"Next," Sacks said. "Is Marigold," he pointed at Birthmark. "Her Dad was Merle. Merle was," Sacks pointed at Tank Top. "Also, JD's dad. Oh and," Sacks pointed at Fonda. "Walter's son. Say hi."

Fonda came down and fed Spaceman and I the butt of his rifle. I didn't want to give him the satisfaction of spitting out my teeth, so I swallowed them.

Tank Top walked down, stood in from of me and swung his table leg. The razor wire nearly sent my cheek into the next county. I blinked. I still had both eyes. My jaw and chin, however, were anyone's guess.

Tank Top stepped in front of Spaceman.

"Don't be a pussy now," Spaceman said.

Tank Top swung for the fences. At the last second Spaceman pulled his head back. The full blow would have killed him, only this time the razor wire just took off the tip of his nose. Spaceman fell forward on his stomach in agony. Dragon Tits and Fonda grabbed Spaceman by the collar and set him back up on his knees. Dirt and dry leaves were stuck where the tip of his nose used to be.

"Anybody want to be funny now?" Sacks said. "Mock me? Make jokes? Anybody?"

"You gonna introduce me?" Denny said.

"No more. We gotta keep 'em alive for the tale."

"So, still to be fair you oughta intro-"

"Jesus," Sacks said. "This is Denny. Jed's boy. Now everybody shut up."

The women were struggling and sobbing against the fence. Karen was out of her mind looking at Brian slumped over next to Shively.

"You wanna pay attention here now, Sheriff. This is far too rich a tale to miss moaning on your stomach." Sacks slowly ran his tongue over his greasy smile. "Which reminds me of ramming into your skinny little ass down in that mud that day. Course had to break your arm to do it. Scrappy little bastard."

There were gasps amongst some in the group.

"Oh, you didn't tell nobody about that did ya?"

"I'm going to kill you," Spaceman spat.

Sacks laughed. "He ain't gay folks. I just got in a pump or two."

Fonda walked up to Sacks.

"What in the hell is going on here, Vernon? You said these people-"

Sacks raised his pistol and held it in front of Fonda's face.

"Back off, old man. This is my show."

Fonda did as he was told.

Amber shook and trembled. Yelled something behind her gag. Tears ran down her cheeks. Sacks walked up the hill and pulled her gag out.

"Got somethin' to say there, Fatty?"

"You sick bastard," Amber cried.

Sacks raised his hand above his head and swung his flat palm down hard on Amber's stomach.

Amber let out a scream.

"Damn," Sacks laughed. "My beer gut is big, but at least it's firm. What you got there is world class jelly belly. He poked the red spot where he had hit her.

"You piece of shit! You-"

Sacks shoved the gag back into Amber's mouth. He pulled out his pistol and ran the barrel along the top of her panties.

"You want something hard up there? How about this gun? I bet you've slid worse up there on your own accord." Sacks snickered.

"Leave her alone," Shively bellowed. One eye swollen shut. The other blood red. His mouth a mush of teeth and lip.

Sacks turned. "Ah, yes. There he is. The lover boy. I start making fun of your old piece and you get brave."

Karen's eyes got big.

"Let the women go," Shively said.

"Or what?" Sacks laughed.

"Just kill me," Shively said, "and let the women go."

"Are you crazy? Then they'll miss story time," Sacks said. "I guess there is one that doesn't deserve to be here."

Sacks walked over to the fence. Looked at Cherry and eyed her body.

"So sorry you got dragged into all of this sweetheart. Man, you are a peach."

Sacks kissed her cheek.

"Take it easy," Denny said. "I found her. Brought her here. She's mine when this is over."

Sacks laughed. "Yours huh? Looks like we'll be drawing straws."

"What in the hell you doin', Vernon? I don't know about all this. You said they killed-"

"In cold blood," Vernon said. He lifted his gun at Fonda again. "Cold blood it was, and in cold blood I'll do you now. Now, does everyone want to shut up and hear the greatest story that ever came out of this county, because I'm tellin' you, I think you do."

Sacks walked over and pulled a pack of cigarettes and a lighter from Spaceman's shirt pocket. He fired one up and shoved both items into his jeans.

"We're from out in the sticks. Woods people. For us redneck is a step up.

"Didn't matter none. We were taught how to hunt and fish. Plant vegetables, grow weed, make moonshine. My grandad built our cabin. Momma made our clothes.

"Wasn't until my teen years that me and Jed wanted more. That's when we started stealin'.

"First gas stations, little corner stores. Then after that it grew. We got popped. Were in and out of different prisons through the years. As the crime grew, the time grew.

"I don't give a shit how tough you are. You never want to go to prison. Things happen in there you can't unsee. There are no do-overs. Some men fold up. It just made me meaner. Smarter.

"I ran things on the inside. Got some leverage on a couple high level screws. Got Jed transferred to Statesville where I was. There was a work program through the state. Got men out of our cages and into the fresh air.

"I didn't think we stood a shot, but I had this clerk under my thumb agreed to fudge a few things on our paperwork. We made it in. It was some kind of work something, something program. And that's where we met Mr. Barnes."

Sacks pointed his pistol at Shively.

"Didn't matter the work. We were just happy to be outside. Detasslin' corn, hanging tobacco, mending fences, running all kinds of equipment out on Mr. Barnes' land. We was happy to do it all."

I looked around the clearing. Everyone was listening, some sobbing, but still tuned in. I worked on the zip ties.

"Course view wasn't bad to take in while we were workin'." Sacks looked up and pointed at Amber and Karen. "You two splashing around in the pool, shakin' your asses in your bikinis. Laughin' and drinkin'.

"I knew Mr. Barnes was engaged to you," Sacks pointed at Karen. "So, you can imagine my shock one day when I got to the barn to get some gloves and spied ol' Barnes giving some turkey neck to Fatty."

"Don't listen to him, Karen," Shively cried. "He's lyin."

Karen struggled against her restraints.

"Oh, I am? Am I, Mr. Barnes? I'm lyin'? Am I lyin' when I saw you plowin' Fatty in the hayloft, down at the wells, in the machinery shed? What about those times you had her bent over that skid of herbicide?"

Karen's dark eyes were darting back and forth between Shively and Amber. She was seething with rage.

"Great, right? What good friends." Sacks laughed. He looked at Karen. "You know sometimes I couldn't get it straight which one he was engaged to, you or your friend. I mean you should seen 'em. Real passion."

Shively's sobs were louder now. His body shook.

"Please, please, Karen. Don't listen to him," Shively said.

Karen looked down in shock from the fence where she was bound.

"Oh buddy," Sacks laughed. "One afternoon I get up the sand to ask Mr. Barnes why he's screwing the best friend of his fiancée. He tells me it's complicated. He's heard rumors about his girl being unfaithful. Says Fatty up there is really putting the pressure on for a ring herself or some crazy thing."

Amber spat the bandana out of her mouth.

"It's Amber, you son of a bitch. And I'm sorry. I'm so sorry Karen, but-"

"Shut-up Jelly Belly," Sacks said. "Anyway," he went on, "at this point Mr. Barnes has come to like me. I'm a good listener he says. He tells me how he's kind of torn between the two women. Much as he cares for Karen," Sacks turned and pointed at Amber, "Amber, here is telling him his fiancée is cheating on him. Is it true? What if she's lying for no other reason than spite and jealousy. Good friends huh? Remember what you said Mr. Barnes? Man, what an ego. You said, she wanted you all to herself and would step over anyone to get you."

Amber looked down from the fence. The big tears started rolling.

"Anyway, Mr. Barnes says, he's kind of stuck between the two women. I tell him he needs to find out for sure before he makes such a big decision."

"You were just supposed to scare them," Shively whimpered.

Karen spit her gag out by sheer will.

"You sent them?" Karen screamed. "But how did you know?"

Sacks laughed, “Now, now, now. Everybody shut up, this is where it gets-”

“I told him,” Amber sobbed. “I told Shively we were going to the spillway that day. You had it all Karen and were throwing it away. You had it all and didn’t care.”

“What?” Karen spat at Amber.

“I needed to prove to Shively the rumors he was hearing about you were true.”

“You sent them to rape us?” Karen yelled at Shively.

“Naw, that was just us improvisin.” Sacks laughed. “Man, that was a weird day. Merle brung my boy out there hopin’ to see his daddy for the first time in years. Well, we all know what happened.

“Anyway, long time later, I’m back in prison and this chaplain comes in to counsel the guy in the cell next to me. I hear him tell the guy that he too done bad. Stabbed someone in a fracas one awful day fishing. The preacher leaves a tiny Bible for the guy. I borrow it one day to tear out a page to roll a joint with. I’m flippin’ through it, and see this stamp. Briarfield Christian Church, Pastor Robert Cole. What are the odds? I try to see if I can get the pastor to visit me, but before I can even put in a request, I get shipped out to another cage for dealin’ dope inside.

“But guess what. The miracles kept on comin’. My new cellie has a Briarfield tattoo and I learn a few things. Of course, I don’t last long there, moved again. But, years later I make parole and guess where I go?

“Briarfield, to find Pastor Bobby Cole. It was easy. Went to his church. Met in his office and told him who I really was. Gotta say he was a man about it. Took responsibility. More than you two bags of shit, but, he said what me, Jed and Merle done was wrong too and that’s when I hit him with a few shots then strung him up.”

My ties finally gave.

I grabbed my knife, stood up, spun around and unzipped Fonda’s throat.

That was when everything went full shit show.

Sacks drew his gun and fired. I held Fonda up in front of me to absorb the shots.

Amber dropped her legs out from under her, snapping her binds with her weight and dove on Sacks taking him down.

Spaceman rocked back on his shoulders and neck and swung his bound hands under and over his feet and legs. He threw his hands over Sunglasses head and started choking him with his restraints.

I picked up Fonda's rifle and fired off three immediate kill shots at Tank Top, Denny and Birthmark. The gun was jammed.

Denny laughed and came at me. The dumbass went with a flying Superman punch. For his trouble, the hot shot got the barrel of a Weatherby Vanguard driven through the skin of his submandibular. I tripped him then rode my weight down on the gun and drove the barrel into his brain.

I dropped and swept Birthmark's leg as she rushed me with the prod.

I cut Shively free as he struggled with Sunglasses. That is when I felt Tank Top's razor wire table leg slice up the back of my thighs. He brought it around again. This time I turned and stopped his second swing with my forearm. The razor wire tore into flesh and bone.

I sent a fifty-yard field goal directly to Tank Top's balls. He dropped and it was my turn with his twisted toy.

Karen broke free from the fence like some kind of insane hellcat. She screamed and dove on the human pile that was Sacks and Amber who were struggling over Sacks' gun.

Karen was pounding her fists on both Amber and Sacks.

"You bitch!" Karen screamed. "You killed Brian."

In the corner of my eye Spaceman and Sunglasses were fighting tooth and nail. One swing, two swings from me with Tank Top's saw-toothed table leg and Sunglasses was down.

Sacks was up now and had the gun.

Shively stood up and speared Sacks.

Sacks spun off balance and squeezed off a shot in Karen's direction, Amber dove in front of her old friend and took the bullet.

"Swim for it," Shively screamed at Karen.

Karen ran to the edge of the reservoir and dove in.

I swung around and looked for Sacks.

Sacks came down the hill firing at me. I pushed Dragon Tits in front of me and watched as hollow points ripped into my poorly tattooed human shield.

Spaceman hit Sunglasses with Dragon Tits prod and watched him ride the lightning.

I ran up and freed Cherry from the fence.

She tried to say something, but there was no time.

"Go!" I yelled.

I felt a knife slice into the scar tissue on my back. It was Sunglasses, bloodied but back up. I pulled the knife out of my shoulder blade, spun around and went Fruit Ninja on his ass. He went down and I fell on top of him and gasped for air

When I turned back around. Sacks was feeding hard fists to Spaceman's face. I tried to get up but slipped.

I heard a splash and saw Birthmark go into the water after Cherry. Birthmark pulled Cherry up on shore. The two fought like alley cats over the last cup of milk. Cherry landed two kicks that put Birthmark down.

I ran to help Spaceman, but when I got there he was alone.

"Where's Sacks?" I yelled.

"Stop right there hero."

I turned around. Sacks had a buck knife to Cherry's throat.

I looked in Cherry's eyes. They were wide open, but strangely composed. She brought her heel up and drilled Sacks in the balls. He fell forward and the blade got all of Cherry's cheek.

"Swim!" I pushed Cherry into the water towards the other side.

I heard water splash behind me and ducked.

Sacks just missed me with the knife. I spun around exhausted. I got him with two punches that didn't have much behind them.

Sacks stepped a foot or so down into the water.

"Gonna be fun," he said. He took a swing. The knife just missed my chest.

I ripped off my shirt and loaded it with water. When Sacks lunged I swung at his wrist and missed. He took another swing, then another. On the third he lost his balance. I crouched down and crashed into his knees like a linebacker. I heard one snap and hyperextend.

I got both of my knees on Sacks shoulders and brought fist after fist to his face. I had his massive head under water, maybe just an inch or two when his hands came out and he began digging his thumb nails into my tear ducts. He brought his head up gasping for breath. I grabbed hands full of silt and started shoving them down his throat.

I felt his nails begin to force their way into the orbs of my…

POP- POP- POP.

Sacks hands fell away. I fell over on my side.

I lifted my head out of the water and blinked my eyes. I shook my head clear and saw Dallas holding a smoking Colt Python.

Cherry was almost to the other side of the reservoir now. Maybe ten feet from shore.

And then. A sickening laugh. Birthmark had somehow righted herself and now held both cattle prods in front of her directly over the water.

"An eye for an eye," Birthmark said. "This is for Guthrie."

Birthmark lifted the prods up in dramatic fashion over the water.

"Don't do it," Dallas said drawing on her.

"Why not?" Birthmark sneered.

"Because you'll die too," Dallas said.

Birthmark let out a strange laugh and plunged the prods down into the water. Nothing.

Spaceman walked up behind her with his pistol drawn.

"Already squeezed all the juice out of 'em, didn't ya?"

"Shit," Birthmark said. "This is better anyway. The world is going to love my story."

"What story?"

Spaceman pulled the trigger.

75

I didn't take my eyes off Cherry until she was met by a first responder.

Dallas and Spaceman crashed into the water and grabbed me.

It felt like pieces of me were loose. I coughed up a mouthful of blood.

"Take it easy, Arch. We'll get you to the hospital."

"Over here," Dallas screamed. "Over here."

"No," I said. "I can't be here."

"But, you'll die," Dallas waved. "Over here, help."

"I can't be here," I said.

I could feel it, my body teetering on the brink. All I had to do was close my eyes and drift away. It was as easy as laying my head down on a pillow and turning off a lamp.

I wasn't afraid, but I wasn't ready.

I opened my eyes.

Spaceman's face looked like he'd been making out with a cheese grater.

"We got 'em, Arch. It's over."

"We got 'em," I said.

"Over here," Dallas waved.

"Let him go," Spaceman said to Dallas.

"But Sheriff-"

"Let him go."

Dallas did.

"Go Arch," Spaceman coughed. "Go and don't come back." He gave me a push.

I swam towards the spillway. Each stroke was slow, deliberate, purposeful.

Seconds seemed like hours.

The spotlight from the state police chopper hit the water.

I made it up the rusted rungs to the top of the concrete structure and grabbed the rope. It took every ounce of strength I had left in me to slide down and not fall. I made it to the bottom. The water crashed and knocked me to my knees.

I looked down the long black canal.

Some believed a man could be born again.

I wondered if it was true.

I waited for the water to rise then removed the board.

6 months later

If there was a number in the title of the news show, you can bet they each ran a package on what had been dubbed the Shoal County Shootout.

48 Hours

60 Minutes

20/20

After V's team of federal and local fixers and lawyers arrived with truckloads of cash and pre-written sworn testimonies, the story went like this:

Vernon Sacks, a known felon and former convict had gone back to Southern Illinois to even scores for slights he believed were exacted by members of a traveling meth production ring. Caught in the crossfire between violent criminals, rival drug gangs and Sacks known associates were a number of innocent citizens from the tiny town of Briarfield.

Survivors of the ordeal had little to say, instead choosing their previously sworn testimonies to tell the tale for them.

In short, methamphetamine production continues to be an epidemic that ruins more lives than just its users.

Nowhere stated or mentioned in the entire case file is the name Arch Moses or a woman going by the name of Cherry.

After a long period of rest in a hospital bed and a number of surgeries and procedures, I am slowly getting back into the game.

While I'm almost a hundred percent, V has me taking baby steps. No hits just yet. Mostly doling out tune ups and teaching painful lessons.

The sports teams are lousy here, but the food is good. I've always enjoyed staying at the Four Seasons. However, I'm not in Philly for fine dining or to take in athletic contests. I'm here because this city is chock full of schools and universities.

You know who rich white college boys rape? Sometimes anybody, but oftentimes it's rich white college girls. Do you know what rich white girls have? Dads. Do you know what happens when rich white boys rape rich white girls and the only thing that comes out of it is a slap on the wrist?

I get a phone call.

And do you know what I do?

I go to work whistling.

Coming in 2019!

A BUSTED GOLD TOOTH IN THE SMILE OF FORTUNE

another Arch Moses novel

by Chris Craig

Acknowledgements

Thank you to my dear wife, Phoebe, who no matter what kind of book I am writing at the time, is always supportive, encouraging and understanding. For my kids, Parker and Oscar, thank you for your patience and allowing me time to pursue a passion.

To all my readers, family and friends, a sincere and humble thank you for your enthusiasm and interest in my work. Your readership is a blessing that I do not take for granted.

A special thanks to Gretchen Kren, Chad Main and Kate Pastorelli for their eyes and edits.

Mad gratitude to Jimmy Parker for putting the trailer together.

Thanks to Josh Brogadir for the narration.

Lastly, to the Greenwood, Mississippi boys who took me down the real Teoc tube that crazy summer between junior and senior year.

What a rush. Thank you for the unforgettable ride.

73537714R00183

Made in the USA
Lexington, KY
09 December 2017